FINDING DESTINY

The Destiny Series Book 5

EMMA EASTER

Finding Destiny
by Emma Easter

Paperback Edition

CKN Christian Publishing
An Imprint of Wolfpack Publishing

6032 Wheat Penny Avenue
Las Vegas, NV 89122

This book is a work of fiction. Any references to historical events, real people or real places are used fictitiously. Other names, characters, places and events are products of the author's imagination, and any resemblance to actual events, places or persons, living or dead, is entirely coincidental.

Paperback ISBN: 978-1-64734-709-3
Ebook ISBN: 978-1-64734-708-6

FINDING DESTINY

ONE

Davina Brooks bit her lip as she listened to her fiancé, Daniel, talk about their upcoming nuptials. As usual, he was beyond excited and wore a huge smile on his face as he went on about their wedding and the prospect of starting a family immediately after. But she felt trapped. She loved Daniel, but the more she thought about marrying him, the more encaged she felt. And she realized she'd started feeling this way on the same day he proposed.

"Vina!" Daniel blinked and stared at her. "What's the matter? You look really troubled. Did I say something wrong?"

"No, you didn't say anything wrong," Vina answered, and avoided his eyes.

"But you were not listening to what I have been saying." Daniel's eyes searched hers. "I asked if you wanted our wedding reception to be held in the House of Refuge or maybe one of the empty houses around Fallow Creek."

"Oh." Vina gathered up a smile for him. "I don't think it matters where we hold our wedding reception. You can choose wherever you want it to be."

Daniel frowned and took her hand. "Tell me what's really bothering you, Vina. You've been distracted for a few days now."

She shrugged as though he was overreacting. What could she tell him? That she was getting cold feet?

"Vina, tell me what's on your mind. What is really going on with you?"

"What do you mean, Dan?"

He sighed loudly. "Every time we are together, I feel like you're somewhere else." He took her other hand and squeezed both. "You always seem troubled about something."

She bit her lip.

"Whenever I ask you what the problem is, you tell me it's nothing. 'Just a bit of stress about the wedding' is what you always say. But I think it's more than that. I need you to trust me and tell me what the problem is."

She didn't speak, and he groaned. "Won't you tell me what's wrong, Vina?"

She sighed deeply and turned away from him. How could she tell him that she was beginning to have serious doubts about marrying him? Their upcoming wedding, the constant talk about the children they would have in the future... it was all his dreams, what he'd always wanted. It wasn't really what she wanted.

She had been married before, and at only twenty-two she was a widow who was about to get married again. Her marriage to Mike had been a disaster. Even though she had not loved Mike when she married him and had done so because her parents had arranged everything, she had tried to give the marriage the best she could. Unfortunately, she had been in a losing battle.

Mike, of course was already married to someone else, but at the time she'd married him, that had meant nothing. Polygamy had been a common practice in Fallow Creek then. It should have occurred to her that he was a terrible person by the way he treated his first wife, Olivia. It had taken him almost wiping out everyone in the House of Refuge because of his jealousy and pride to realize the kind of person he was. She regretted ever being married to a horrible man like him. Though she had not been given a choice on who to marry at the time, she could have fought her parents' decision, or at the very least, protested. But she'd accepted things the way they were.

She felt guilty for being relieved when Mike had died, but she was glad she wasn't married to him anymore. Now that Fallow Creek had changed and she didn't have to get married if she didn't want to, she felt confused about her upcoming marriage to Daniel. It felt strange that she was soon going to enter an institution that had brought her nothing but regret and pain. She'd accepted Daniel's marriage proposal because she truly loved him and had been caught up in the moment, but she didn't think her love for him was enough to give up her freedom. Besides, she had plans for her life now that did not include being married. She wanted more. So much more. Plus Daniel had a jealous streak in him that sometimes reminded her of Mike.

"Vina! You are doing it again."

She tilted her head toward Daniel and frowned. "Doing what again?"

"You're looking at me, but I can see you are not really seeing me. It's like you're not here," Daniel said. He placed his hand on her arm and looked tenderly into her eyes. "Tell me what the problem is, Vina. Please."

Vina took a deep breath and searched his eyes. She pressed her lips together and said, "Dan, do you sometimes feel like you want more?" She stared at the House of Refuge in front of her and then turned around and looked at the gate behind her. Finally, she focused on Daniel again. "Do you ever feel like you want more than this?" She pointed at the House.

He frowned. "I don't understand. More than what exactly?"

"More than Fallow Creek. More than the life we're living here, the life we grew up living. Don't you want something different? More?"

He moved closer to her and placed his hands on her cheeks. Smiling tenderly, he said, "You're all I want, Vina. I want to marry you and have lots of children with you. I want to raise our children here in Fallow Creek with you by my side. That's all I've ever dreamed of since we were thirteen."

She shut her eyes briefly and then opened them again. Looking at the ground, she bit her lip and sighed wearily. She and Daniel had been close since they were thirteen. Before then she had seen him around town but hadn't paid any attention to him, but one day at the general chapel, their eyes had met while everyone was standing and singing a hymn, and she was immediately smitten. She could see from the way he looked at her that he felt the same way. They had gravitated toward each other after the service and when her late parents were not looking, she'd left the chapel with him.

They had become friends, and as the years went by, they became closer and closer until they were inseparable. But even then they could not confess their love for each other, which had grown in leaps and bounds. They understood their love would come to nothing and in fact would bring only heartbreak if they tried to explore it in any way.

When she turned eighteen and her father began to talk about her being old enough to get married, she knew she had to squash her feelings for Daniel. In Fallow Creek, she was not allowed to choose the man she would marry and there was no point in continuing to harbor feelings for him when she would soon be given away to another man. Even their friendship had to be broken, or they would both be left devastated when she got married. Especially Daniel. She began to avoid him after that, which clearly left him confused. He accosted her one day and, with a voice laden with emotion and hurt, asked her why she'd stopped speaking to him.

She told him why, but he refused to understand. However, she knew it was the right thing to do. She got married to Mike when she was nineteen, almost twenty. That was the year her parents died. Daniel had come to Mike's to commiserate, but Mike had refused to let him in. When she finally realized Mike was a horrible person and she didn't want to be married to him anymore, she had known Daniel was the right person to help her and Olivia escape

Mike's clutches.

Daniel, however, had left Fallow Creek during the mass exodus. She had sent a message to him asking him to return, and he had immediately come back. After that, they finally confessed their feelings for each other, and when Mike died, she knew she wanted to be with Daniel. But that was until she began to realize she had spent her whole life in this tiny town, wasting away. She wanted to be her own person and live her own life. Daniel, on the other hand, wanted the opposite of what she did now.

Slowly, she pulled away from him and said, "I have to go back into the House of Refuge, Daniel. Rachel might need me." She began to walk away, but he grabbed her hand and gently pulled her back.

"Rachel does not need you right now, Vina. I know that."

She frowned. "How do you know? She chose me to be her assistant so I could be there to help her out with whatever she needs. I can't assist her if I'm here with you."

He shook his head. "I know she doesn't need you because I saw her leave the House of Refuge with Keith some time ago. I think they said they were going to see Amanda Larson, who just returned to Fallow Creek. I don't think they will be back for a while."

Great! She had tried to use her job as Rachel's assistant to avoid telling Daniel what was really going on with her, but it hadn't worked. Right now, she did not feel like being with Daniel... or anyone else. All she wanted was to be alone with her thoughts.

"Let's take a walk," Daniel said. He wove his fingers through hers and gave her a bright smile.

She let him lead her down the road toward the town hall. They stopped in front of the town hall briefly and Vina listened impatiently as Daniel talked about the possibility of holding their wedding reception there. He kept talking about their wedding day and how excited he was to see her walk down the chapel aisle. They soon moved away from the front of the town hall, and he wound his arm around her waist as they strolled around Fallow Creek.

The more he spoke about how thrilled he was to soon be married to her, the more irritated she became. How could someone be content to remain in this tiny town, especially someone as young as Daniel? Someone who had spent his whole life here and who, like her, should be longing to see more of the world. Surely Daniel knew there was more to life than Fallow Creek.

She tuned him out as he continued to speak. Her dream was to explore the world, and maybe that meant that they would have to hold off on this marriage. She not only wanted to explore the world, she also wanted to find herself; to find what exactly it was she wanted to do and become in this life. Remaining here and simply getting married to Daniel and having a bunch of children would not help her do that. She slowly removed Daniel's hand from her waist.

He turned and looked at her. Frowning, he studied her face and said, "Am I boring you, Vina?"

She said nothing for a brief moment as she gazed at him. He looked slightly angry. Finally, she spoke.

"I'm sorry." She took his hand again. "I just have a lot on my mind."

"And that's why I asked you to share what exactly has been bothering you. You have a lot on your mind, and clearly, whatever it is has made you absent-minded. We will soon be husband and wife. We shouldn't hide things from each other. Tell me what has you so troubled. Maybe I can help." He stopped and turned her to face him fully. She remained silent, and he pleaded. "Please, Vina. Talk to me."

She reached out and ran her fingers through his beard. He was so handsome and completely devoted to her. She felt guilty for not feeling as devoted to him as he was to her.

His eyes softened, and he cupped her cheeks with his hands.

She felt a strange panic rise up in her as she realized he was about to kiss her. The last thing she wanted to do was to kiss him, which was really strange to her. They had kissed a hundred times since the day they realized they wanted to be together, and she had never felt like this before. For some weird reason, she felt as though she would be giving up on her new desire to find herself and surrendering her dreams to his if she kissed him. She backed away before their lips met, and he frowned again.

He looked really hurt, and once again she felt guilty for causing him pain. She quickly took his hand so he would not feel completely rejected.

They walked on in silence, and she was glad he didn't speak about their future marriage anymore. Clearly, he had finally realized she did not want to talk or even listen to him talk about their wedding day.

As they walked hand in hand around Fallow Creek, she studied their hometown. It was totally different from the town she had grown up in. For one, it was quieter. A few people who had left when Rachel took over from Dennis Hamilton had returned, but most had not. Many of the houses were still empty and the street she and Daniel were passing now was completely deserted. The empty town only increased her desire to leave. There was nothing here for her. She glanced briefly at Daniel and felt guilty again.

Daniel. Remember him, Vina. He was right here beside her. If she left Fallow Creek, she would also be leaving him.

But Daniel didn't have to remain here. Neither of them had to stay here any longer. They could explore the world together.

She glanced once more at him and sighed softly. On the other hand, it probably wasn't a good idea to leave town with Daniel, if indeed he agreed to leave. He wasn't interested in exploring the world like she was. All he wanted to do was get married. He would probably hold her back from going after her dreams of finding herself if he agreed to leave town with her, which he probably wouldn't.

He had a strong personality, and one of the things she was afraid of was that all her dreams and desires would be swallowed up in his; that she would be swallowed up in him if she got married to him. Not that she knew exactly what her dreams were, but that was the reason why she had to discover her purpose and find herself. Whatever she discovered her purpose to be would not be realized if she married Daniel. She would end up doing only what he wanted; never what she wanted. Even though he had never been as disparaging of women as most of the men who'd lived in Fallow Creek, and had become even less so after Rachel and Keith took over, he still had a few of those characteristics. He believed that he was to be the ruler of his household and his word was law.

Her mind traveled back to her marriage to Mike… or what she realized now wasn't a marriage, but an abominable union. One that should never have happened. Olivia, Mike's real wife had two children for Mike and all her life was devoted to her family. But Mike never really returned Olivia's love and mostly ignored her, especially after Vina married him.

Vina sighed. It was not like she believed Daniel would treat her the same way Mike had treated Olivia. They lived in a new Fallow Creek, where Rachel and Keith had purged from their minds most of the erroneous beliefs they had all been raised with. Plus Daniel truly loved her. Still, he was a man's man and the product of this town, at least the way this town used to be. She wasn't sure she could live with that. Not now.

They finally turned around and made their way back to the House of Refuge.

A short distance from the House, they met Rachel and Keith. They fell in step with the couple and the four of them walked toward the House of Refuge. Rachel asked Vina how her wedding plans were going, and Vina held back a weary groan. She was tired of talking about the wedding. Without looking at Rachel she said, "The wedding is still a month away."

Rachel chuckled. "The time goes by really fast. I promise. It might seem as though it's dragging on, but the wedding day will be here before you know it." Rachel put her arm around Vina's shoulder. "I felt almost as impatient as you when Keith and I were going to get married."

Vina wanted to scream. Why did everyone think her recent restlessness was because she couldn't wait to get married? She turned to look at Rachel and Keith. They had their arms around each other and looked totally in love. Rachel had had quite an adventure before she married Keith. She'd been married to Mike but had had the courage to leave him and marry the man of her dreams. She had risked everything by leaving Fallow Creek for Keith, but they had returned because the Lord told them to. Vina did not feel like God wanted her to remain in Fallow Creek and she'd had none of Rachel's adventures. She wanted to have hers before she got married.

Keith was laughing. "Rachel, remember we got married in a hurry. We didn't want to wait for long."

Rachel shook her head and smiled. "One month isn't very long." She looked at Vina and Daniel. "Though I know both of you have been waiting to be together for years."

"Maybe we should move our wedding date forward," Daniel said, sounding excited.

"No!" Vina shook her head and turned to Daniel. He looked disappointed, and she immediately added, "I need a full month to plan for our wedding."

"So you're not in a hurry then," Rachel said. "I

guess that's good. You will have enough time to talk about the kind of marriage you want to have. Though you will have a lifetime to talk about that."

They reached the gates to the House of Refuge, and as they walked in Vina faced Rachel. "Can I speak to you about something?"

"Of course," Rachel answered.

She looked back at Daniel and gave him a small smile. "I'll see you later."

Once again, he leaned toward her, clearly planning to kiss her. When she backed away, he winced, obviously hurt.

She sighed and turned away from him. Rachel held out her hand and she took it. She walked back to the house with Rachel.

The common room was empty, which was not unusual for this time of the day. Just like her, some of the women had left the house to stroll around Fallow Creek. Others had gone out of town to visit friends and relatives, which had not been possible before Rachel took over the running of the town from Dennis Hamilton. Rachel had changed everything for the better good and they were all grateful to her. She turned and gave Rachel a wide smile.

They climbed up the stairs and walked to Rachel and Keith's small apartment at the end of the wide hallway. The apartment had belonged to Margaret, the woman who had been in charge of the Restoration House before Rachel. Vina sat next to Rachel on the couch, and Rachel focused her gaze on her.

"So, tell me... what's wrong, Vina?" Rachel asked. "You look really troubled today."

Vina took a deep breath and began to speak. She told Rachel everything she had been feeling lately. How she wanted to find herself, to explore the world, to find exactly what she was put on this earth for.

"And you don't feel you can find it in Fallow Creek?" Rachel asked, and smiled sympathetically at her.

"No," Vina answered. "I feel trapped here. I mean, I enjoy working with you and I love Daniel, but I feel guilty because I'm not sure I want to marry him yet. I do want to marry him one day… but it's just that I have been through a bad marriage, and the thought of getting married again scares me."

Rachel gave her a knowing smile. "I understand. I was 'married' to Mike too. But I'm married to Keith now, and I love him with all my heart. I can't imagine not being married to him. Marriage can be such a beautiful thing if you are married to the right person. The kind of person you can't wait to wake up to every day."

Vina quickly said, "I want to marry Daniel…"

"Just not now," Rachel said, finishing her sentence. "I understand why you think you need to leave Fallow creek in order to find yourself, but I don't think it's necessary. If you think you must leave, however, I think you should talk to Daniel about it. I know how much he loves you. He might be willing to leave with you."

Vina shook her head. "You know how Daniel is. He won't want to leave."

"But he left Fallow Creek when I took over as leader of this town."

"That was because he was one of the leaders of

the security squad at that time and thought he had to leave. But you know he came back as soon as he knew he could. And if he realizes that we're not going to get married immediately or in the near future, he might think I'm rejecting him. I don't see him agreeing to leave town with me if he knows we won't be getting married anytime soon. When I tell him I don't want to get married now, he will be terribly hurt. I don't know how to tell him, Rachel."

"Just pray about it," Rachel said, and she smiled. "I know that sounds like the usual cliché advice we Christians give whenever there's a problem, but you know how important it is. Prayer works. Tell the Lord everything and after that talk to Daniel. Also search your heart and make sure leaving town is really what you want to do. What are you going to do when you leave? Where will you go? Do you have any relatives outside Fallow Creek?"

"Yes. My mother's sister and her husband," Vina said. "They moved to a town outside Prospect." She recalled her stern aunt and her husband, who had three more wives, and shuddered when she thought about living with them. "But I really don't want to go and live with them. Doing so would be even worse than staying here."

"So you don't have much money, you have no place to live, and right now you have no real qualifications to get a job."

Vina said nothing.

"What are you going to do for a living when you leave Fallow Creek? It's much harder out there than you think. Trust me. I know."

"Yes, Rachel, I know you do. That's why I'm talking to you about it. You survived when you left

Fallow Creek. Why can't I?"

"I was beyond lucky to have met Keith when I left town. He took care of me after I left Mike and gave me everything I needed. But that might not happen for you. Especially since you're still with Daniel. You wouldn't want to have another man take care of you unless you're planning to break up with Daniel. Are you?"

Vina looked away. She sighed when Rachel turned her back to face her.

"Are you planning to break up with Daniel?" Rachel asked again.

"No, I don't think so." She felt so confused. A few months ago she was sure that all she wanted was to marry Daniel and live here in Fallow Creek. But now, it wasn't the same. She wasn't sure her love for Daniel was strong enough to make staying here bearable. She might end up having to break up with him. Even thinking about it flooded her heart with pain.

Rachel took her hands and closed her eyes. She began to pray that God would give Vina wisdom to know what to do. When she finished, she smiled. "I'll keep praying for you. You have a very tough decision to make, but I would ask that you make the decision quickly. As much as Daniel will be hurt if you decide you don't want to be with him, it's better not to string him along. I hope that you will decide to stay with him, because I love you two together."

Vina nodded and hugged Rachel. "Thank you," she said.

Rachel smiled again. "I don't know how much help I've been. I pray you will make the right decision, Vina." She's squeezed Vina's hand encouragingly. "I guess I'm a bit selfish because, as I said, I like you and Daniel together. Most of all, I want my awesome assistant and friend to remain here in Fallow Creek with me."

Vina smiled brightly at Rachel. They had become close over the last few months, and she would miss Rachel if she decided to leave Fallow Creek. She would miss the House of Refuge as well and all the women here. In a way, she would also miss this town because this was where she'd grown up. But she could feel the desire to explore the world outside Fallow Creek growing in her even as she sat looking at Rachel. She wasn't sure where her desire would take her, but she knew that she could not remain here much longer.

She stood up after she had thanked Rachel again and left the apartment. She went back to her room and sighed with relief when she found her roommate, Lisa, was not there. She and Lisa were good friends, but she wanted to be alone and pray, just as Rachel had told her to do. She sat on her bed, closed her eyes and began to commit all her worries and concerns to the Lord. She did not pray for direction as Rachel had asked, because she was certain God wanted the same thing for her that she did — a life much bigger than marriage and kids... and tiny Fallow Creek. His dreams and purpose for her exceeded that.

She prayed instead that the Lord would reveal that purpose quickly. She also prayed that the Lord would give her the courage to tell Daniel how she felt. As for whether she would stay with Daniel or break up with him, she held off praying about that. The way everything unfolded and how God answered her prayers would determine whether she stayed with Daniel or not.

Once again guilt gripped her. She pictured Daniel's face; the way he would look if she broke off their engagement. He would be devastated.

She blinked as she immediately felt smothered. Without a doubt, this feeling would remain if she married Daniel now. She would feel smothered and trapped. She sighed in confusion. This was the decision she had to make — break up with him and be filled with guilt or marry him and live feeling like she was trapped in a tiny box. Whatever decision she made, it had to be made now, and she would have to live with the consequences of her decision.

She stood up from her bed to go to Daniel's house. She already knew what her decision was. She pictured him again, how he would feel when she told him. Sighing, she sat back down. She didn't have to say anything to him today. They would talk tomorrow, once she gathered her thoughts and decided on the right words to say.

TWO

Daniel Bacon walked into the House of Refuge and made straight for the stairs. He got to the top and paused, wondering whether to stop by Vina's room before he went to see Keith. When she'd left him yesterday, he'd felt like she wanted to be alone. But these days, it felt like she always wanted to be alone. It was why he was going to see Keith. Vina seemed to be pulling away from him more and more. It troubled him greatly. Whenever he brought up any talk about their wedding, she always grew quiet. Sometimes she looked troubled. If he did not know better, he would think she didn't want to marry him anymore.

Fear gripped him. Surely, she was not thinking about ending their relationship. She knew how much he loved her. He sighed as he walked past her room.

Worry and fear warred in him as he reached Keith and Rachel's apartment and knocked on the door. A few seconds later, it opened and Rachel peered at him.

"Hey, Daniel!" she smiled at him and opened the door fully. He walked in, and she pointed at the sofa and told him to sit down.

"Is Keith in?" he asked.

"Yes, he is," she answered. "Let me go get him for you." She left, and Daniel pressed his lips together as once again his heart thudded with worry. All he'd ever dreamed of since the first time he'd laid eyes on Vina was to marry her, but back then the possibility of that happening had been zero. When Mike had died and Rachel and Keith took over Fallow Creek, they had been able to declare their love for each other. She had been ecstatic when he'd asked her to marry him and had seemed thrilled when he'd told him he was looking forward to building a life with her right here in Fallow Creek. He wanted to help Rachel and Keith make his hometown the best possible place to be. But Vina's question yesterday about wanting more had shaken him to his roots. He couldn't help worrying that what she meant, added with her recent reticence, wasn't just that something random was bothering her, but that she was tired of him.

"Please, Lord, let it not be so," he whispered.

Keith walked into the living room and gave him a bright smile. "Daniel, how are you?"

Daniel was too troubled to smile back.

Keith sat next to him and put his hand on Daniel's shoulder. "You look awful, Daniel. What's the problem?" He frowned. "Did anything happen in town? Any threat of danger?"

"No," Daniel immediately said. The events of last year, when Mike Cadwell had nearly killed everyone in the House of Refuge, had not been forgotten. Most people in Fallow Creek, especially the women in the House of Refuge who had gone through it, were mostly sunny and happy again. But once in a while, when a dog barked too loudly or something heavy crashed to the floor, people jumped, with dread on their faces. Most thought the same thing he did — that it was a gunshot, that someone as wicked as Vina's ex-husband had shown up in town. Now he acted as the town sheriff, and it was his job to protect everyone.

It was a job he knew how to do well, having been a security squad leader for years during Dennis Hamilton's time. Once in a while, he carried his rifle with him, the one he'd been given as a member and leader of the security squad team. But most times, he left it in his house. He smiled slightly to put Keith at ease. There were no threats — at least not the kind that Keith was thinking about. The only threat was to his emotions and his dreams of a future with the love of his life.

"What is it then?" Keith asked.

"It's about Vina," Daniel answered. "Me and Vina. Our relationship is in trouble. I think Vina might be getting cold feet." Daniel bit his lip as pain ran through him. The thought that Vina might be on the brink of breaking off their engagement weighed heavily on him.

"What makes you think that?" Keith asked, looking intently at him. "I know how much Vina loves you. Are you sure you're not just feeling nervous about the wedding and reading too much into things? Vina might just be stressed out because of the wedding planning and other reasons that don't include your relationship. That doesn't mean she is thinking about breaking off your engagement."

"I don't know, Keith," Daniel said. "Every time I try to talk to her about the wedding and all the things we still have to do and plan, she either becomes strangely quiet or ignores whatever I say and changes the subject."

"Have you talked to her about it?" Keith asked. "She might not know she's doing it. Maybe she really does just have a lot on her mind."

"I was talking to her about the wedding yesterday, and she said something that has been bothering me. She asked if I wanted more than the wedding. More than our marriage here in Fallow Creek. I didn't really understand what she was saying at the time, and I told her that all I wanted was her. But that seemed to make her look even more troubled."

"I think you should sit down with Vina and have a heart-to-heart," Keith said. "You need to talk about your relationship and make sure you're both on the same page. But I know Vina loves you, and I don't think she has any plans to break off your engagement."

Daniel was scared to ask exactly what was in his heart, but he did anyway. "Did you ever feel like Rachel was having second thoughts about your relationship or your upcoming wedding when you were engaged?"

Keith frowned. He didn't say anything for a few seconds, and then he leaned back on his seat and sighed. "You know, I don't think I remember her being concerned about our engagement." He added quickly, "But Rachel and Vina are two different women, Daniel. Besides, the circumstances in which Rachel and I got married are totally different from yours and Vina's. You definitely need to sit down and have a serious discussion with her about all this. I'm sure talking it through will help you know exactly why she has been down and troubled. Maybe you will be able to help her."

"I'm just worried and concerned about her. I've tried so many times to get her to tell me what the problem is, but she always tells me it's nothing or she's stressed but will be okay. I don't know if she'll agree to sit and talk to me about what has been bothering her.

"Well, you will definitely need to insist that she talk to you. How else will you be able to help her if she doesn't?" Keith tilted his head toward Daniel. "Knowing you, I know you'll want the problem resolved quickly so you can move on. But you'll have to be patient with her and hear her out. Don't put it off until tomorrow. Get to the bottom of it now."

"I will," Daniel said, with grim determination. He wasn't sure how he would get Vina to open up to him and tell him exactly what the problem was, but he would have to try. He had to get her to talk to him today. He would move heaven and earth to try to help her with whatever was troubling her, but he had to know what it was first.

He left Keith's apartment and went immediately to Vina's room. Knocking on the door, he waited for her to open it. A few women passing in the hallway stopped to make small talk. Though he didn't feel like talking to anyone, he answered their questions politely. They wanted to know how he was doing and if he'd noticed any problems while on his daily patrol. When they moved on, he turned back to Vina's locked room door and frowned.

Where is Vina or her roommate? He knocked again and tapped his feet impatiently.

The door finally opened, and Vina appeared. She frowned as she looked at him, and his heart sank. She usually had a warm smile for him whenever he visited. This was new. Keith was wrong. Something more than wedding planning stress was troubling her. Hopefully, it wasn't him or their relationship.

"Can I come in?" he asked.

"No," she said. She turned around and looked back at her room and then faced him again. "Lisa is away."

He nodded in understanding. They had made a joint decision that they would not be alone in her room unless her roommate was there. It was too risky. They'd made the decision the very day Daniel had proposed to her. After they announced that they were engaged and everyone had congratulated them, they had talked for a long time in the common room about their future together as husband and wife.

Vina had yawned as it was getting late and told him she was tired. He had walked her to her room. When she'd invited him in, he had sat down beside her on the bed and they had continued chatting. They were alone as Lisa was out of town visiting relatives.

Before long they were kissing passionately. Their passion for each other had grown so intense as they kissed that Vina had pulled him down on the bed beside her. He'd known they had to stop or they would be in trouble and weakly tried to pull away, but she held on to him.

They continued kissing and then, just as it was getting out of hand, Lisa opened the door and they quickly separated. Vina smiled at Lisa, guilt clearly written on her face, and he was sure he looked just as guilty as she did. When he'd suggested the next day that they never be alone in a room or house unless someone else was there, she'd immediately agreed. Now though, it seemed as though she did not want him in her room, not just because her roommate wasn't there, but simply because she did not want to talk to him.

"Can we go and talk somewhere?" he asked.

She looked reluctant as she glared at him. She finally sighed. "Okay then." She closed her room door firmly and led the way down the stairs to the common room.

They sat in the large common room where a few other women sat chatting. Daniel shifted closer to Vina on the loveseat near the entrance to the room. When she moved slightly away from him, he sighed loudly.

Oh, Lord, please help me. I am about to lose her. "We have to talk, Vina."

"Yes. I agree. I also have something to tell you."

Fear gripped him again. She looked so serious. What did she want to tell him? Maybe that she had grown tired of their relationship and wanted them to break up. Before she could speak, he said, "Can I go first?"

"Okay."

He began. "Vina, you've been really troubled about something for a while now. I keep asking you what the problem is, but you never tell me. I know the problem isn't with our relationship, but we seem to be growing apart lately and I'm afraid that if we don't get to the bottom of this soon, it might be too late. That scares me. I need you to talk to me."

She turned away, and he frowned. "I am not going to take no for an answer. And don't tell me nothing is wrong because I know something is definitely wrong." He took her hand, and when she did not pull it away, he sighed with relief. He wove his fingers through hers and looked into her eyes. "Please, Vina, tell me what's wrong. Are you worried about the wedding or is the stress of the wedding planning getting to you? You know we don't have to have a big wedding and invite everyone in Fallow Creek. I can talk to Keith and Rachel and they will make sure that we have our wedding with just the two of us. Keith will marry us and Rachel will explain to the women later why we wanted it that way."

"It's not stress, Daniel," she said.

"Then what is it, love? If the wedding planning is too much for you, I could take over completely. In fact, I can do all the planning. I just want you to be happy." He smiled at her. "I can't wait to marry you, Vina."

She pulled her hand from his and snapped. "I just said it's not stress from the wedding planning!"

He blinked in surprise, and she pressed her lips together.

"Vina, this is unlike you. Please tell me what's wrong. I am not going to let you go until you do."

She looked at him again. "I don't think I want to get married."

Daniel gasped. His heart crashed down to his feet and he briefly shut his eyes. *No, Lord. This can't be happening.*

She added, "I mean, I want to marry you one day, just not now."

Daniel opened his eyes and looked at her. "When then, Vina? When do you want us to get married? I can wait." He did not want to wait, but he would because it was better than completely losing her. Hopefully, he would not have to wait too long. Hopefully, she would let him help her sort out whatever confusion and trouble she was going through that had led to her wanting to postpone their wedding date.

"I don't really know when we'll get married, Dan, but it won't be in the near future."

Daniel leaned back in his seat as pain and worry ran through him. The way she'd just told him that she didn't know when she wanted them to get married sounded like she was saying she did not want them to get married at all. He took a deep breath and asked, "How far in the future are we talking about? Three or four months?" That was as far as he could bear.

She shook her head

He grimaced. "Six months?"

"More, Dan."

Surely she couldn't be asking them to postpone the wedding to a year from now. He said slowly, "You want us to get married next year?"

Please Lord, let it not be so, he prayed. But then he knew if that was what she wanted to do, he would have no choice but to agree. It was definitely better than her breaking up with him.

She shook her head again. "Farther into the future than that. I'm not sure when I want to get married. Right now, I want to find myself and explore the world." She turned away from him and then faced him again. "I don't want to live in Fallow Creek anymore. I think I will leave town soon and see what the world has to offer." She looked away again.

He could not breathe. She didn't know when she wanted to marry him and she wanted to leave Fallow Creek. She was actually saying in a roundabout way that she didn't want him at all. His worst fears were coming to pass. Even though she wasn't saying it directly, she wanted to break up with him. Anger burned in him, and he struggled to suppress it. Since they'd gotten together after Mike's death, she had made him a better man and his quick temper had subsided greatly. Before then, when he was in the squad, he had been quick to lash out at anyone who offended him. And the worst thing was that his quick temper had not been curtailed in any way but actually encouraged, because as a leader in the security squad it came in handy. But he had left that behind. Falling in love again with Vina had helped him put his anger away. Now, he could not help feeling angry because he felt like she had betrayed him. But the last thing he needed now was to let his temper get the better of him. If she was telling him in a roundabout way that she wanted to break up with him, she would say it directly if he let his anger take over and raised his voice at her — something he had never done.

Finally, he managed to get control of himself and said, "What do you mean by 'wanting to find yourself,' Vina? I don't understand."

Vina looked him in the eye. "I mean I want to discover why I am on this earth. I want to live a full life, and I don't think it can happen in this small town. I want to see the world, and I want to live my dream." She chuckled. "If I can figure out what exactly my dream is."

He blinked and stared at her. She was directly saying that he was the obstacle to her finding herself and living her dreams. Again he felt angry but tamped it down. "We don't have to postpone our wedding because you want to find yourself and live your dream. You can do all that right here in Fallow Creek. You don't have to leave."

"Yes, I do," she told him.

Daniel glared at her. "So you want to leave me? What about our love for each other, our relationship, our wedding? And where are you going to go if you leave Fallow Creek, Vina?"

"I don't know," she answered. "But I can't keep staying in this small town."

He narrowed his eyes in anger. "All you talk about is your dream and that you want to leave, but you haven't answered my question. You haven't told me what I should do about my broken heart if you walk away. How do I bear missing you every day?"

She sighed. "I don't know, Daniel. What you're saying is that it's not important for me to find why I was put on this earth. I love you, Dan but…"

He cut in. "But not enough to stay here with me. Not enough to marry me."

"I didn't say I don't want to marry you, but…"

"But you don't know when. And you don't mind leaving me here while you go off to discover yourself." His anger erupted. "All I want — all I've ever wanted — is to marry you, but that isn't what you want, is it? What you are actually saying is that you don't want to be with me, isn't it? Just come out and say it, Vina."

Daniel groaned after he'd spoken. Why on earth had he just said that? He opened his mouth to say something else that would distract her from his last statement, but Vina shook her head.

"Okay, Daniel. No, it's not what I want. Is that what you want to hear? I love you, but I don't know if that is enough for me to marry you right now. Like I said before, I will get married to you eventually, but I don't know when that will be."

Daniel laughed harshly. "Do you hear yourself, Vina? So you want me to wait here for you, while you gallivant around the world or wherever it is you want to go."

"I am not saying that."

"So what are you saying?" he stared straight into her eyes. "Are you saying you don't mind if I find someone else?" He winced after he'd spoken and mentally berated himself. *Daniel, please, just stop talking. You are making everything worse.*

She looked like he had just slapped her, and then she squared her shoulders and nodded her head. "Is that what you want to do, Dan? If it is, then you can go ahead and find someone else!" She stood and stormed off.

What have you done, Daniel? He had let his anger get the better of him and had said things he didn't mean. Of course he didn't want someone else. He wanted only her. Now he risked losing her forever. He immediately stood up and went after her.

She was already at the top of the stairs when he reached the bottom. "Vina," he called out. "Please stop." He raced up the stairs to catch up to her before she could enter her room. When he did, he took hold of her arms and turned her around to face him.

She glared up at him. "Please, let me go."

"I'm sorry, Vina. You know you're the only girl I want." He still didn't understand why she wanted to leave, and he was terribly hurt at the fact that she didn't love him enough to marry him now, but he wanted to understand her point of view.

"Daniel, you know I've been married before, and the thing is… I don't want to rush into another marriage."

"But we've known each other for so long," he said. "We won't be rushing. Besides, I am not like Mike Cadwell. You know that."

"I want to explore the world and find my life's purpose before settling down. It would be great if you waited, but I would never insist that you do."

He felt weak with hurt and worry again. He really had to do something before he lost her forever. "I will wait as long as it takes, Vina. I know it will be hard, but if you want to find yourself and explore the world, I will wait for you."

She stared at him for a long moment, and then she said, "I don't know how long it will take for me to discover myself or my dreams and, like I told you, I don't even know what my dream is yet. I will have to find out. It would not be fair of me to ask you to wait, Dan."

"I want to wait," he said to her.

She sighed loudly.

He ignored the wary expression on her face and reached out to hug her. He was not surprised when she backed away.

"I'll see you tomorrow," she said, and then walked away from him. She reached her room, opened the door, and went inside without looking back.

He stood in the middle of the hallway, his emotions boiling as he stared at her door. She didn't want to marry him.

"Not now," she'd said. Some day in the distant future. She did not think it was fair to ask him to wait for her, she'd said. But in fact, she was effectively breaking up with him.

I won't let her, he said to himself. Not unless she came out and told him directly that she did not want him anymore, that she did not want them to be together. As long as she had not said that, he would hold on. And just like he'd promised her, he would wait for her to come back to him, no matter how long it took.

THREE

Daniel opened the gate of the House of Refuge just as Keith stepped outside the door. He smiled and hurried up to Keith.

"Hey, Daniel! Are you going to see Vina?"

"No, I spoke to her yesterday evening. I don't think she even wants to talk to me right now. I came to see you, to talk to you about her, but if you are heading out, I will come back later."

"No, you can walk with me," Keith said, and began walking away from the House of Refuge. Daniel fell into step beside him, and Keith added, "I am on my way to see Dennis Hamilton."

Daniel frowned. "Dennis Hamilton! You want to visit him after everything he did to you and Rachel? Why?"

"Trust me, I never feel like going to visit him whenever the Lord tells me to, but I obey the Lord and go anyway. Besides, Dennis is a changed man now."

"I don't know how changed that man can be. I don't trust him."

"But you worked for him as one of the leaders of his infamous security squad," Keith said. "If you don't like him, why did you do that? Why did you join his squad?"

Daniel sighed, remembering his time as a leader of the security squad. That had been just over a year ago, but it was a time he didn't want to remember. He said to Keith, "First, it wasn't like I had a choice to join the security squad. Dennis Hamilton hand-picked whoever he thought would be a good addition to the squad, and we were made to understand that he was our leader and could not question him."

"But you enjoyed being in the security squad and being a leader of that group," Keith said. "At least that was what I thought from watching you."

Daniel shrugged. "Well, maybe I did enjoy it… at least a little. But I'm definitely glad I'm not part of that kind of group anymore. Most of all, I am glad that Dennis Hamilton isn't the leader of Fallow Creek any longer. I just wish you and Rachel had not allowed him back into this town. He's dangerous, that man. Like you said, I know him well since I worked closely with him as a leader of the squad. You never know what he's planning."

"As I told you, I think he's a changed man. I've been visiting him, talking to him about God because he wants to know how to build a close relationship with Christ. You know some of the old squad members live with him in the house Taylor lets him use. They also join our small prayer meetings."

Daniel frowned. He wanted to tell Keith to be careful but decided to let it go for now. "Well, I didn't come to talk to you about Dennis Hamilton."

"You came to talk to me about Vina, right? Did you have that talk with her?"

"I did," Daniel said. He clearly recalled the discussion he'd had with Vina the day before, and his heart flooded with worry again. Right now, their relationship was hanging by a thin thread. He had to do everything in his power to change that before the thread snapped and he lost her permanently.

"What did you decide to do?" Keith asked, looking inquisitively at Daniel.

"Nothing," Daniel said. "We ended up fighting, and she stormed off. I went up to her to apologize, but it seems she doesn't want us to be together." He pressed his lips into a thin line and took a deep breath to try to let go of his anxiety.

"Oh no, I'm sorry, Daniel. What exactly did you say to her?"

"I asked why she was always so troubled lately, and she told me she wasn't ready to get married right now. She said the same things she had told me before — that she wanted to find herself and explore the world, that she didn't want to stay in Fallow Creek. When I asked when exactly she wanted us to get married, she said she didn't know. I was angry and asked if she expected me to wait forever for her, and then I said something stupid. I asked if she expected me to find someone else. She got angry and said I didn't have to wait at all. She said I could move on and find someone else if I couldn't wait for her. That broke my heart."

Keith stopped briefly and put his hand on Daniel's shoulder. "I'm sorry," he said.

Daniel shook his head. "I'm not going to give up

on her or our relationship. That's why I came to talk to you. She didn't say directly that she wanted us to break up, so I told her that I would wait as long as it took. But I really don't want to. I want to marry her now. I don't want her to leave Fallow Creek."

"So what do you plan to do? It's not like you can hold her physically down to prevent her from leaving."

"I want to try to find a way to show her how much she means to me. I haven't really given her anything special since we got together after Mike's death. I haven't even asked if she has *a wedding dress*, but I don't think she does."

Keith looked at Daniel thoughtfully. "I think I heard her talking to Rachel about that. But it was weeks ago. I can't remember exactly what she said."

Daniel stared curiously at Keith. "Don't you remember anything they talked about?"

"Umm… I think I remember her telling my wife that she was going to wear her old wedding dress. The one she wore when she married Mike. She said she would adjust it and change it somehow so it would be different."

Daniel shook his head slowly. "No, no, that will not do. Maybe that was one of the reasons why she was so hesitant to marry me. What bride would want to get married in her old wedding dress, especially when she'd married a man as evil as Mike? I was thinking about getting Vina a more expensive engagement ring than the one I gave her when I proposed, but maybe a brand new wedding dress will be better."

"I think she would love that," Keith said.

"Yes, I think so, too." Daniel smiled, picturing

Vina in a white wedding dress, looking as beautiful as ever, walking down the aisle of the small chapel near the town hall. His heart swelled with love for her even though she wasn't there. With everything in him, he wanted to make her his wife, and he would. He was not going to let anything come between them. But the problem was that he didn't have money right now to buy her the kind of dress she deserved. "I need to ask a favor, Keith."

"Anything."

"I want to buy Vina that beautiful wedding dress that she deserves, but I don't have money to buy it right now." He had been paid wages as a member and leader of the security squad, but he'd decided that since the money had been made out of terrorizing and forcing people to conform to ungodly rules, he would give everything he'd saved to the poor. He hadn't done that yet, but he planned to. Now that the squad had been disbanded, he had been living on the stipend that Keith and Rachel paid him for his job as the unofficial town sheriff. He never lacked for food and the basic things he needed, but a wedding dress, especially the type he had in mind, was a luxury he could not afford right now. He felt ashamed about asking Keith for money to buy his bride-to-be a wedding dress, but he had no choice. He would pay Keith back when he could.

"About how much do you need?" Keith asked.

"I'm not sure how much a wedding dress will cost. Can you help me ask Rachel without letting Vina know? I would love for it to be beautiful but affordable so I can pay you back as soon as possible."

"Okay. I'll ask Rachel and get back to you," Keith said. "Don't worry about paying back the money,

Dan. It can be my wedding gift to you and Vina."

Daniel hugged Keith and smiled at him in gratitude. It was the first good news he'd heard this week. "Thank you so much, Keith." He looked down at the ground as they walked, feeling too ashamed to ask his next request.

"Out with it, Daniel!" Keith said. "You have something else to ask me, don't you?"

Daniel sighed. "How is it that you know what I am thinking before I say it? Did the Lord tell you this one as well?" He grinned.

Keith laughed. "The Lord doesn't have to tell me anything for me to know that you have something else to say. You have something to ask me, and you're too embarrassed to do so. Tell me what it is."

"Okay. You and Rachel have been so good to me, Keith. You did not have to pay me monthly to be the town's sheriff as Fallow Creek is so peaceful and actually needs no policing..."

"But..."

"But if my plan goes well, Vina and I will soon get married. I need to provide for her and for the children we will have in the future by God's grace. I want to ask for a raise. I know I don't really deserve it as I don't have much to do here. There has been no threat or any kind of crime in Fallow Creek since last year when Mike died, but I..." He stopped talking as he realized how wrong his request sounded. It had been a good idea when he was thinking about it before he came to Keith. Now it sounded ridiculous. He was asking for a raise for a job he hardly did and for which he was only paid because of the goodwill of Keith and his wife. He said quickly, "I will understand if you can't give me a raise."

Keith stopped walking and placed his hand on Daniel's shoulder again. "Listen, Daniel, you might not think that your job as sheriff is important, but I want you to know it is. You certainly helped us greatly when Mike wanted to wipe out everybody in the House of Refuge, and you definitely have the skills to protect everyone here... at least to show us what to do in order to protect ourselves. So I will grant your request and increase your wages as you've asked."

Daniel's heart soared with joy, and he smiled. "Thank you so much, Keith," he said. You and Rachel have been so kind to me."

"I understand the need to provide for your family, Daniel. Whenever you do get married." Keith frowned slightly. "You really need to make sure that you and Davina are on the same page. Are you sure she will appreciate the wedding dress you buy for her, especially after she told you she doesn't want to get married yet? You know you cannot force her to do what she doesn't want to do. She might feel offended that you bought her a wedding dress. It might seem like you disregarded everything she said and went ahead with what you wanted."

Daniel's heart began to pound as he thought about what Keith had just said. Would Vina think that he didn't care about her opinion if he bought her a wedding gown? He did want to show her how much he loved her and try to get her to change her mind about postponing their wedding, but it was only because he did not want to lose her. And he knew she loved him, too. Even if they were not getting married next month, hopefully, with all he planned to do for her, she would agree that the best thing was for them to get married in the near future. If not next month then at most in three months' time.

Keith was staring curiously at him, and he said, "I think she will understand that it's a gesture of love. I don't think she will see it as me trying to impose my will on her."

"Ok then," Keith said. "I'll let Rachel know about your request, and then I'll tell you what she said."

They walked on in companionable silence until they reached the old pharmacy, which was now empty. The house where Dennis Hamilton now lived was a short distance away. Daniel stopped and told Keith this was as far as he would go with him near the viper's, Mike Cadwell's, dwelling. Keith went on while Daniel turned around.

For a brief moment, as he walked, he thought about going to see Vina at the House of Refuge, but he changed his mind. A little distance would help Vina feel less stifled by their relationship. A thread of pain ran through his heart as he thought about what she had said about not wanting to get married to him yet. Hopefully, his gift to her would help make her know that marrying him was not such a bad idea. Now, all he had to do was wait for Keith to get back to him. He hoped it would be today.

Some hours later, he was in his small living room when his phone rang. He looked at it. It was Keith calling, probably to let him know what Rachel had said about the wedding dress.

"Hey, Keith!" he said as he answered the phone call.

"I spoke to Rachel, and she agreed with me that

giving a wedding dress as a gift for you to give to Vina is a good idea." He paused for a few seconds and then went on. "Actually, she said she was not going to give you the money."

Daniel frowned in confusion. "I don't understand. I thought you said that Rachel told you it was a good idea to give me the money as a gift."

"No... I said Rachel told me it was a good idea to give you a wedding dress as a gift. She also said it was a bad idea to let you go wedding dress shopping for Vina, as you will not know the right kind of dress to buy. She said she would help you buy the dress today, box it up, and wrap it before giving it to you so you don't see it. You can present it to Vina after that." Keith chuckled. "Rachel said she knows exactly where she can get a dress that will be so beautiful that Vina will want to get married in it immediately."

"Oh, that's great!" Daniel grinned. "Rachel always has the best solutions for everything. You said she told you she would get the dress today?"

"Actually, she has already left Fallow Creek to buy the dress in a small shop in the town outside Prospect. You know how Rachel is. Once she has a plan, she puts it into motion immediately."

Daniel laughed. "Well, remind me to talk to Rachel anytime I need something important done quickly. She's definitely the woman for the job."

Keith laughed along with him and said, "She should be back from her wedding dress shopping in a few hours. You can come by this evening to get it."

Daniel thanked Keith profusely again. "What would I do without you and Rachel?" he said. "You are lifesavers."

For the next few hours, he went on his daily patrol around Fallow Creek, looking for any kind of threat or suspicious activity, even though there was never any. He walked past the House of Refuge a couple of times and each time he thought about going in to see Vina. But he always changed his mind. It was not a good idea. Vina would probably send him away or refuse to see him after the discussion they'd had yesterday. He would wait until he had the wedding dress with him in order to surprise her.

The hours seemed to go by slowly, and he kept watching out for Rachel every time he walked past the House of Refuge, hoping she would come back quickly with Vina's wedding dress.

He was patrolling the border when Rachel's new white Prius crawled toward him. His heart soared with joy and relief, and he grinned.

She stopped just before she reached him and stuck her head out the window. "I see you're here at the edge of town waiting for me." She shook her head and chuckled. "So impatient, Daniel."

He laughed. "And I can see that you're still going at two-point-five miles per hour even though you learned how to drive years ago."

"Better safe than sorry," Rachel said, grinning. She whispered, "I have your package."

He looked back to see if anyone was coming and took the wrapped package from her. He laughed as he tucked it under his arm. "Why are we acting as though we are secret agents on some covert mission?"

"Get into the car, Daniel, and I will drive you to

the House of Refuge. You can give your beautiful fiancée her gift when we get there."

"Yes, ma'am," he saluted, and then got into the car.

Rachel drove the short distance to the House of Refuge, and Daniel took the wedding dress, which was boxed up and neatly wrapped, out of the backseat. He stepped out of the car and followed Rachel into the house. Hopefully, Vina was in her room and would want to see him because if she refused to speak with him, he would not be able to surprise her today. He blinked as an idea came to him. Turning to Rachel, who was climbing up the stairs behind him, he said, "I have a plan, but I need your help. I'll tell you when we get to your apartment."

At the apartment, he asked her if she could send for Vina. "We had an argument the last time I saw her. She might refuse to see me if I go to her room."

Rachel frowned at him, but she nodded. She picked up her phone from the coffee table and called Vina. After she told Vina she had something to show her in her apartment, she ended the call and looked at Daniel again. "I hope your plan to surprise her will help you iron out the troubles you have in your relationship."

A few minutes later, the front door opened and Vina walked in. When she saw him, she frowned deeply, but the frown melted off her face as quickly as it had appeared. "Dan, you're here."

"Yes, Vina." He stood, and went to her, hiding the wedding dress behind his back. "I have a surprise for you." He looked at Rachel and then turned back to Vina.

"So Rachel is not the one who wants to see me. It's you, Dan."

"Yes." He brought out the package from behind his back and handed it to her. "My gift to you, Vina."

She took it from him and stared at it. "What is this?"

"Open it," he told her.

She began to unwrap it with a curious expression on her face. She put the wrapping paper away and carried the box to the sofa. She sat and opened the box, and then she blinked rapidly. Her mouth dropped open and she gasped. She brought out the wedding dress from the box and stared at it, speechless. Covering her mouth with her hand, she looked at Daniel as her eyes filled with tears.

Daniel held his breath, praying she liked his gift and would not be offended by it. She seemed to like it, but...

"Daniel, it's beautiful!" Tears ran down her cheeks, and Daniel smiled knowing they were tears of joy. "It's lovely."

Daniel's heart soared as she walked over and hugged him tightly. "Thank you," she said. "Nobody has ever given me something so beautiful." She pulled away from him and went to pick up the dress again. She gazed at it and said, "I still have my first wedding dress. Mike had all the money, but he didn't even bother to buy anything half as special as this."

Daniel said, "I have to admit that Rachel helped me pick the dress."

Vina looked at Daniel again, and he noticed the question in her eyes. He knew exactly what she wanted to ask him. Where did he get the money to buy a dress this beautiful and clearly expensive? He took a deep breath and sighed with relief when she turned away again and did not ask her question.

Rachel stood and went to hug her. "It's a beautiful dress, Vina. Daniel truly loves you, and he wants you to have the best wedding you could possibly have."

Daniel held his breath again, worried. Would she think he was trying to manipulate her into marrying him? He did not want her to marry him out of pressure. When she came and threw her arms around him again and kissed his cheek, he smiled brightly and the worry fled.

"I love you, Dan," she said. "I'm so sorry for making you feel like I didn't. Because I really do. And I want to marry you."

Daniel's heart soared with joy again, and he kissed her. He was thrilled beyond words when she returned his kiss. She pulled back slightly and smiled at him. "I can't wait to try the dress on." She pulled away completely, squealed, and snatched up the dress from the sofa. She began to leave the living room with it and Rachel followed her out.

Daniel sat on the sofa and couldn't help grinning happily. And then he sobered some when a slightly troubling thought crossed his mind. He'd wanted her to say she would marry him now rather than in some unknown future, and that she would stay in Fallow Creek. But she had said none of that. He sighed. Still, she had told him she loved him and she'd seemed very happy and definitely wanted their relationship to continue. He had to be satisfied with that, at least for now. Hopefully, he could show more gestures of his love for her in the coming days, and in due time she would come to realize that all she needed was here in Fallow Creek. Him and the children that God would bless them with in the future.

FOUR

Vina furiously jotted down the list of items Rachel was dictating to her. Items she had to buy for the House. Since she'd become Rachel's assistant four months ago, she had spent hours every day with her and Keith in their home, just like today, and had become very fond of them. She counted Rachel as not just a friend, but an older sister.

As she wrote down the things Rachel wanted her to purchase, her mind circled around Daniel and the beautiful wedding dress he'd given her yesterday. She had to speak to Rachel about that. In the euphoria of receiving such a beautiful and thoughtful gift from Daniel, she had probably given him the impression that she'd changed her mind about leaving Fallow Creek.

She had definitely not. She just didn't know when exactly she would leave. Already, she had started to save money from the wages Rachel paid her as her assistant. Soon, it would be enough to leave this town and discover other places. Rachel, who she also considered her mentor, had made a successful life for herself outside Fallow Creek before she'd finally returned here. If Rachel could do it, then she could as well.

"Vina! Why are you so distracted today?" Rachel stared at her.

"I'm sorry," Vina said.

"You stopped writing about a minute ago. You need to buy another carton of milk and also detergent. We are running out."

"What about olive oil?" Vina asked. "The cook mentioned yesterday that the one I bought last week was finished. And she also said she needed fresh spices."

"Okay, write them down as well," Rachel said.

She wrote down the things she needed to buy for the cook and then turned to look at the front door when someone opened it. Susan, a freckled-faced redhead with a constant smile walked in. She had entered Rachel's apartment as usual without knocking. Every time she did, she was scolded for it and apologized. She always said she would not do it again, but she always forgot and did the same thing next time.

Rachel chuckled. "I've told you to knock before entering my apartment, Susan. You know that this is a private home, don't you?"

Susan apologized, an impish smile on her face. She started to back away but Rachel waved her back in. "You're already in the house," Rachel said. When she came in again, Rachel asked, "What is it, Susan?"

"There is a man at the gate who says he wants to see you and Keith," Susan answered. "I've never seen him before, so I think he's from out of town."

"A stranger," Rachel murmured. "Did he say what he wanted to speak to me and Keith about?"

"He only said it was something important."

"Is he alone, or did he come with someone else?"

Vina looked at Susan, who was now looking at the ceiling with a thoughtful expression on her face. Vina understood why Rachel was asking all these questions. Since the frightening events that took place last year with Mike and his hired goons, everyone in town, especially the women in the House of Refuge, had become wary of strangers.

"I think he is alone," Susan said.

Rachel pressed her lips tightly together and then told Susan to let the stranger in. "Tell him to wait in the common room. I'll be downstairs soon."

Susan left, and Rachel continued to dictate to Vina everything she needed to buy later in the day. Since the two stores where everyone in Fallow Creek did their shopping had closed down after most people left, they had to go to Prospect or the next town to purchase everything they needed for the House. Most of the time, Hailey, the cook, bought the ingredients she needed to prepare their food. Rachel's former assistant, Cecilia, bought the other things needed in the House, as she had always done so when Margaret was in charge of the Restoration House.

But last month, Vina had had to go to Prospect to purchase some things when Hailey had fallen ill. Since then, she had done the shopping for the entire House. Whenever she had to leave Fallow Creek to go to Prospect, she was excited, especially those times when Rachel came with her and she got to ride in Rachel's new car. She always imagined them both as women of the world, independent and free to do whatever they wanted. That was a privilege she hadn't grown up with, but now enjoyed. Those trips probably added to her desire to leave Fallow Creek and explore the world; because why go only as far as Prospect now that she had the freedom to come and go as she pleased. As excited as she was for another opportunity to leave Fallow Creek, if only for a few hours, she was also a bit nervous as she was going alone today. But it would be a nice practice for her for when she finally left Fallow Creek for good.

She thought about Daniel and how sad he had been when she'd told him. The usual guilt she felt whenever she thought about Daniel and leaving him rose up in her, but she pressed it down. She had to live her life, and he had to live his. If he could wait for her, she would come back one day and they would get married. But if not, then there was nothing she could do about it. She would miss him terribly, but without a doubt, she would regret it if she did not try to find herself and what her purpose in life was.

Rachel stood up and straightened her dress. "Will you wait here for me, Vina, or will you come along?"

Vina stood up. She was curious to know more about the stranger who had come to see Rachel and Keith. "I'll come with you."

"'Kay! Wait here. Let me go and get Keith and Emily. You can help me watch Emily while Keith and I speak with our out-of-town visitor."

She left the living room, and Vina walked to the door to wait for her. Her mind went back to Daniel again. She would have to make it clear to him sometime today that she had not changed her mind about leaving Fallow Creek. She was not looking forward to that. The look on his face when she'd told him she was going to leave and wasn't sure she wanted to get married now remained etched in her mind. She didn't want him to try to convince her to marry him right now. A month was too soon to get married. His remark that he could find someone else if she was away for too long had left her shaken. She had been angry and had told him he could go ahead and find someone. She regretted saying that, but she would not be surprised if it happened. After all, she didn't expect him to stay alone forever waiting for her.

The thought that he might move on when she left frightened her a little.

You know he loves you too much to do that.

She bit her lip. He did love her a lot — sometimes she thought a bit too much. Still, there was only so much time anyone could wait before they had to move on in a relationship. She would have to accept that.

Rachel and Keith came out of their bedroom. Rachel carried Emily in her arms.

Vina smiled at the toddler, who was rubbing her eyes. Clearly, Emily had just woken up. She looked slightly grumpy and terribly cute. Vina felt a tug in her heart. When would she have her own little one?

She immediately pushed the thought away. She wasn't ready to have a child of her own. She reached out eagerly and took Emily from Rachel. Kissing Emily's chubby cheeks, she smiled and said to the child, "How are you today, Em?"

Emily turned her face away and rested her head on Vina's shoulder.

Vina laughed. "So I'm not good enough to talk to, but my shoulder is good enough to act as your pillow, right?"

The toddler snorted as though Vina had said something incredibly stupid. Her parents laughed out loud, and Vina shook her head and chuckled.

Vina followed Rachel and Keith out of their apartment and climbed down the stairs slowly as she was still carrying Emily.

They walked into the common room, which was empty except for a man sitting at the far end of the room. Vina's heart skipped a beat when he turned in their direction. He was a handsome man, more handsome than anyone she'd ever seen. He looked about ten years older than her, which meant he was probably in his early thirties. He had dark blond hair, and as she reached him, she noticed his eyes were startling blue. He was not dressed like most of the men who lived or had lived in Fallow Creek who constantly wore flannel shirts and plain, dark pants. He wore a crisp white shirt underneath a black jacket. She felt herself blushing when she noticed the shirt buttons were open halfway, revealing part of his chest. This was something else that no man in Fallow Creek ever did. The visitor was not only handsome, he was mysterious… at least to her. His shirt was unbuttoned to his chest and he had on a black jacket. She blushed again when he looked at her, and then she quickly turned away.

He shook hands with Rachel and Keith. When he held out his hand to Vina, she nervously held on tightly to Emily with one hand, and shook his extended hand with her left.

Rachel and Keith sat on the sofa facing the stranger while Vina went to sit on the couch near the door so she would not be intruding on their private conversation. But she could still hear them clearly from her seat.

She played with Emily, who sat on her lap, while she listened to what the handsome stranger was saying to Keith and Rachel.

"I learned about this place from a friend of a friend," he said. "When he told me about Fallow Creek and the life here and showed me a few pictures, I really couldn't believe there was such a place. I had to see it with my own eyes. I've gone around town and I really love what I see."

Rachel and Keith looked at each other and then at the man, curiosity shining in their eyes.

"The town is a bit deserted, though." The man looked up with a thoughtful expression. "I wasn't expecting that. But that will probably work better for what I have in mind."

Rachel frowned and Keith leaned forward and studied the stranger's face. "What exactly do you have in mind?" Rachel asked, suspicion creeping into her face.

The man laughed softly, causing Vina's heart to thud. She sighed, angry at herself for reacting to this man the way she was. *Get a hold of yourself, Vina.* It was not as if she had not seen a handsome man before. Her Daniel was handsome after all. Though not as handsome as this stranger.

"I'm sorry," the man said. "All I have seen and learned about this town has left me so excited, I didn't properly introduce myself and tell you why I am here. I apologize." His smile widened. "My name is Trent Radar. I'm a movie producer and director, and I've been looking for the perfect setting for a movie I just started shooting. We have already shot several scenes, but there are scenes that call for a particular kind of setting. We scouted several locations in the country, but we didn't find exactly what we were looking for. Some of the places we found were good enough, but none as perfect as Fallow Creek."

Rachel and Keith looked at themselves again, but this time there was understanding in their eyes.

"That's why I came to speak to you. Someone in town told me you were in charge. I want to ask you two if we could use your town as one of the settings in our movie."

Rachel leaned back on the sofa while Keith folded his arms across his chest.

Vina's heart began to beat very fast. She'd hardly watched movies growing up because it was not allowed in her house and was largely discouraged in Fallow Creek, especially for children and young people. But she had watched a movie or two, and she had heard a lot about Hollywood and movie producers from a rebel friend of hers who had found a way to connect her phone to the internet, even though that hadn't been allowed in Fallow Creek. Her friend Leah had told her a lot about Hollywood actors and directors and producers, and about models and fashion shows. Leah had also found a way to smuggle fashion magazines into Fallow Creek, and they both studied the models in the magazines, their designer clothes and makeup, and the designers themselves. They had also watched some movies and TV shows on Leah's phone. Vina had been utterly fascinated by the actors in the movies and the people who actually made the movies.

But all that was before she'd married Mike. He'd stopped her from having friends over or even seeing them. She'd lost contact with Leah, who she heard had left Fallow Creek with her family during the mass exodus. The movies she had seen with Leah had planted a seed in her heart even though she had not known it then. It was probably the main reason why she wanted more than Fallow Creek could offer her. Even though she had never experienced the world that she and Leah had seen in the movies, she had seen enough to be hungry for some of that life. Now, a real-life producer and director was sitting just a few feet away from her. And what was most exciting was that he wanted to shoot a movie right here in Fallow Creek. She thought she would die of excitement.

Her heart sunk as Rachel shook her head and said, "No, I don't think that shooting your movie here would be a good idea."

The mysterious stranger nodded. "I understand that you may have some misgivings about having a movie cast and crew seemingly invade your town to shoot a movie, but I promise that we would not destroy anything or get in the way of anything important in your town. We would try our best to be respectful and at the end of our shoot leave it better than when we came here."

Keith looked up with a thoughtful expression on his face and then looked at the director. "What kind of movie are you planning on shooting here?"

"It's a family film about a movie star who escapes to a small town in order to avoid the paparazzi and all the publicity he's been getting lately. And that was why I wanted a small town that would be both charming and mysterious at the same time. Somewhere everyone watching would fall in love with. Fallow Creek is that place, Mr. and Mrs. Thorn. I'm ready to pay a good amount of money to both of you in order to use your town."

"It's not about the money," Rachel said. "I don't know much about movies and all that, but from what you've said, we will have more people — strangers — coming into our town. I don't think I want that, at least not now. Most of the people here are wary of strangers because of some events that have happened recently."

The director did not seem fazed by her refusal. He looked intently at her and then turned to Keith.

Keith looked like he was at least considering the director's request. Vina felt a slight hope spring up in her heart again.

"I understand my wife's concerns, and I share them. I know about movies and Hollywood... at least some things. I don't think we want to be a part of any of that."

The man suddenly turned in Vina's direction, and she blinked in surprise. "What do you think?" he asked her. "Wouldn't it be exciting to have a Hollywood movie shot somewhere you know? You would be able to watch a movie shot in your town."

Vina's heart drummed. She was taken aback by the fact that the man had even asked for her opinion. For some seconds she could not speak, and then she said, "I'm not sure." She groaned inwardly after she'd spoken. Of course she was sure of what she wanted. She wanted the man to shoot his movie here in Fallow Creek. In fact, she had not wanted anything more in a long time. Still, she couldn't just blurt out what she wanted when it went against what Rachel and Keith wanted.

The man gave her a small smile and turned to Rachel and Keith again. "Like I said earlier, I am ready to pay whatever you want in order to use this town for our movie. I promise that by the time we wrap up shooting, we will leave it even better than when we came."

Rachel shook her head. "I'm sorry," she said to the director, "but what you're asking will not be possible. We've had a very difficult time in this town. I don't want to put the people through more difficulty. Even though you say you will not get in the way or pose any problems, I cannot trust that that will be entirely true, especially since I don't really know you." The man began to say something, but Rachel stopped him. "I'm sorry. You will have to find some other town to shoot your movie in."

Vina sighed with disappointment and gently patted Emily's back. Emily had rested her head on Vina's shoulder again and seemed to be fast asleep. Vina looked at the director again, hoping he would turn his gaze in her direction once more but knowing she would be embarrassed if he did. He did not.

"Can you both just think about it?" He dug his hand into his jacket pocket and brought out a small card. Handing it to them, he added, "I am staying at a small guest house in the next town. If you change your mind, please give me a call. I need to know your answer quickly as I can only spend a few days here before I have to leave since I have other engagements in Los Angeles."

Keith took the business card from the director and shook the man's hand again. They got up, and Rachel gave the director a thin smile.

The man walked past Vina, and her heart began to race again. She gasped when he turned and looked straight into her eyes. He smiled and said in his sophisticated, probably Californian, accent, "I hope to see you soon."

Once again she could not speak, and he walked past her. She immediately followed Rachel and Keith as they walked the director to the gate and watched as he entered his expensive-looking car and drove away.

Vina sighed. A mixture of excitement and disappointment warred in her heart as the handsome man's car disappeared from view, and then she turned to Rachel and Keith. With all her heart she wanted to see the man again and she wanted Fallow Creek to be the setting for the handsome director's movie. It would bring some much-need excitement, something new to Fallow Creek. Rachel and Keith were already walking back into the House of Refuge, and she followed them again.

In the house, Rachel took the sleeping Emily and began to head up the stairs. Keith was already at the top of the stairs when Rachel got to the middle and beckoned to Vina to follow her.

Vina hurried up the stairs, and Rachel handed Emily to Keith. He went on to the apartment while Rachel stood in the hallway and turned to Vina.

She said, "Out with it, Davina. When that director asked you what you thought about them shooting their movie in Fallow Creek, you said you were not sure. But I know you. You want the movie to be shot here, don't you?"

Vina tamped down the desire to tell Rachel exactly what she thought — that Fallow Creek was boring and needed the movie to liven things up. She shrugged and said instead, "You and Keith are the leaders. You know what's best for this town. It doesn't really matter what I think."

"Of course it does," Rachel said. "Keith and I might be the leaders, but it's the people of this town who will be affected if a movie is shot here. I need to know what everyone thinks. The director asked us to think about it, and I need to be totally sure that Keith and I made the right decision not to have that movie shot here. But if you, as part of this town, feel like you want the movie shot here, then maybe we need to at least consider some different opinions"

Vina nodded. "Okay... yes, Rachel. I like the idea of a Hollywood movie being made here. It will bring something new to Fallow Creek, and I think the younger women like me and you would enjoy something as exciting as having a Hollywood movie shot in our small town."

Rachel nodded and smiled. "I'll see you later, Vina," she said. "You can take the rest of the day off after you have bought all the items on our lists."

Rachel walked away, and Vina ran her hand nervously through her hair. Had she offended Rachel by clearly stating how she felt? Rachel had asked her opinion, after all. But from the look on

Rachel's face and how adamant she and Keith had been when they'd spoken to the stranger, it was unlikely that the director's movie would be shot in Fallow Creek.

Vina turned around as disappointment flooded her heart. She had come face-to-face with a director today and had believed that something exciting was going to come to their small town. Maybe something that might have changed her mind about leaving and at least kept her here. Unfortunately, that would not happen. She understood Keith and Rachel's concerns, and in a small way shared them. But nothing good came without risk. Besides, how risky was a bunch of Hollywood actors and movie crew?

She walked back to her room to prepare to leave for Prospect. All she could think about as she changed into another dress in preparation for her shopping trip was the missed opportunity for something exciting in town, and most of all, that she might not ever see the handsome director again. His face was etched in her mind. When he smiled at her, it had melted her insides. She began to imagine what it would be like to be in the arms of such a handsome, exciting man.

She finally controlled her wayward thoughts and scolded herself for them. Guilt flooded her as she remembered Daniel. She tried to press the director's face from her mind, but she couldn't... or maybe she didn't want to. For the first time in a long while, she'd felt everything in her come alive. Even though it had only been for a short time, it felt great. Maybe there would be a miracle and Keith and Rachel would agree to let the director shoot his movie here. But it was unlikely.

She left her room again telling herself she had to put the director and his movie out of her mind permanently.

Or I can try again to convince Rachel that it would be a good idea to have a movie shot here. Maybe she could even speak to a few other women about it and get them to try to change Rachel's and Keith's minds.

She changed her mind immediately about that. Rachel would not like that at all. Rachel had had her listen in on their conversation because they were close and she was her assistant. She would not abuse that privilege.

With all her heart, she wanted Rachel and Keith to change their minds, but there was no way to have that happen. She thought about praying about it, but knew it was not a very good idea. She was already thinking about the handsome director in a not-so-pure way. It was unlikely the Lord would grant her request. The only thing she could depend on now was luck, with maybe a small prodding on her part.

The exciting, handsome, director remained in her mind all through the day, even when Daniel visited her briefly that evening. She went to bed and even dreamt of the director smiling at her and telling her she would be perfect for his movie.

FIVE

Two days later, Vina walked into Rachel and Keith's apartment and found them in the living room making a call. Rachel had the phone on speaker.

Vina sat across from them and listened as Rachel told the person on the other line that they could come to Fallow Creek in a week's time. Her heart soared with happiness as she listened. She immediately knew who the other person on the line was. It was the handsome director. When his deep, mesmerizing voice came on the other end and said he was looking forward to coming back to Fallow Creek to start shooting, she could not help smiling.

The call ended, and Rachel looked at Vina. "I can see you're very happy about the fact that this movie is going to be shot here. Keith and I are still not totally sure about it, but I asked some of the women in the House what they thought and they all said the same thing. That they could not wait to have a movie shot here. A few even thought they would appear in the movie." She chuckled.

"We also had Barb check out the director and his movies online," Keith said. "You know Barb is great with the internet and all that."

Vina nodded. Barb was one of the only women in the House of Refuge who had not been born in Fallow Creek but had come here about five years ago.

Keith continued. "Barb said she didn't find anything out of order and that the director usually shoots clean family movies. I think I've seen one of his movies before, but that was years ago. We decided to call him and let him know he can come and shoot his movie here."

Rachel nodded. "I also think it might be great for the women's morale since most haven't forgotten what happened last year. They all seemed so excited, and we haven't had anything exciting happen in Fallow Creek in a while, except for the bad kind of exciting."

Vina could not help laughing with joy. "I told you guys, it will be so much fun to have all the movie cast and crew here." Soon her mind strayed, and she began to dream about Fallow Creek being overrun with handsome actors and beautiful actresses, camera equipment and operators. She could not wait. Most of all, she longed to see the handsome Trent Radar again. "When exactly is the director going to come back?" she asked Rachel. "Is he going to come before the crew and cast arrive next week?"

Rachel and Keith gave her curious stares, and she sighed softly in embarrassment. She had asked way too eagerly about the director. Maybe Rachel and even Keith could see that her eager questions were more than just her excitement about having a Hollywood movie cast and crew in her hometown. They might guess that she was enamored with the movie director. She sighed again and stared briefly at the floor as her embarrassment increased.

"We will have to tell everyone in the House and even the rest of Fallow Creek about this," Rachel said. "They need to be warned about the deluge of people coming to town soon before the Hollywood gang arrived."

Vina chuckled. "I am pretty sure that the women you told about the movie will have spread it around the rest of the House, if not around the whole town. There aren't many people living outside the House of Refuge anyway."

"Yes, but they don't know that Keith and I have accepted to have the movie crew shoot their movie here," Rachel said.

"Everyone will be so excited." Vina smiled widely.

"I'm not so sure about that," Keith said.

Vina ignored his words. She stood up without thinking and began to leave the apartment, eager to tell someone the good news. And the one person she wanted to tell above all was Daniel. He was the first one she always shared her happy or sad news with.

"Where are you going, Vina?" Rachel asked just as Vina reached the door.

Vina turned around slowly as she realized she had just been about to leave without telling Rachel and Keith. It was not yet time for her to go back to her room. She worked for Rachel now. She couldn't just up and leave whenever she felt like it. In her eagerness to tell Daniel her news, she hadn't even remembered she was still at work. She came back and sat down on the sofa again, feeling embarrassed once more. "I'm sorry," she said.

"I understand." Rachel laughed softly. "You're filled with excitement about this movie, and you just can't wait to tell everyone. But please let me and Keith be the ones to tell the women about it."

Vina nodded. "I was only going to tell Daniel."

"Okay then, but let's finish up here before you go," Rachel told her. "I have a few errands for you to run for me."

Vina nodded again. She grinned when Emily tottered into the living room and climbed into Keith's lap. He put his arms around her and kissed her curly blond hair. "How's my little princess doing today?" he asked, his voice filled with laughter.

Emily smiled and nodded her head, and Keith kissed her cheek.

Vina felt another tug in her heart. Keith clearly loved his adopted daughter deeply. Anyone looking at them would not know that Emily was not really his. Vina had taken turns with Olivia to watch Emily and take care of her when Mike had barred Rachel from seeing her daughter. Emily was a beautiful little girl, easy most of the time, but she could be a handful. Vina loved her as well, and seeing her with Keith made Vina think about Daniel and how he would be with the children they would have one day.

But once again, she shoved the thought out of her mind. She was nowhere near ready to marry Daniel or have a child. And yet she could not deny the longing in her heart as she watched father and daughter together. Confusion flooded her. How could she yearn to leave Fallow Creek and be free, yet at the same time crave for children of her own?

She sighed and tried to think of something else. She was very sure she didn't want kids yet. But it was all Daniel wanted; her and the kids they would have in the future. But that was if they ever got married, and that depended on if she remained in Fallow Creek or if he could wait for her to come back when she left.

There were so many ifs. Months ago, when she was sure she wanted to marry Daniel soon, she'd been excited by the thought of starting a family with him in Fallow Creek. But that was before he'd actually asked her to marry him. When he did and she'd said yes, the doubts had begun. She had probably been excited about the fairy-tale — marriage to her prince and a houseful of children. But when reality had come calling, after Daniel had proposed, she'd remembered married life vividly, and even Olivia's with kids, and had known it wasn't what she wanted in the present. When she'd realized that, the relaxed certainty she'd felt about her path in life had evaporated. She knew she had another path to take. She just didn't know what that path was. Now, everything seemed up-in-the-air. But even that brought its own excitement. She was on a path of discovery rather than a clear one set in stone.

She began to think again about the director and the movie that would be shot in Fallow Creek. It would be a good distraction, and maybe, for now, she wouldn't have to decide on what to do about her life and her future. She could just enjoy having a Hollywood movie crew here. Maybe by the time they left, she would have gained clarity on the path she was meant to take.

She blinked when Rachel snapped her fingers and called her name. "Yes, Rachel." She shook her head. Her mind had strayed far away again. "I'm sorry," she said.

Rachel frowned. "You're always so absentminded these days, Vina. I think you need a break. You can go now. I'll handle everything that needs to be handled today by myself."

Vina winced. She apologized again. "Rachel, I'm sorry. I'll pay attention from now on."

Keith shook his head as he looked at Vina with an amused expression on his face.

"Don't worry about it," Rachel said. "Go and see Daniel. I insist."

Vina sighed, stood up slowly, and left the apartment, mentally chiding herself for her absentmindedness. But by the time she got down stairs, her excitement had returned. She hurried out the gates of the House of Refuge and almost ran to Daniel's small house. She paused briefly in front of the tiny, single-story house where Daniel lived. He fully expected her to move into this house with him once they got married. She had thought she would months ago, but now it was one of the things she couldn't imagine doing. Even though Mike had not been a very good person, he had been a great provider. She had lived lavishly, and as much as she would never have gone back to Mike if he were alive, not for all the money in the world, this was not how she envisioned starting off her married life.

She entered the house and looked around the living room. For a brief moment, she considered asking Daniel if he did not want more from life than this. He was smart, responsible, and hardworking. Maybe they could leave Fallow Creek together, go to a big vibrant city, and get jobs that would bring them satisfaction.

But Daniel already had a job he loved, and most of all, he loved living in this town. He would not want to live somewhere else.

She looked around his living room again. It was furnished simply, completely different from Mike's two lavishly outfitted living rooms. She sighed and called Daniel's name.

A few seconds later, he walked out and gave her a huge smile. "You came to my house today, Vina! You haven't come here in a while."

She nodded. "I have good news." She took his hand and began to pull him out of the house. Their joint decision never to be in an enclosed space alone also included his home. Especially his home.

He laughed and followed her out. "What has gotten you so excited, Vina?" He took both her hands. "You know, it doesn't really matter." Before she could say anything, he added, "I just love that you are so happy. I haven't seen you smile this way in such a long time." He grinned at her. "I don't know whether to be jealous of whatever has made you so happy or to simply be glad you are. I wish I were the one who has made you so happy."

"Stop talking, Dan." She grinned. "Just like I said, I have great news."

He winked at her and enfolded her into his arms. "What news, Vina? Have you decided that we should get married next week?"

She rolled her eyes and pulled away from him. "No! But there's definitely something huge taking place in town next week."

Daniel raised his brows. "What is it?"

She told him everything about the discussions Rachel and Keith had had with the movie director. "I was in their apartment when they called the director to tell him he could shoot his movie here. Imagine, Dan! Our town is going to be the setting for a Hollywood movie! Isn't that the most exciting thing you have heard in a long time?"

Daniel frowned. "So Keith and Rachel have agreed to let that director shoot his movie here?"

Vina blinked in surprise. "You knew about it all this time, Dan?"

"Yes, but I was hoping that Rachel and Keith would refuse the director's request. They will turn the town into a jamboree for the duration they are here."

She shook her head and laughed at the worried expression on his face. "Can't you see, Daniel? That is exactly what Fallow Creek needs. A jamboree. This town is so boring. The only exciting thing that has happened here in a while was that awful incident with Mike."

"No, that's not true," Daniel said. "What about when Rachel and Keith took over as leaders of this place?"

"Yes... that was great... but that didn't really happen for the whole town."

"Of course it did. Their takeover changed everything, especially for the women, Vina. You know that.

"Okay, that's true," Vina agreed. "But that was a while ago." She studied his face. "How come you're not excited that a Hollywood director chose our town as the setting for his movie?" She hit his arm playfully. "Come on, Daniel! You cannot say you are not thrilled. Even a little."

He said nothing for a while and then sighed loudly. "You are forgetting something, Vina. Apart from Rachel and Keith taking over leadership of this place, something really exciting happened months ago. Something much more exciting than this Hollywood thing you are so thrilled about."

She frowned. "What, Dan? What is that exciting thing that happened here in Fallow Creek that I cannot remember?"

Daniel stared at her with a worried expression on his face. "Really, Vina? You really don't know, or are you just pretending not to?"

She said, "I really don't know, Daniel. Are you going to tell me or not?"

The worried look on his face turned to anger. "I asked you to marry me, Vina! We got engaged! We pledged to spend the rest of our lives with each other."

Again she felt guilty for not considering their engagement as momentous or exciting enough. Daniel looked incredibly hurt and angry. She began to apologize, and then she stopped herself. Why should she apologize? This was how she felt. She had been happy on their engagement day, but she could not say she was really excited, especially as excited as she was now. She couldn't lie about that. Even if it wasn't what Daniel wanted to hear.

"It's not even as if we are going to be in the

movie," Daniel said. "I don't know why you're so excited about it."

She began to grow angry herself and then pushed her anger away. Daniel got angry or frustrated over little things. She had noticed he had a temper when they were much younger, but now it was beginning to grate on her. Well, if he thought he could control her emotions with his anger, he had something else coming.

"You are always angry and never excited about anything," she said, glaring at him.

Well, that wasn't true. He was excited when he talked about their upcoming wedding or having kids with her. That irritated her now. She felt even more smothered by the thought that the only thing that truly made him happy was her and the thought of the kids they would have in the future. She did not want that kind of pressure. Not now.

He looked more hurt than angry now. "It's not true that I'm never excited about anything." He reached out and pulled her into his arms again. "I am excited about you and..."

"Stop it!" She angrily pulled away from him. "I don't want you to be! There are other things in the world to be excited about. Look around you, Daniel. Look beyond this town. Think about having a Hollywood..."

"I don't care about Hollywood!" he cut in. "Or the stupid movie they are going to shoot here! None of that matters to me."

"Well, it matters to me! I feel stifled, Daniel!" she said before she could stop herself. Daniel blinked and stepped back, overwhelming hurt in his eyes, and she sighed, regretting her outburst.

"I'm sorry," she said, guilt flooding her at the look in his eyes.

He shook his head slowly. "We are always fighting these days, Vina. It shouldn't be this way. We are going to get married soon. We should go back to focusing on the things we loved about each other. We have so many disagreements now."

"Dan, I think our constant fights are telling us something. We don't agree on a lot of things because maybe we are just too different."

He took her hands again and stared into her eyes. "Don't say that, Vina. We love each other, and we have a great time when we are together." He sighed. "At least we did until recently. We will soon get married and have a family together. We belong to each other. We always have."

She winced as he gazed at her. An uncomfortable feeling settled in the pit of her stomach. She loved Daniel and he loved her, but his love seemed a bit too obsessive. She felt as though she were in some sort of prison, and she wasn't even married to him yet. How would she feel if they got married? Everything in her screamed for her to break the relationship off, but she could not bring herself to do it. Daniel would be so hurt if she did. And she still loved him and didn't want to see him hurt. She bit her lip, feeling terribly confused by it all.

He pulled her closer and kissed her. "I love you so much, Vina. Please, let's get married now."

She pushed away again. "No, not now." His eyes grew terribly sad, and she stammered, "Maybe… maybe… after the movie cast and crew leaves." Hopefully by then she would have decided on exactly what she wanted to do with her life.

He smiled, looking relieved. "Really, Vina? We will get married as soon as the Hollywood people leave?"

"No, no, I didn't say that, Daniel. At least that is not what I meant. I mean that we will talk about when exactly we should get married after they leave Fallow Creek."

"But you just said…"

"Please, Dan, let's not talk about this right now."

Daniel narrowed his eyes. "What you want to talk about is that Hollywood movie, but you cannot find time to talk about something as serious as our future together."

Anger welled up in her again, and she bristled. "Stop it, Daniel! I'm so tired of your whining."

He narrowed his eyes. "So I'm whining now. I love you and can't wait to spend the rest of my life with you. Am I the only one that cares about our relationship? You tell me you're not sure you want to get married and that you want to leave Fallow Creek and explore the world, and you expect me not to complain. You expect me to just sit and take it and say nothing."

"I don't expect anything of you, Daniel! I told you before. If you can't wait for me, you're free to move on! You say you care about how I feel, yet you don't care that I feel empty because I feel like I have no purpose in life." She glared at him and then turned around and stormed off.

She headed toward the House of Refuge, fuming. Daniel thought he could control her the way Mike had. She would have to show him that she would not be controlled. She was a different person now. Fallow Creek was different now. He had no right to lord it over her.

She looked back to see if he was following her the way he had last time. This time he wasn't. She turned around again, still angry. As she neared the House of Refuge, she noticed a familiar figure entering the gates and saw the expensive-looking car. The handsome director's car. She hurried toward the House of Refuge as the front door opened and he entered.

Her excitement began to grow again, and her frustration and anger fled. She walked briskly through the gates and entered the House. She was going to enjoy everything that was coming to Fallow Creek and immerse herself in it. She would not let Daniel stop her from living her life to the fullest.

SIX

The handsome Trent Radar looked at Vina and smiled before sitting down on the sofa across from Keith and Rachel. With her eyes fixed on him, Vina sat on the couch near the entrance to Rachel and Keith's apartment. When the director smiled at her again, she melted on the inside. He was so handsome.

He looked at Keith and then at Rachel and said, "So the crew will be arriving first, and the cast will follow. I have worked with most of them before. We shot our last movie partly in a small town in Connecticut, and they were respectful of the people living there. They are all professionals, and so are the actors. There will be no problems at all."

Keith nodded, while Rachel gave him a small smile. She still did not look convinced that it was a good idea to have a movie shot in Fallow Creek, but Vina was glad she had agreed to let it happen. A fresh wave of excitement went through her, and she turned once more to the director. She could not hold back a gasp when she saw his eyes were on her.

She felt herself blushing and quickly turned away in embarrassment, hoping he had not noticed how flustered she was.

Trent Radar told Rachel and Keith what to expect when the shooting of the movie started. They had already shot part of the movie somewhere else, and they would be shooting the rest of the movie in Fallow Creek for about a month if everything went well.

Vina hid a smile as waves of anticipation ran through her. She hadn't known they would be here for that long. For a full month, the cast and crew would be in Fallow Creek, shooting their movie, breathing life and excitement into the town. Most of all, Trent Radar would be here. She could gaze at his handsome face as many times as she wanted.

She sighed as she realized how obsessed she'd become over this director. *Pull yourself together, Vina.*

She tried to focus on Rachel as Trent talked about his movie and about how excited he was to use Fallow Creek as its setting. For a minute or so, her eyes remained fixed on Rachel, but her gaze soon traveled to the handsome producer and director.

Once again, she caught herself gazing intently at him and silently scolded herself. Guilt gripped her as she thought of Daniel. How would he feel if he were here while she was gazing longingly at Trent Radar, or if he found out she had a huge crush on the director.

She averted her gaze again and once more tried to focus only on the conversation in the living room. But her eyes kept moving to Trent and her mind kept straying to thoughts she felt ashamed of.

She chided herself over and over again. *Stop looking at him, Vina.* And yet not only did she continue looking, she also longed for him to look at her. But he didn't look at her again, which didn't surprise her. Why would someone like him find her attractive when he was constantly surrounded by beautiful actresses. Once again her thoughts traveled to Daniel, but this time she tamped down the guilt rising up in her. Her crush on this director meant nothing and would come to nothing anyway. She had no reason to feel guilty. She just admired Trent Radar, that was all.

But if Daniel knew, he would not understand at all.

She brushed the thought away. That would be his problem, not hers.

A few minutes later, Trent got up to leave, and Vina felt a rush of disappointment run through her. Keith and Rachel walked the director out of the apartment and Vina followed. They kept talking as they walked out of the House of Refuge.

Trent finally bid Rachel and Keith goodbye and then walked to his car. This time he had not said goodbye to her. She bit her lip as her disappointment grew. She watched as he opened his car door, while Rachel and Keith walked back into the House. And then her heart skipped a beat as he turned and looked directly at her. He smiled and she grew hot. When he waved his hand to call her, she hurried over to him, her heart beating with anxiety and delight. She stood before him, drinking in his handsome face and a warm smile.

For a long moment, he gazed at her and said

nothing. She looked down at the ground feeling flustered and wishing she had something smart to say to him.

"What's your name?" he asked her.

She looked up at him again. "Davina, but most people here call me Vina." She groaned after she had spoken. *Most people here call me Vina? That sounds so...*

"Your name is as gorgeous as you are."

Her eyes widened and her heart rate increased. Did he just say she was gorgeous?

"You have the kind of face that should be in front of a camera," he said.

She blinked in surprise. "Me?"

"Yes, Vina. You." The expression on his face turned thoughtful. "Would you like to be an extra in my movie?"

She frowned in confusion. "What is an extra?"

"Well, an extra is someone who appears in a movie but isn't one of the major characters. Usually, that person doesn't have a speaking role but still adds depth to the film."

She stared at him, not fully understanding what he was saying but too ashamed to ask him to clarify.

"Well? Will you act as an extra in my movie?"

She could not believe he was asking her to be in his movie. She didn't fully understand his explanation about extras, but she knew as an extra she would appear in the movie, even if for a short time. She couldn't imagine herself being in a movie, and yet it felt so deliciously exciting.

"Yes, I would love that very much," she said. "But I don't think I know how to act. I have never acted before."

He smiled. "Don't worry about that. You don't really need to know how to act to be an extra. You don't have any lines." He turned thoughtful again. "Well, maybe a line or two, but nothing you won't be able to handle, I am sure."

She felt flattered and surprised that he believed that she could actually act. Most of all, he thought she was gorgeous. She hadn't forgotten he'd said that. She couldn't wait to tell someone what he'd said. The first person that popped into her mind was Daniel, but she immediately knew it would be a bad idea. He had a jealous streak and would probably be angry that another man had told her that.

Trent said, "I have to go now, but I will be back in a few days."

She watched him leave, her heart racing. When he got into his car and drove off, she squealed in excitement and resisted the urge to do a jig when two women passed by her and gave her curious looks.

She started to walk through the gate and jumped when someone touched her shoulder. She turned around and stared at Daniel. "You scared me," she said, and gave a nervous chuckle.

Daniel looked angry, but that wasn't new these days. "I saw you talking with that director," he said. "What were you talking about, and why do you look so excited?"

She considered not telling him about what Trent Radar had just told her, but there was no point keeping it from him. He would find out soon enough. Her excitement returned and she said,

"Trent asked me to be an extra in his movie."

Daniel narrowed his eyes, clearly angry. "Trent! So you're on a first-name basis with him now."

"Is that all you heard from what I just said to you?"

"He said he wants you to be an extra in his movie," Daniel waved his hand dismissively. "Surely, you are not considering that. You're not an actor, after all."

Anger bubbled up in her, but she refused to give in to it. Anger was Daniel's thing, not hers. "He said I'm gorgeous and have the kind of face that should be in front of a camera. He also said I don't have to know how to act because I will just be in the background mostly and only have a line to say."

"I don't like him telling you you're gorgeous..." Daniel frowned at her. "And I don't like the look on your face as you're talking about him."

She could not hold back her anger anymore. "And I don't like how jealous you can be over nothing. I am trying to tell you something great that happened to me; something I am very excited about, and all you can think of is that another man called me gorgeous. When was the last time you complimented me like that?"

"What are you talking about?" Daniel stared at her with an incredulous expression on his face. "I tell you that you are beautiful all the time."

"Being gorgeous is different from being beautiful. Beautiful is common. Gorgeous isn't."

"Vina! Just listen to yourself and look at how excited you are just because some movie director says you're gorgeous."

"It's not about that, Dan. I've been bored out of

my mind in this town and looking for something new. I've just been offered a role in a Hollywood movie, even if it's a small one, and of course, I am excited. I thought you would be happy for me, but all you are is jealous and ready to pick a fight. I'm tired of it all!" She started to march away and then paused. She frowned. Hadn't she been doing that for the past few days? It seemed as though they fought every single time they were together, and she always left him in anger. She turned around and walked back to Daniel. She wasn't going to run away whenever they had a fight so she would not change her mind about following her dreams... just because he did not want her to. She would stand her ground in every way.

"Vina, I'm sorry," Daniel said, and took her hand. "I didn't mean to make you think I'm not happy for you. I just wanted us to talk about our relationship, and I didn't think you were interested in acting or anything like that. If it makes you happy, then I'm happy."

She bit her lip but said nothing.

Daniel took her hand again. "Please forgive me," he said, sounding anxious.

She looked up at him in surprise. Why did he look so worried? She sighed and laid a hand on his cheek. "I forgive you," she said. "I don't want you to be so jealous or concerned every time I tell you about something that interests me other than you and our future together. I want you to be happy for me. I would be happy if you found another passion outside our relationship. I wish you would, Daniel."

He turned away from her, but she turned his face back towards her. "I love you, Dan. Nothing is going to change that. You don't have to be jealous of that director."

He chuckled. "I am not jealous."

She raised her brows. "Really? You were angry because the director said I was gorgeous, and now you are saying you are not jealous of him?"

"I'm sorry," he said again. "And yes, you are gorgeous. I just keep remembering what you told me about not being ready to get married and wanting to leave Fallow Creek. That is what really worries me."

"It's just a temporary thing, Daniel. Yes, I am going to have to leave Fallow Creek soon, but that doesn't mean I never want to marry you or that I won't come back." He opened his mouth to say something else, but she laid a finger on his lips. "Stop worrying so much, Dan. We still have each other now. I'm still in Fallow Creek. I don't even know when I will leave."

"Yeah, that especially worries me," he said.

"It will be fine," she told him. Once again, he started to say something, but this time she pressed her lips to his, stopping his words. She kissed him deeply, hoping he would forget about his concerns and his jealousy about the compliment the director had paid her. She was getting weary of his ever-present desire to hold on to her so tightly, thereby trying to convince her to let go of her dreams for his sake. She was also getting tired of having to constantly placate him like she was doing now.

He held her tightly as they kissed, and she knew it was his unconscious way of trying to hold on to her, hoping that she wouldn't leave him. But in her mind, she was already letting go of him and maybe already had. The more he tried to hold on to her emotionally, the more stifled she felt. It was time to tell him they couldn't be together anymore. And yet, she still couldn't bring herself to say it to him. Not directly anyway. She pulled away from his embrace and hurried back into the House.

SEVEN

Vina stood in front of the town hall with a group of women from the House of Refuge, staring with open-mouthed fascination as men and women in black outfits set up cameras and film equipment. Everywhere around Fallow Creek, white vans threw up film-making gear and even film crew. Since Trent had said the crew would arrive first, she knew none of the cast had arrived yet. She'd not known that so many people worked behind the scenes during movie productions.

She and the group of women she was with had been walking around Fallow Creek, watching everything that was happening around them with growing excitement. She still hadn't seen Trent Radar and still waited with bated breath to catch a glimpse of him, but all she had seen held her attention. It made her even more excited at the fact that soon she would be one of the people starring in the movie. Yes, it would be a very small role, but it was a role all the same.

Her heart began to drum as Trent's car sped past

the town hall. She turned to one of the women and told her she was leaving. Before the woman could ask where she was going, Vina walked away. She wasn't sure where Trent was heading, but she had to see him, if not speak to him.

And what are you going to say to him when you see him? She sighed. She had developed an annoying condition of not being able to speak whenever they met. Maybe she would ask him about her role again. That would give her an opportunity to talk to him without seeming like she was stalking him.

She hurried to the House of Refuge hoping he had gone there first to see Keith and Rachel. When she got to the front of the house, she huffed in disappointment. His car was not there.

Where can he be?

She looked around the area, hoping to spot him, and then smiled in self-mockery. That was silly. Since he was going to shoot his movie in Fallow Creek as a whole and not just the House of Refuge, he could be anywhere. She thought about going in search of him and quickly changed her mind. That would definitely be stalking.

Still, she could not stop herself from moving away from the House of Refuge and wandering about the town. She told herself she was just taking a stroll around Fallow Creek, but she knew that wasn't really true. She was hoping to see Trent somewhere. She wanted to see his handsome face again.

She groaned when instead of Trent, she spotted Daniel walking toward her. She looked to her left and then her right, wondering if she could escape him, but there were no houses to hide behind in this part of town. If she turned back, Daniel would know she was avoiding him. She squared her shoulders and continued to walk.

Daniel smiled and hurried toward her. He reached her, and she sighed wearily.

"I was just coming to see you at the House of Refuge," he said.

She frowned when she noticed the rifle hanging on his arm. He hadn't carried that thing since the unfortunate incident with Mike last year. "Why, Daniel?"

He frowned. "Why what?"

"Why do you have your gun with you today?"

Daniel shrugged, but she could see from the look on his face that he was anticipating some trouble. That worried her. Not because she thought the movie cast and crew were going to make any trouble, but because she was certain if there was any, it would come from him.

"I was just patrolling the town as usual. I decided to take my gun along with me today."

She shook her head. "Yes, you just decided to patrol the town with your gun today. It has absolutely nothing to do with the fact that the film crew have arrived in Fallow Creek. What are you trying to do? Run them out of town?"

Daniel chuckled. "I wish I could." When she frowned, he sighed loudly. "I did not mean that. It's just that it's my duty to guard this town, and these people, these Hollywood people, we don't know them. You don't know what kind of trouble they might stir up here. I have to make sure there's order in this town and that no one gets hurt, especially by strangers coming into our town."

"Oh, Daniel! They are cameramen and film equipment operators and actors and actresses. They are not hired assassins."

Daniel arched his brows and stared at her. "Film equipment operators. Hired assassins. Where did you learn all that?" He shook his head. "No, don't tell me. I already know. It's from your friend, Leah, isn't it? That girl is something else. I'm glad she..."

"You're glad she has left Fallow Creek," Vina said accusingly. "Of course you are. Because now there's no one to teach me anything new. Anything that will challenge me to be my own person and not rely on you for everything."

His jaw stiffened. "Where is all this hostility coming from, Vina? Why do we always have to quarrel every single day? I don't like it."

She sighed. It was definitely time to tell him they had to go their separate ways. He had finally noticed how they fought constantly. They had very little in common. She opened her mouth to speak, but he took her hands again and stared into her eyes. The look in his gave her pause.

"Vina, I'm so sorry for everything. I know I have been a bit touchy, and maybe even needy, these past few weeks. Please forgive me. I promise, from today I will let you be yourself and do whatever you want to do. I just want you to be happy. You can even leave Fallow Creek today if you choose in order to find yourself. I will be waiting here for you when you get back." He squeezed her hands. "I promise not to pick a fight with you anymore and to listen whenever you want to talk about your dreams and plans for the future. I know I really want to marry you now and want a future with you, but I will keep that on hold if that is what you want and wait until you're ready. Please, just give me a chance to show you that I truly care about you and that I want the best for you."

She looked deep into his eyes. He looked really sincere. Maybe they didn't have to break up after all. As long as he did not try to smother her and he gave her some space to be herself, they could go on with their relationship. He had said they didn't have to get married now, and she was pleased about that. Hopefully, he meant all that he had said to her. She gave him a small smile and whispered, "Okay, Dan. We can still be together as long as you mean everything you just said."

"I do." He beamed at her. "Thank you for not giving up on me... on us. And again, I am sorry for not being attentive enough and making you think I am not interested in your dreams." He took her hand and led her to the front of one of the empty houses a short distance away. He leaned against the house, folded his arms across his chest, and looked at her again. "Tell me all about the acting role the director gave you. I'm all ears."

Her heart soared with happiness. Her friend Daniel, the one she always told everything to; the one who was a good listener and her constant encourager, had shown up again. She began to tell him about everything the director had said, about how excited she was, and about her dreams of leaving Fallow Creek to discover the world, starting with the towns near their own.

He seemed to be listening attentively, and she went on talking.

And then she blanched and stopped as shame

flooded her. She had been talking about herself for a long time, but she hadn't asked him about his own dreams and plans for the future. She opened her mouth to ask and then shut it again. She pressed her lips tightly together. Of course she knew what his dreams and plans for the future were. He'd told her more times than she'd cared to hear. He wanted them married as soon as possible, start a family immediately after, and raise their children here in Fallow Creek. That was definitely not the plan she had for herself. His plans were the direct opposite of hers.

"What is wrong, Vina? Why did you stop talking?"

"Nothing is wrong." She mustered up a smile for him, but on the inside, she felt awful. She had insisted that he listen to her dreams and plans for the future and had been angry that he did not care enough to. Now that he was listening and had promised not to try to stop her from going after her purpose, the right thing was to listen to his dreams. Because why should he be the only one to take an interest in her dreams and her future plans? The problem was that already knowing what his dreams and plans for the future were, she wasn't interested in listening to them again and definitely not in supporting them. Which meant that there was no way they could be in a relationship. This wasn't going to work.

"What's the problem, Vina?" Daniel asked, placing his hands on her arms. "Talk to me."

"It's nothing, really," she said. She looked past him toward the road. "Can I talk to you later, Daniel? I think I need to get back to the House of

Refuge. Rachel might need me."

He smiled. "I guess I need to get back to my patrolling, too."

She turned around and hurried away. She was halfway to the House of Refuge when she recalled he had stretched out his hand to hug her, but she had not let him because she was in such a hurry to get away. She could still see the hurt look on his face when she had moved away just before he could gather her in a hug. She groaned. What was she really doing anyway? One minute she was thinking about breaking up with him, and the next she was accepting his apology and thinking about a future with him. But there couldn't really be a future with him when they both wanted different things.

She got to the House of Refuge still feeling confused. Just as she started to climb up the stairs, she blinked in surprise. And then her heart began to race. Trent was coming down the stairs alone... if she didn't count the women at the top of the stairs ogling him and giggling. He didn't seem to notice them. He looked as self-possessed as anyone she'd ever seen and even more handsome than the first time she saw him. She stood transfixed in the middle of the stairs until he reached her.

"Hi," he said, smiling widely.

"Hi," she whispered.

He gazed at her with a question in his eyes.

Don't just stand here gazing at him. Say something to him, Vina.

"So, about your role as one of the extras," he said. He continued down the stairs, and she followed him. "I will talk to the casting director and let her know you're to act in the movie. All the roles have been filled, but she will find a small one for you and maybe call you for a quick audition tomorrow."

Vina gasped and shook her head. "A quick audition?" Her hands shook and grew clammy. "I thought you said as an extra I didn't really have to act."

He touched her arm as they got down the stairs, sending sparks through her entire body. "Don't look so scared." He smiled. "I'm pretty sure whatever she chooses for you will be perfect. Don't worry about it." He gave her an encouraging smile, and she could not help smiling back.

They walked to the gate in silence, and she kept telling herself to say something to keep him from getting into his car and driving away. She wanted to keep talking to him, but her mind seemed to freeze up in his presence. He intimidated her a little. He had said she was gorgeous but she didn't feel so pretty beside him, especially knowing he had worked with some of the most beautiful women in the country. He had probably complimented her looks that day because he was a nice person and thought it was an appropriate thing to say to her.

Just before he got into his car, he turned to Vina and said, "Can I see you this evening?"

She blinked, and her heart began to race again. When he added, "To talk about your role and what to expect," she nodded and her heart sank in disappointment. He got into his car and drove away, and she sighed in embarrassment. What had she thought he meant when he'd said he wanted to see her this evening? Did she really think that someone like him would be interested in going on a date with her? And why was she even thinking of going on a date with him when she had just promised Daniel to give him another chance?

She sighed again and walked back into the House of Refuge.

For the next few hours, she stayed by Rachel's side, walking through the house, listening and jotting down whatever Rachel said needed to be replaced or bought. She and Rachel went back to Rachel's apartment after they had gotten Emily from Nettie, the woman who had volunteered to babysit Emily today. Keith had gone out to visit with a family who had returned to Fallow Creek about a week ago

While she ran around the living room chasing Emily, at the back of her mind, Vina kept thinking about Trent and then about Daniel. She had no business thinking about Trent, at least not in the way she was, but a girl could dream.

You have no business dreaming about the man, especially when you're still with Daniel, she scolded herself. But that did not stop her from doing so.

She reached out, caught Emily, and lifted her up on her shoulder. The toddler screamed with laughter, and Vina could not help laughing out loud.

Minutes later, Vina was sitting on the floor playing with Emily when a knock sounded at the door. Rachel was on the couch dozing, and Vina looked at the door and then at Emily. She smiled when Rachel opened her eyes.

Rachel stood and swept Emily off the ground. "Go and open the door, Vina."

Vina went to the door and opened it. She smiled at Susan who was standing there, her freckles looking more prominent than usual.

"What a surprise!" Vina grinned. "You didn't forget to knock today, Susan. I'm impressed."

Susan rolled her eyes and laughed.

Vina held the door open for her to enter the apartment. Susan walked in and greeted Rachel.

"What is it, now?" Rachel said grumpily. She was sitting on the couch, trying to keep an eye on Emily and focus on Susan at the same time. Emily was standing unsteadily on the couch beside her mother, looking out the window and mumbling.

Rachel sighed, looking weary. Throughout the day, one messenger or another had been sent to ask her about something pertaining to the film crew and cast. They needed to know a lot of things, like where the best place was to store some equipment or the other, or what empty house was best for a particular actor or actress to reside in. Vina smiled slightly. She didn't blame Rachel for being a little snappy today. She was tired and probably still sleepy.

Susan shook her head. "Nothing, Miss Rachel. I don't have any message for you." She turned to Vina. "I have one for you, Vina."

Vina's heart began to thud again. Maybe Trent wanted to see her. He had said he would see her this evening, after all. It wasn't yet evening, but still...

"A woman is looking for you at the gate," Susan cut into her thoughts. "She said it's urgent."

Vina frowned. "Did she tell you why she wanted to see me?"

"Umm... I think she said something about being a casting director?"

"Oh... okay."

"The casting director wants to see you?" Rachel

asked.

"Yes, Trent told me she would send for me. I thought I would have to go and see her." She stood up, about to ask Rachel if she could go downstairs to meet the woman, and then blinked. Rachel was looking at her with an incredulous expression on her face.

"So... Trent, Vina? I didn't know you and the movie director were friends now."

Vina shrugged as though Rachel's words had not affected her at all. "I cannot say we're friends, Rachel. But we've talked some. He's nice."

"Nice?" Rachel smiled. "I hope that is all you think he is, because Daniel will not be pleased if it were more."

Vina frowned and said, "There isn't more. How could there be? He's a huge Hollywood director, and I'm just..."

"A beautiful, impressionable young woman who lives in the tiny town he'll be living and shooting his movie in for weeks. I'm not going to tell you what to do, but you should be careful. I saw the way he looked at you the other day."

"Really? He was looking at me?" Vina blurted out, and then she regretted speaking at all. She waved her hand as though what Rachel had said about the director meant nothing to her. "Can I go and speak to the casting director downstairs?"

"Sure," Rachel said. "When you finish with her, I want to know why she wants you. Is our Vina going to be a movie star soon?" She smiled.

Vina laughed and shook her head. "I'll be back soon," she said to Rachel, and then left the apartment.

She met the casting director at the gate. The woman was much shorter than Vina had imagined. She had short curly dark hair and wore a white pheasant dress. There were multiple ivory necklaces on her neck and more bracelets on both her hands than Vina could count. She found the woman's look both funny and fascinating.

"So, you're the girl that Trent was talking about. I thought he was exaggerating when he said you were a beauty, but you truly are."

Vina grinned, feeling terribly flattered by the woman's words and the fact that Trent had been raving about her.

"Trent was right. You do have a face that belongs in front of a camera. But I don't know if you can actually act."

Vina felt worried again. "Trent... umm... The director told me I was only going to act as an extra."

The casting director looked Vina over from the top of her head to the soles of her feet. "I think when we get you out of this plain gown and into something more suitable, you will be perfect to act as one of the groupies stalking our lead actor's character. You won't need to say more than a few words. All you have to do is follow our lead actor around, throw yourself at him at various points in the movie, and kiss him."

Vina's mouth fell open, and her stomach flipped.

The casting director stared at her. "What is it?"

"Trent didn't say anything about me kissing anyone. I cannot do that."

"Well, you will have to. Every other role has been filled and that is all we have for you. It's either you take it or you don't get the part. We already have enough groupies for the movie. I'm only doing this for you because Trent spoke highly of you." She looked Vina over again. "You will truly be perfect for the part," she shrugged, "but it's up to you."

"I don't feel comfortable..."

The casting director shook her head. "No! You're either taking the role as a groupie, which involves kissing the lead actor, or you don't act in the movie at all." She gave Vina a patronizing smile and then turned around and walked away.

Vina watched the woman leave, and all her excitement and anticipation about acting in a Hollywood movie evaporated. There was no way she could act the role the casting director had given her. Not only did she not feel comfortable with it, but Daniel would also definitely find out about it and he would be furious. Knowing him, he would not listen if she told him it was just acting. He had been jealous and angry because the director had said she was gorgeous. How would he react if she told him her role in the movie involved kissing the lead actor? She had to accept the fact that she would not be in the movie anymore.

But she had been looking forward to acting. Surely, there had to be a way to avoid kissing anyone. Maybe she could go to Trent and talk to him about it. He could find another role for her or remove the love scene altogether.

With determination, she headed off to find Trent. Hopefully, he would be able to help her, because she really wanted to be in this movie. She knew she would be asking a lot of him by requesting that he find her another role, and she wasn't sure he would agree to it. But she had to try.

She found Trent in front of the house that had been Mike's. He was with a group of cameramen and two other men who looked like actors in the movie. One of them looked about her age or a little older, with dark, longish hair, a chiseled jawline, and the kind of physique that made women swoon. She guessed he was the lead actor.

But his good looks did not capture her attention, nor did Trent's for the first time. Instead, she stood staring at Mike's house, the house she had lived in for about a year until Mike was killed. Fear, shame, and loathing filled her and she bit her lip, distressed by the images that ran through her mind. She recalled living in this house with Mike, trying to play the role of a good wife. She shuddered as she thought about what her life would be like if Mike were still alive. Why were all these people in front of Mike's house? She felt like turning around and hurrying away. The house brought back bad memories. A few good ones, but mostly bad. She hadn't been here since Mike died.

She jumped when someone touched her shoulder. Turning around, she saw it was Trent.

He smiled brightly at her. "You're here, Vina."

"Umm... Yes. Actually, I came to see you." She had been distracted for a brief moment with memories of this house, Mike, and the trouble he had brought to the whole town. She gritted her teeth. And the awful fact that she had been married to such a man.

"You look troubled about something," Trent said, and followed her line of sight. He faced her again and frowned, looking concerned. "Do you know the people who live here or used to live here? The house looks deserted, but Rachel and Keith assured me we could shoot a scene of the movie in front of this house."

She blinked. "I used to live here."

His eyes widened in obvious surprise. "You did? It's a pretty big house. Did you live here with your parents?"

"No," she said, frowning. "I lived here with my..." She stopped herself just in time. She didn't want to talk about Mike, especially not with Trent. She fixed her gaze on him. "The casting director came to see me at the House of Refuge. She told me I'm supposed to play a role as one of the lead actors' groupies or something like that. She said I had to kiss him."

Trent laughed. "Is that why you look so troubled? You do know it's just acting. You won't really be kissing him. Your character will be kissing his character."

She shook her head. "Still, I don't feel comfortable doing that. Isn't there any other role for me?"

Trent arched his brows and studied her face. "All the roles are filled, and we actually have enough groupies as it is. I decided to add one more so you could be in the movie, but that's all I can do." He briefly turned around and pointed at the handsome actor some distance away. "That, Vina, is Garret Fletcher, the lead actor and the guy you will be kissing. Just look at him. Women fall over themselves all the time just to be noticed by him. It won't be so hard to kiss him, will it?"

She looked at the actor again and then looked away. He was handsome, but that didn't change her mind. She still wasn't comfortable with the idea of kissing a stranger.

And yet you have been fantasizing about kissing Trent since you first saw him.

She pushed the thought away and said to Trent, "It's not about the way he looks. I know I am asking a lot, but if there is any way you could switch roles for me..." She sighed. "I'm sorry to be asking this of you. It's just... apart from the fact that I am not comfortable with the role I was given, my boyfriend will also not want me kissing someone else."

Trent frowned. "I don't know what your dreams are, Vina, but whatever they are, they might involve you one day having to do something that your boyfriend isn't comfortable with. This is real life. And in an industry like this, most significant others understand that it's just acting. It comes with the career. Besides, your boyfriend sounds like the jealous type. Are you sure you need that sort of energy in your life?"

Vina sighed wearily. This conversation with Trent was going nowhere. Maybe she had to give this acting part up. She would be violating her conscience and hurting Daniel if she went ahead.

But she would also be killing her dreams of finding her purpose in life, because she was beginning to believe that acting might be her life's purpose. If she gave up this once-in-a-lifetime opportunity just because she was afraid Daniel would be hurt, she might regret it for the rest of her life. And who knew where taking this part would lead her. Just like Trent said, this was real life. She and Daniel would ultimately be fine. She had to do what she had to do in order to follow her own path. And sometimes it would involve doing things that didn't feel comfortable to her or were totally out of her comfort zone.

Maybe you should talk to Rachel about it.

She discarded that idea immediately. She already knew what Rachel would say. "If you don't feel comfortable doing it, then don't." But that advice would not get her far in life. If she was going to explore the world and find her purpose, she had to take risks. She had to grab whatever opportunities came her way, even if it felt uncomfortable. Besides, she wanted Trent to be happy with her, and he would not be if she declined the role he had created specifically for her. Since she had agreed to continue her relationship with Daniel and one day marry him, this might be the most exciting thing that would happen to her before she got tied down with married life.

"Okay, Trent. I will do it."

"That's my girl," he said with a wide smile. "Shooting starts the day after tomorrow."

EIGHT

Daniel's blood boiled with anger as he stood behind a tree watching Vina throw herself at the shirtless man who he guessed was the lead actor. He noticed her outfit — a skimpy skirt and tight blouse — which made him even angrier. When she leaned in and kissed the guy, Daniel felt like running onto the scene and decking that man. Instead, he gritted his teeth and held himself back.

There were all kinds of movie people around the place, most watching the scene playing out in front of the House of Refuge. He wasn't the only one who wasn't part of the cast and crew here. Most of the women from the House of Refuge and some other residents of Fallow Creek stood watching from a distance. He heard the audible gasp from the women as his fiancée kissed another man. Yes, it was just acting, but it still hurt. When the director yelled 'Cut' and told Vina and the actor to do the scene once more, Daniel narrowed his eyes, furious. Why did this director want them to act out the kissing scene again?

The director yelled, "Do it again, but draw out the kiss so it's longer and more passionate."

Vina walked over to the actor and threw herself at him again. Daniel groaned and turned away. He could not bear to watch anymore. He felt his anger growing. He was angry at everything and everyone. Angry at the director who had decided to give Vina this role that involved her kissing another man, angry at the film cast and crew for invading his peaceful town, and angry at Vina for agreeing to play this disgusting role and not caring about how he would feel when he saw it. The director yelled out again, "One more time!" and Daniel felt himself shaking with rage. He stormed away, feeling sick with jealousy and hurt.

Why would Vina agree to take such an immoral part? She hadn't even warned him that her acting would involve a kiss, or he would not have come out to watch it. He had promised to support her dreams in every way he could, no matter how he felt about it. But this he could not stomach. It was unfair of her to ask him to be okay with her kissing another guy. The too-sophisticated-for-their-own-good Hollywood crowd out there might laugh or berate him for being so affected by his fiancée kissing someone on the screen, but he had a right to feel the way he did. It wasn't like she had a stand-in. She had to kiss the actor herself.

"She should have warned me at least," he spat out as he marched away in anger. He had to talk to someone. Someone who would understand. The only person he could think of was Keith. Hopefully, Keith would be able to advise him on what to do.

He turned around again and avoided looking in

the direction where Vina and the actor were making out. Skirting all the film crew until he entered the gates of the House of Refuge, he walked inside. Just before he headed for the stairs, he spotted Keith and Rachel sitting in the common talking with Rita, a young brunette whose room was next to Vina's. He walked over to them, took a deep breath, and said, "I'm sorry to bother you two. Keith, could I speak to you after you're finished here?"

Keith looked at Rachel, and Rachel shrugged. "Keith can talk to you now, Daniel. Rita doesn't need both of us. Just me."

Keith nodded and stood up. "Let's go up to the apartment."

Daniel sat across from Keith in the living room of the apartment and folded his hands on his knees. He pictured Vina kissing the actor and groaned again.

"So, Dan, what do you want to speak to me about?" Keith asked.

Daniel sighed and began to tell Keith about the love scene he'd just watched with Vina and that actor, and how hurt he was by it. "What bothers me is not just the kissing," he said, "but that she could have warned me about it and chose not to. If I had known she would be kissing another guy, I would have not gone to watch." He continued to tell Keith about how the director had made her do the scene over and over again. When he finished talking, he ran his hands through his hair, frustrated. "I wish she'd told me..." he said again. "I told her I would support everything she did from now on. That was why I went to see her play her role in the movie. I should have stayed home."

Keith gave him a sympathetic smile. "Would you have approved if she had told you?"

Daniel shut his eyes briefly and tried to shake the memory of Vina kissing the actor from his mind, but he couldn't. He looked at Keith and shook his head. "Definitely not!"

"Then that was why she didn't tell you. You already know this, Dan, but I think you need someone to remind you that it's just acting."

Daniel felt anger racing through him again, and he blurted out, "If it was Rachel kissing another guy in an acting role, what would you do? Would you say it was just acting?"

For a split-second Keith looked taken aback, and then his sympathetic smile returned. "If that was what she wanted, what she felt was the part she had to take, then I would try to support her." Keith sighed and raked his fingers through his hair. "I do understand how you feel. To be honest, I would hate it, and I am definitely glad Rachel isn't an actor." He sighed again. "I know I am not really helping… but this is what Vina has chosen to do. You know more than I do that if you try to talk her out of it, it will only make things worse. As you said before, just support her and pray. At least she hasn't told you that this is the career she wants to pursue. After this film is shot, that will hopefully be the end of it."

"But what if it isn't?" Daniel said, frowning with worry. "What if she decides she wants to be an actor?"

"Then you will need lots of prayer and patience," Keith said. "I know it isn't what you want to hear, but you will have to let her find her way and trust that God will lead her on the path he wants her to go. Trying to control her and her decisions will not work in your favor. For now, I say commit it to God and don't worry about it."

Daniel bit his lip. Nothing Keith had said made him feel any better.

Keith leaned forward and put his hand on Daniel's shoulder. "You're getting all worried about nothing, Dan. As I said, this is probably a one-time thing. It's not like she has to do this regularly. However, since it bothers you so much, you could speak to her about it. Tell her how you feel, but please, lose the anger or you might lose her, and that isn't what you want."

Daniel frowned. This was not the advice he'd expected from Keith. Vina was clearly in the wrong in every way, and yet he was being blamed for being angry at what she had done. How could he speak to Vina about this? First, she was growing increasingly stubborn, and if he told her how he felt, that might make her annoyed and even more determined to do things like this without telling him first. That would lead to him getting angry and blowing his top, which would make everything worse. It would be a bad cycle.

"Daniel, you look even angrier than when you came in here. Tell me what you're thinking."

Daniel focused on Keith and sighed. Keith just wanted to help. He trusted the man's advice because Keith was godly and he had a great marriage. Maybe he needed to take the man's advice. He sighed again and tried to let go of his anger. He said, "I think I feel this way not just because of the love scene, but because of the way our relationship has been going lately. She off-handedly tells me to support her dreams of finding herself, which includes leaving Fallow Creek."

He took a deep breath as a thread of pain went through him. "By the way, our wedding is now postponed indefinitely, and I'm expected to be calm about it all. I am expected to wait for her and support her until she finds herself and is ready for us to get married. I don't even know when that will be." Daniel stood up, still feeling frustrated, and went to stand in front of the window. Glancing out, he groaned when he looked down. They were still shooting the movie in front of the House of Refuge. He quickly moved away from the window and went to sit down again.

Keith said, "I know I tell you to talk to Vina about your feelings and your relationship a lot, but it really does help. If you're serious about marrying the girl, then she has to know that you really love her and will always be there for her."

"And shouldn't it be vice versa?" Daniel said.

"Yes, it should. But Vina is going through a lot now, and she seems confused about her life and her purpose. This is the time to support her and be there for her. Trust me, one day it will be you going through it, and you will need her to stand by you even when she doesn't understand fully what you are about. That's life."

Daniel blinked and then took a deep breath and nodded. "I've never thought about it in that way, Keith. I guess you are right. I will try to talk to her, but not now. I am still too angry and hurt to think straight. I need to cool down first."

"That would be the wise thing to do," Keith said.

"Thank you, Keith." Daniel smiled slightly and

stood up.

Keith stood as well and patted him on the back. "I'll be praying for you. Hopefully, it will all work out in the end. I like you and Vina together, and I hope you sort out your problems."

"Thanks," Daniel said again. He left the House of Refuge, and as he had done before, he avoided looking toward the area where the movie was being shot. He moved in the direction of his house, but as he turned a corner, he blinked. Vina's voice floated toward him, and then he heard a male voice. She started laughing at something the man said, and Daniel frowned. He turned toward the sound of their voices and saw Vina standing in front of a house with the lead actor she had kissed earlier. She was laughing hysterically at something the guy had said as though the actor was the funniest person on earth. When the man placed his hand on her hip, Daniel's anger erupted. He rushed up to them, pushed the actor away from her, and took her hand. He pulled her with him and glowered at her when they were far away from the actor.

She jerked her hand away and screamed, "What is wrong with you, Daniel?"

"Vina, are you serious? First, you don't tell me you're going to have a love scene in that movie and I have to watch you kissing another man. Now, here you are alone with that same man, laughing hysterically while he puts his hand on your hip. And you're asking what's wrong with me? Don't you care how I feel?"

"Daniel, why would you push Garret like that and grab me as though I am your property?" She glared at him. "I'm tired of your constant jealousy and neediness. You're so possessive, and I cannot stand it anymore. We won't be able to go on with this relationship if you keep acting like this."

"So I am wrong for feeling hurt because my fiancée didn't tell me she was going to be kissing another guy over and over again. And now you're with that same guy chatting and laughing. How do you expect me to feel exactly, Vina? Please tell me."

"I expect you to understand that the kissing thing is just acting. I expect you to support me and…"

"Stop!" Daniel glared at her. "I'm so tired of you saying that I need to support you. What about me? You've never bothered to consider that I need your support, too."

She narrowed her eyes. "You promised you would support my dreams."

"And I have. But you're being selfish. I have dreams, too. But I guess mine aren't as important as yours are. I'm the one who has to wait for you to figure yourself out and find your—"

"Daniel! I told you that you could move on if you can't wait for me."

"Stop saying that! I love you, Vina. I am not going anywhere, but I need you to show me that you love me, too. It's like you don't anymore." She looked away and he blinked. He turned her around to face him again. "Tell me, Vina. Do you still love me?"

"Listen. This is not a good time. I might be called again to repeat my scene…"

"The same scene that we are arguing about right now? You will have to keep kissing that guy over and over again?"

She started to move away, and he frowned. He gently pulled her back as he remembered what

Keith had told him. "I'm sorry for the way I reacted. I should not have pushed that guy or pulled you away like that. But try to see things from my point of view. First, you postpone our wedding indefinitely, then tell me you want to leave Fallow Creek, and now you're acting out love scenes and kissing actors. How do you expect me to take all that? I'm not a robot. I get hurt and angry."

"I'm not asking you to react like a robot."

"But you keep getting mad because I am hurt by your attitude to our relationship. That is expecting me to act like a robot without feelings."

She huffed. "I am not a robot either. I have dreams. I have plans for my life and the future."

He groaned. "Which I am stopping you from achieving, right?"

She shrugged. "Maybe. I mean here you are, jealous over a simple kiss. What would you do if I had to act a full-blown—"

"Don't even say it, Vina! Tell me you're not considering doing anything beyond what you've already done. You're supposed to be a Christian."

"And I also think I want to be an actor," she said. "And if I am to act, I have to take riskier roles."

His mouth fell open and he stared at her. Finally, he said, "When did you decide you wanted to be an actor?"

"Not too long ago. Just within the last few days, I began considering it, and shooting today has made me realize that this might be what I want to do. Of course, that would mean I might have to go to Hollywood."

"What are you saying, Vina? You want to take up acting and go to Hollywood and start taking riskier roles?"

"Yes, that is what I just said."

"And how do you expect me to accept that?" He held up his hand when she opened her mouth to speak. "And please don't tell me you are not expecting me to accept it or wait for you. That is what you say every time we argue about you leaving. I might accept you temporarily leaving Fallow Creek to find yourself or whatever, but deciding you want to act even more sordid roles than in this movie," he shook his head, "is something I cannot accept. You will have to choose between that and our relationship."

He groaned after he had spoken. A week ago, he would have been certain that it was a no-brainer. Of course, she would choose their relationship. She would choose him. Now, however, he wasn't sure so sure. In fact, from the way she had been acting these past few days and what she had been saying, she would probably choose the acting over him. He shouldn't have given her the ultimatum. He quickly took her hands to try to rectify what he had said, but she snatched them away.

"You want to know which I choose, Dan?" she asked, frowning. Before he could answer, she said, "I choose acting."

Pain flooded his heart as she glared at him, turned around, and walked away. The farther she walked, the more panicked he became. She was walking out of his life forever. He had to do something quickly before he lost her. He ran and caught up with her. Apologizing again, he asked her to give him another chance.

She shook her head and said angrily, "I have been

doing a lot of that lately, giving you one chance after another. This relationship isn't working, Daniel. There is no point in keeping it alive any longer. Please don't try to follow me anymore or change my mind." She left him and disappeared around the corner.

He groaned. He had to do something. And yet he had no idea what to do.

"Help me, Lord," he whispered as he made his way back to his house. There had to be something he could do, not only to win her back but to put this troubling idea about leaving Fallow Creek to go to Hollywood out of her mind. There had to be a way to show her how much he loved her and renew her love for him and her dedication to their relationship.

An idea began to form. It was a long shot, but it was all he could think about right now. Hopefully, it would work or he had to come up with something else as soon as possible. Before he lost her completely and forever.

NINE

Daniel paused in front of Keith and Rachel's apartment, and once again thought about what he was about to do. He was about to lie to the couple he considered his friends and mentors.

Maybe you shouldn't do it, Daniel.

He took a deep breath and knocked on the door. He had to do it. It was the only way he could think of to save his relationship with Vina. He didn't know if it would work, but he had to try.

The door opened, and Keith smiled at him. "Daniel, you're here. Come in." He opened the door wide, and Daniel stepped into the apartment.

Keith looked surprised as Daniel sat on the couch and told him he needed to speak to him. Daniel understood why Keith was surprised. They had talked not too long ago.

Keith sat facing him and leaned forward. "It's about Vina, isn't it?"

"Yeah," Daniel said. "At least about our wedding. I know I told you we're postponing it to an unknown distant future because Vina wants to find herself, but something has come up, and I need to convince Vina that we have to get married now. You're the one to officiate our wedding, so I have to give you a heads up."

"What has come up, and how soon are you moving the wedding forward?"

Daniel took a deep breath. "Well, you know my elder brother, Steven — the one I told you I lost contact with some time ago when many people moved away from Fallow Creek?"

"Yes," Keith answered, looking at him with a curious expression.

An uncomfortable feeling settled in the pit of his stomach. He was about to lie to Keith, but hopefully, he could soon turn the lie into the truth. "Well, I got a call today, and it turned out to be him. He told me he's coming to Prospect to visit some of his wife's relatives in a week's time, but he is also coming with his wife and sons. He asked if I could come and see them there."

Keith smiled. "Oh… that's great."

"Yes. The thing is he cannot stay for long, and because I really want him and my nephews to be at my wedding, I told him about Vina." Daniel paused for a brief moment and then went on. "I told him I was getting married next week as well, and I want him and my nephews to attend the wedding in Fallow Creek."

"What?" Keith stared at him in disbelief. "Why would you do that?"

Daniel sighed. Hopefully, this lie would not swallow him up. "I told you, Keith. He won't be able to stay in Prospect for long, and he will only be coming to Fallow Creek because of the wedding. I really want him to witness my wedding before he leaves, because I don't know when I will see him or my nephews again. It is the one chance I have to share something this great with my brother."

Keith frowned. "I don't know if that will be enough to convince Vina to marry now, but I will always be ready to officiate your wedding. So you are serious about getting married next week?"

"Yes," Daniel said.

Keith chuckled. "How about tomorrow?"

"That would be a dream come true if I could get married to Vina tomorrow, but she will never agree."

Keith looked slightly shocked and then shook his head and smiled widely. "I was only kidding, Daniel. Even Rachel would skin me alive if I agreed to that. She is a little more excited about your marriage and wedding than I am. I would say that between her and Vina, I am not sure who's more excited about the wedding."

Daniel sighed sadly. "I am pretty sure Rachel is more excited about it than Vina."

"It's a long shot, Daniel. Convincing Vina to get married next week will be hard but not impossible. Vina might understand since it's about your family, about your brother who you haven't seen in a long time. You have to try to get her to see how important it is for you to have your brother, your only surviving relative, at your wedding."

Daniel pressed his lips tightly together, worried about what Vina would say if she found out he was lying. His brother hadn't called. He still didn't know where Steven and his wife and kids were. Steven was his only surviving relative. When he had up and left Fallow Creek with his wife and children without telling Daniel anything, Daniel had been angry. His pride had prevented him from going to look for his brother. Steven hadn't even bothered to let him know where he was. But if he was to convince Vina to marry him now, he had to go looking for his brother and find him no matter where he was.

"I hope she understands," Keith said to Daniel.

Daniel stood up from the sofa. "I have to go and talk to her now." He was at the door, about to open it, when Keith tapped him on the shoulder. He turned around and looked at him.

"Daniel, I am in full support of you getting married now, but tell me the truth. Your brother didn't really call, did he? You still don't know where Steven is.

Daniel winced and stepped back slightly. He should have known he could not hide anything from Keith. The man had a sixth sense, or more accurately, he heard God's voice clearly, which sometimes scared Daniel. He sighed and nodded as guilt flooded his heart. "I'm sorry, Keith. Telling you my brother called and wanted to attend my wedding was the only thing I could think of. It was the only idea that came to me when I was trying to figure out a way to save my relationship with Vina. Do you know that she broke up with me yesterday?"

Keith's mouth dropped open, and he shook his head slowly. "Daniel, you cannot force Vina to stay with you by lying to her or trying to manipulate the situation."

Daniel went to sit on the sofa again. "I'm not really going to lie to her, Keith. And I only partly lied to you." Keith arched his brows, and Daniel groaned. "Okay, I did, but I still intend to try to find Steven. I have to anyway if Vina will agree to marry me in a week's time. Knowing her, she might call off the wedding on our wedding day if Steven doesn't come."

Keith came and put his hand on Daniel's shoulder. "You said she broke up with you? It will be hard to win her back, but even if you do by telling her what you told me, what will happen if you go in search of your brother but don't find him? What if she truly calls off the wedding on your wedding day? And that is if she even agrees to marry you in a week."

"And that is why I must find Steven." Daniel groaned again. "But I don't want to think about what will happen if I don't find him."

"Maybe you should look for your brother first of all, and then when you find him and are sure he will come back to Fallow Creek for your wedding, then you can tell Vina about it."

"I have thought about that, Keith, but I think it will be better if I told her now. It will give me the drive I need to find Steven, knowing that my marriage to Vina will be on the line if I don't. Besides, I miss my brother and nephews very much, and going to look for him now is the right thing to do."

"Do you have any leads on where to find him?" Keith asked.

"I know where his good friend Alan moved to when he left Fallow Creek. Alan's younger brother was one of the first people to return earlier this year, and he told me Alan was in Tucson. He said he didn't know where Steven was, though."

"So you're actually going to look for your brother. How long do you think you will be away?"

"I don't expect to be away for more than three days. I certainly don't want to be away from Vina for much longer than that."

"But what will you tell her before you leave?"

"I don't know yet," Daniel said frowning. "I will have to figure that out soon." He stood up again and gave Keith a tight hug. "Thanks, Keith. I'm so glad I have someone like you to talk to." He grinned. "Though it can be a little intimidating sometimes, as I know I can never lie to you. I would have gone crazy with all these problems with Vina if I didn't have you to tell my relationship woes to."

Keith smiled and patted his shoulder. "I still think it would be better if you found your brother before telling Vina he will be coming to your wedding." He shrugged as Daniel looked away.

"I have to go and speak with Vina now," Daniel said, and smiled before walking out the door. He took a deep breath as he raced down the stairs. He had not seen Vina or any of the cast and crew this afternoon, but he knew they were somewhere in Fallow Creek shooting their movie. His stomach turned with anger as he remembered the scene Vina had acted with that actor yesterday. Hopefully, they had finished shooting that scene and she didn't have to do it again.

He walked out of the gates of the House of Refuge and looked to his left and then his right. *Where can she possibly be?* He had gone past her room on his way to Keith and Rachel's apartment and she wasn't there, which meant she was likely with the film crew. But what part of Fallow Creek was the film crew in now?

He walked through the streets of the town searching everywhere for Vina and the film crew. He knew it was a long shot to find her and he couldn't possibly search every single part of Fallow Creek on foot right now. For all he knew, she was in one of the empty houses in town with the film cast and crew shooting a scene in the movie.

He kept walking. Where on earth was Vina? He had to find her.

He continued past several empty houses wondering if Vina was in them, but surely if she was with the film crew in one of the abandoned homes, he would see signs of them outside the house.

He kept searching for her as he approached the town's border, and then he saw some of the film crew from a distance. He sighed with relief and then frowned when he saw her standing a few feet apart from everyone else talking with that slick director, Trent Radar. Anger burned in him at the way the director was looking at her.

He blinked in shock. It was not just the director who was looking at her as though he wanted to devour her; she was looking at him in the same way. He felt his body shake with fury and he marched toward them. And then he paused, took a deep breath, and told himself to calm down. He could not afford to do anything stupid, or his plan would not work. Not only would she never agree to marry him, but she would never speak to him again.

Lord, please help me get control of my anger.

He took deep breaths, gathered himself together, and approached them slowly. They did not notice him coming toward them as they seemed absorbed in the conversation they were having. He felt his anger begin to rise again, but once more he pressed it down. He reached them, ignored the director, and called her name.

She jerked her head around and turned to him. Her eyes widened slightly, and then she glared at him. "What is it now, Daniel?"

Pull yourself together. Don't let your anger get the best of you. He sighed, refusing to give in to his anger and frustration, and then said slowly, "Can I speak to you, Vina? I have something very important to tell you."

She narrowed her eyes and glowered at him.

"Please, Vina!"

She sighed loudly and turned to the director. "Please excuse me." She gave the director a sweet smile that burned Daniel on the inside, but he refused to react.

Waving her hand, she beckoned to him and then walked away from the director.

Daniel resisted the urge to glare at Trent Radar and immediately followed her.

When they were far away from the director and film crew, she turned and faced him. "What do you want, Daniel?" she asked, scowling. "I thought you said I had to choose between you and acting, and I chose acting. I thought we were over."

He sighed and looked deeply into her eyes. "I was wrong. I have been wrong so many times during these past few weeks. I know I have been asking you to forgive me almost every day, but I am asking again. I never should have asked you to choose between me and your dream. I understand how important it is to you." He sighed again. Their relationship should be more important to her than anything else, he thought, but he did not say it out loud.

She groaned. "I don't think we can do this, Daniel. This relationship. We've been fighting non-stop for a long time."

"That's not true, Vina. We started fighting two weeks ago, when you told me you wanted to postpone our wedding."

"I explained why," Vina said. "I told you it was because I have been married before and I felt trapped in that marriage. I know you're not like Mike, but sometimes your anger and jealousy scare me."

"I'm really sorry for making you scared of me," he said.

"I didn't say I was scared of you." She studied his face. "I said your anger and jealousy scare me." She sighed wearily. "You know I got married young. I didn't even know what I wanted to do with my life, or who I really was. I still don't really know now. I need to discover all that before I get married again. It's very important to me. I thought you would understand and we could still be together and get married later, but you clearly don't."

He didn't speak for a short moment, and then he said, "I can't lie. You are right. I don't fully understand, but I want to." He took a deep breath. He had to win back her heart before he could tell her that he wanted them to get married now. How would she take it when he did? He wasn't sure, but it scared him. Still, he had to. It was the only way to stop this constant cycle of breaking up and getting back together. And it was the only way to keep her from leaving Fallow Creek and losing her forever. "Please, can you give me another chance?" he asked.

"I have given you way too many chances lately," she told him.

"I know. But I'm still asking for another, because I love you and I know you love me too. Please, Vina."

She turned away. "I love you, but I cannot give you another chance. I am sorry, Dan."

"Please. I am working on my anger and jealousy, and I promise to do better."

She sighed and then nodded. "Okay, Daniel, but you have to promise that you will stop being jealous and that you will give me time to find myself. Also, you have to stop trying to get me to stay in Fallow Creek. I am leaving. I just don't know when."

He pressed his lips tightly together as worry and fear washed over him. He couldn't promise her that. With the way she and the director had been looking at each other just now, he would definitely lose her if she left. She was asking him to give her unlimited time to discover herself, but he was about to ask the very opposite of that.

"Daniel?" She frowned. "I am waiting."

"Vina, I have something to tell you." He exhaled and went on. "My brother, Steven. He called."

Her eyes widened in obvious surprise, and she shook her head. "Steven called?" she stepped closer to him and a huge smile broke out on her face. "Oh, Daniel, I'm so happy for you! You finally got to hear from your brother after so long." She put her hand on his arm. "When did he call?"

"Umm…yesterday." He raked his fingers through his hair, guilt running through him. He'd never lied to her, and it wasn't easy lying now, even if it was all he knew to do. Soon, he could hopefully turn it into the truth. He said. "The thing is… Steven told me he was planning to come to Prospect to visit some of his wife's relatives next week, and he said he would be coming with his wife and sons. You know he swore never to step foot in Fallow Creek again, but I told him we were getting married and convinced him to come for the wedding. He agreed to come but said he would leave immediately after the wedding"

Vina's mouth was wide open, and she didn't speak for a long moment. He shuffled his feet, worried by the silence. What was she thinking? He added, "You know Steven is my only living relative and how close we were before he left. I really want him to see me get married."

At last, she said coldly, "You told your brother we were getting married in a week? How could you, Daniel?"

He said anxiously, "I did it because this might be the only opportunity I have to get Steven to come to Fallow Creek with his entire family to see me get married. I miss him so much and miss the close relationship we had. This will definitely help mend our relationship and open the door for me to bond with my nephews again. I know I am asking a lot, but it is important to me."

She glared at him, her eyes flashing with anger. "I told you I wasn't ready to get married yet! How could you lie to your brother like that? How could you ask me to get married next week when I told you I don't want to get married anytime soon?"

Daniel sighed and nodded. "I understand how angry you feel, but please can you see things from my point of view? It's my brother, Steven we're talking about. You know Steven well. You know how close we were growing up. You know how much I miss him and that I would have gone searching for him if it weren't for my stupid pride. Now I have an opportunity not only to see him and my nephews again, but to share a once-in-a-lifetime event with them. Won't you do this for me?"

Vina folded her hands across her chest and studied his face. "You did a really stupid thing, Daniel," she murmured. "I told you I felt trapped in my first marriage, and now I feel exactly the same. If I marry you now, that's all I am going to feel."

"I cannot believe you're saying you will feel trapped if you marry me. I am not Mike, Vina. We love each other. We are best friends. You can't feel trapped when you are married to your best friend."

"You don't know how marriage changes relationships, Daniel."

"But we don't live by those old rules anymore, where you get married and are suddenly in a master-subordinate relationship. Most of the men who enforced all those stupid marriage rules have left Fallow Creek. I promise you, Vina. You can do whatever you want even when we get married."

"You don't know what you're saying," Vina told him. "If we get married now, I will have to remain here with you in Fallow Creek as your wife. That will be the end of my dreams to explore the world and to find myself. And it will be even worse once we have children."

He felt incredibly hurt that she was speaking about being married to him as though it were a prison sentence. What had gotten into her lately?

When he had proposed to her, she had seemed so excited to marry him. What changed that? He pressed his hurt and anger away and said, "You'll be able to do whatever you want to do, Vina."

"Really?" she stared incredulously at him. "I'm free to leave you here and go wherever I want for as long as I want?"

"Maybe not."

"You see what—"

He cut in, "I might just have to leave Fallow Creek with you."

She laughed and shook her head. "You, Daniel? You would never leave Fallow Creek."

"For you, I would. I would go wherever you wanted to go."

"Are you just saying that, or do you really mean it?" she asked, a surprised expression on her face.

He sighed. "You really don't know how much I love you. I would do anything for you."

She blinked and searched his eyes. Finally, she said, "But a week, Dan. It's such a short time. Why not the previous wedding date we set? A month from now?"

"Actually, our previous wedding date is about two weeks away. But like I said earlier, Steven will only be able to come to Fallow Creek next week."

"But planning a wedding in a week, Daniel. How will I be able to handle it all? And why can't Steven come next month?"

"First, you don't have to do everything alone, Vina. I will help, and so will Rachel. You know that. The other women in the House of Refuge will also help out. Second, I just told you Steven can only come to Fallow Creek in a week. I want my brother and nephews to see me get married." He gave her a wide smile, and his heart soared with hope when she smiled back. His heart began to race. "I know you love me, Vina. Surely you want Steven and my nephews to witness our wedding."

"I do," she said. "I just wish it didn't have to be now." She searched his eyes again. "But you promise that when we get married and I'm ready to leave Fallow Creek, you will come with me, no matter where I decide to go?"

He did not want to leave Fallow Creek, but he nodded. "Yes. I will go anywhere with you and for you."

He held his breath, anxiously waiting for her to speak.

She looked up with a thoughtful expression on her face and then sighed loudly. Finally, she nodded. "Okay. I will marry you in a week's time."

His mouth fell open and joy like he had not felt in a long time flooded his heart. He lifted his hands in triumph and swept her into his arms, lifting her off her feet.

She giggled as he spun her around, and then he placed her back on the ground.

"Oh, Vina, I am so happy. Thank you." He hugged her tightly again and kissed her cheeks. He placed his hands alongside her face and looked deep into her eyes as his heart overflowed with happiness. And then he felt a little anxious as he searched her eyes. She had not allowed him to kiss her in a while. Would she let him now?

He threw caution to the wind and kissed her. He expected her to draw back at any moment, but she didn't. Instead, she wrapped her arms around him and kissed him deeply.

He sighed in joy and contentment as they separated for a brief moment, and then he swept her into his arms and kissed her once more with everything in him. They finally separated again, and he took her hand in his. Weaving their fingers together, he walked with her toward the House of Refuge. He paused as he remembered that he would have to produce his brother before the week ran out or it would be the end of his plans to marry her.

"What is it?" Vina asked him.

He smiled. "Nothing, sweetie."

They began to walk again, and he silently calculated how long he would be away from Fallow Creek. He had to leave early the next morning and pray with all his might that he would find his brother. Because if he didn't, Vina would call off the wedding, leave Fallow Creek, and cut him out of her life. And then he would never see her again.

TEN

Daniel got out of Keith's car in Prospect and waved to his friend and mentor.

"Remember what I told you," Keith said, sticking his head out of the car window to look at Daniel. "If you don't find Steven by this time tomorrow, you need to return to Fallow Creek and tell Vina the truth."

"Okay." Daniel nodded. "Thanks for driving me here, Keith."

"No problem." Keith waved to him and drove off.

Daniel looked around the bus station where Keith had brought him. There weren't a lot of people in the Prospect station. The last time he'd been here was when Vina had sent for him to come back to Fallow Creek and help get Mike under control. No one could have predicted how much things would get out of hand after that.

When Vina had sent for him, he had returned without delay because he loved her and he loved Fallow Creek. He had only left the town during the mass exodus because everyone, especially members of the Squad, were leaving. A few of the guys from the squad team had stayed with Dennis Hamilton to help him fight his wicked war to try to hold on to the leadership of Fallow Creek. Daniel was thankful that he'd not been called on to join in that. Some of the men were dead, mostly from their battle with Mike and his men. The ones remaining were still living with Dennis in the house that Rachel and Keith had given them, or more specifically, the house Taylor, Rachel's brother, had given them.

Thinking about Mike made him angry. That man had done a number on Vina. First of all, because he was wealthy her parents had arranged for her to marry him even though they didn't have feelings for each other. She'd simply been Rachel's replacement. Also, because of Mike, Vina now hated the thought of marriage. He looked around the bus station again. Hopefully, his mission to find his brother would be successful and Steven would agree to come to Fallow Creek for the wedding.

Doubts assailed him as he stood waiting to get on his bus after he had paid the fare. He brushed aside the doubts and focused his thoughts on finding his brother once he got to Tucson. He could not afford to dwell on these negative thoughts. He brought out the piece of paper with Steven's friend Alan's address written on it and scanned it over. As he did, his mind filled with doubts again. *What will happen if I don't find Steven? What if I cannot convince Steven to come to Fallow Creek for the wedding since he vowed never to return again?*

He stared out the window throughout the trip to Tucson, but he barely saw the houses or cars that flew by as the bus sped on. His thoughts buzzed around finding his brother and what he would say when he saw him. Until now, all he had worried about was whether he could find his brother and convince him to come to the wedding. Now though, he could not help praying that Steven would agree to see him. Before Steven had left Fallow Creek, they'd had a fight. That might have added to the reason why Steven hadn't told him where he was going.

The events that had led to their big fight came back to him. He had promised to help Steven's wife watch their two boys so she could go and see her mother who was ill. Steven had gone to work. Daniel had gone to babysit the kids as he'd promised, and Steven's wife had left for her parents'. But someone had come to the house and told him Dennis Hamilton had called for all security squad members to gather at his house for an important meeting. Anyone that didn't show up would lose their squad membership and be severely punished. Since there was no way to contact either Steven or his wife, as they'd had no phones then, only radios, he'd left the children alone, praying that the meeting would be a short one. But it had dragged on with no way to escape. Steven had returned to find his kids alone in the house, hungry and grumpy. The house looked like a war-zone, wrecked by the young kids.

Enraged, Steven had confronted him. "What if they had hurt themselves?" he had barked. "And you left them hungry. I will never forgive you, Dan."

It wasn't the first time he'd had to cancel on his brother because of a squad engagement, but that had been the final straw. He had felt horrible and had pleaded with his brother, but Steven had refused to listen. To this day, Daniel loathed himself for what he'd done, especially as he now hated thinking about his time as a squad member and leader. Steven's anger had been justified.

Still, when Steven had left without telling him where he was going, he had been angry. Yes, he had messed up, but was that enough reason for Steven to cut off his only brother? Steven had of course taken his wife and sons with him, making sure Daniel would not get to see his nephews grow up. Daniel sighed sadly. Hopefully, Steven's friend Alan knew where Steven was, or he might not see his brother again.

Lord, please help me find him.

It was so wrong that it took his intense desire to marry Vina for him to finally let go of his foolish anger and decide to search for his brother. He shut his eyes as he remembered them growing up. They had been so close until he'd been scouted to join the security squad. Slowly, they had grown apart, but not enough that they hadn't visited each other or stayed in each other's lives. Now, he wanted a close relationship with his brother again.

Please, Lord, let me find Steven and let him agree to see me.

There were so many reasons why he had to find his brother. Not only was Steven the only family he now had, but his brother was also his only hope to have a family of his own, which he'd always wanted.

He dozed off a little after some time and then awoke with a start, afraid he had missed his stop. He blinked and then looked out the window and sighed with relief. They weren't there yet.

He thought about what Keith had told him. If he

didn't find his brother by this evening, he had to return and tell Vina the truth — that he still didn't know where his brother was. But how could he do that? If she discovered he had lied to her, she would never give him another chance. Keith seemed to think that telling her the truth, no matter what, would make everything all right in the end. But he seriously doubted it. Telling her the truth would make things worse and would forever destroy any hope he had of marrying her.

And you think lying to her will give you a better chance? What will happen when she finds out? Fresh guilt assaulted him, but he pressed it away. If he found Steven and could convince him to come to the wedding, what he'd told Vina would not be a lie anymore.

You know it still would.

He sighed and once more brushed the troubling thoughts from his mind.

Leaning back in his seat, he closed his eyes, not meaning to fall asleep, but when he opened his eyes again, the bus was driving into the bus station in Tucson. He sighed with relief and waited for the bus to stop. When it did, he got out.

Once again, he pulled the piece of paper with Alan's address out of his pocket as he made his way out of the bus station with his small duffel bag. Like many people in Fallow Creek before the mass exodus, Alan did not have a phone or Daniel would have called him in Fallow Creek to ask about Steven.

He kept walking until he found a taxi and then showed the driver the address to Alan's house. The driver nodded, and Daniel got in.

The driver drove for a short time and stopped in front of a ranch-style home. For a short moment, Daniel stood in front of the house, staring at it and praying that Alan was home. Alan's brother told him that Alan and his family were staying with relatives until they could get their own home. Since Daniel had not told him he was coming, Alan wasn't expecting him. That meant he might not be home. If he wasn't, Daniel would have to find a cheap motel and come back the next day.

"Lord, please let him be home," Daniel whispered. He took a deep breath and moved toward the front door. He knocked on the door and waited. Seconds later, the door opened and Daniel could not help smiling widely. Alan stared at him with a look of surprise on his face.

"Daniel? Daniel Bacon? How come you're here?"

Daniel laughed.

Alan laughed along with him and affectionately pounded Daniel's back. He opened the door wide and stepped back to let Daniel in.

Daniel sat on the sofa, and Alan sat across from him. He chuckled as he looked at Daniel. "If it isn't the assistant leader of the infamous security squad," Alan said. He looked down at Daniel's duffel bag and raised his eyebrows.

Daniel smiled. "Don't you worry, Alan, I'm not going to stay here. I will find a motel in town."

Alan grinned and shook his head. "Still as direct as ever. I would have loved for you to stay here, but this isn't my house."

"I know. Your brother told me." He looked around the spacious living room. "Talking about your house, where are your wife and kids? And the relatives you are staying with? This house looks empty."

"They all went out for the day." He shook his head. "People outside Fallow Creek apparently have a lot of leisure time. The children wanted to go out, so everyone takes the opportunity to go out with them." Alan ran his fingers through his thick dark hair. "So I guess it was my brother who told you where to find me. He told me a while back that he was going back to Fallow Creek, and even though I tried to talk him out of it, he still went back. I don't understand how he could go back there with his wife and children when everything has changed." Alan came, sat next to Daniel, and tilted his head forward. "Tell me, Daniel, you also went back there, right? How is the town now that a woman is in charge?" He frowned. "A woman who left her husband to marry another."

Daniel shook his head and laughed. "You know, Alan, it's way better than when Dennis Hamilton was in charge. In fact, I don't think the town has ever been this free and great to live in."

"That's a lie!" Alan said. "I hear that the town is now occupied by mostly women. There are hardly any men there. How can you stay in such a place?" He gave Daniel a mischievous grin and added, "Wait, don't tell me. I know why you're still there. You get to have as many women as you want. Tell me, Daniel. How many wives do you have now? Three, four, five?"

Daniel felt rage building inside of him. He itched to deck Alan, but he took a deep breath and controlled his emotions. He could not afford to antagonize the guy who could help him locate his brother, and he was learning that giving in to his anger only made things worse. He said softly, "Actually that's why I came here. You know Vina?"

"Davina Cadwell? Mike Cadwell's wife?"

Daniel pressed his lips tightly together and rubbed his temples. He had not thought about this particular problem before he came to Tucson. Most married women, even if they grew up with the men they later married, were looked on as their husbands' property. If he told Alan that he was marrying Vina, who had been Mike's wife, he might not take kindly to that. Not even if he told Alan that Mike was now dead. Widows got remarried, but not regularly, and most of them were considered used goods. The worst thing was that Steven would share the same silly logic. Still, there was nothing he could do. He had to tell Alan. "She's no longer Mike Cadwell's wife."

Alan's forehead creased as he frowned, clearly surprised. "What happened? Did she rebel like some of the other women in that town? The last I heard, Mike was still living in Fallow Creek and refused to leave with everyone else. Did she leave him and move into that Restoration House full of rebellious women?"

Daniel glared at Alan. It was getting harder to control his anger with everything Alan was saying, but he exhaled and let go of his rage. "She's a widow now. Mike Cadwell died last year."

Alan's mouth flew open, and he shook his head. "I didn't know. That's sad, but then again, not too surprising. He chose to stay in a town where a woman is in charge." Alan turned his nose up. "And worst of all, a woman like Rachel Cadwell, the woman who left him to marry someone else. That would kill any man for sure, no matter how wealthy he is."

"Stop that, Alan!" Daniel barked, unable to control his anger anymore.

Alan frowned, looking confused. "What did I do?"

Daniel sighed and put his anger away. "Nothing," he said. He had to control his anger, or his quest to find his brother would end unsuccessfully. "Anyway, as I was saying, she is a widow now, and if you remember, we were best friends growing up. We are engaged and will be married next week by God's grace."

Alan stared at him with disgust written on his face. "You're going to marry a widow?"

"So?" Daniel narrowed his eyes in anger. He wanted to tell Alan that she wasn't even really a widow because she was never truly married to Mike, but Alan would not understand. He himself would not have understood had he not been living in Fallow Creek under Rachel and Keith's leadership for a while with the benefit of their teaching. He now knew that the polygamous lifestyle they had all thought was normal was, in fact, wrong and a sin. Only the first wives were truly married to their husbands.

Alan raised his hands. "I'm sorry. I didn't mean two annoy you, Daniel. So tell me, why did you come here? What do you want me to do for you?"

"I came because of Steven. Do you know where he is, Alan? I need to find him. I need him to come to my wedding next week."

Alan frowned. "The last time I spoke to Steven,

he was angry with you and said he didn't want you to know where he was. He said he never wanted to see you again."

Daniel's heart ached at Alan's words. His older brother, who he had loved and looked up to for years, never wanted to see him again. That was messed up. "I don't understand why Steven has refused to forgive me," Daniel said, his heart hurting.

"You did a lot of things that showed him that you do not care about him or his family."

"That is not true," Daniel said. "I made a few mistakes, but—"

"A few mistakes? You put everything before your brother, your only living relative. That day you left his children alone in the house to go to your squad meeting was the straw that broke the camel's back."

"I know I did a terrible thing," Daniel said. "I tried to apologize so many times, but Steven refused to accept my apology."

Just like Vina will if you don't find Steven and get him to come to the wedding.

"You may have apologized many times, but he got tired of your apologies because you kept doing the same thing over and over again. Besides, when he left Fallow Creek, he vowed never to go back, just like many of us. I doubt he would agree to come to your wedding."

"But are you absolutely sure he will not want to see me?"

Alan didn't say anything for a long while, and Daniel tilted his head forward and studied him. He said, "Please answer me, Alan. Are you sure my brother doesn't miss me now... at least half as much as I miss him?"

Alan looked up at Daniel and gave him a small smile. "I did hear Steven saying something about how you would have handled a particular situation he found himself in a few months ago."

Daniel blinked. "So you know where my brother is. He is here in Tucson, isn't he?"

Alan nodded. "Yes, he is. But I am not sure I should tell you where exactly. I don't want Steven to be angry with me if he finds out I was the one who told you where he lived."

"Please, Allen. Remember what you said earlier."

"What did I say?"

"You said that Steven misses me… at least a little."

"I never said he missed you." Alan smiled. "I said he talked about you."

"It's the same thing."

Alan raised his brows and shook his head. "Even if I tell you where he is, don't expect him to receive you with open arms. And definitely don't expect him to agree to go to Fallow Creek for your wedding."

Daniel huffed. "Fine, I won't! Just tell me where my brother is."

ELEVEN

Daniel's heart pounded as he stood in front of the tiny bungalow where Steven now lived. He knocked on the door and waited for it to open. And then he frowned when it didn't. Worry flooded his heart. What if Steven wasn't home? What if he had traveled with his children?

He lifted his hand to knock again just as the door suddenly opened. He stared at the familiar-looking blond standing before him. And then he blinked as he recognized her. "Stella? Stella Hunter..." He frowned trying to remember her husband's last name. "Stella Carson, you're here?"

Her mouth dropped open, and then she smiled. "Daniel Bacon. I should be asking you the same question. What are you doing here?" Her eyes widened, and she hit her forehead with her palm. "Oh, I'm sorry." She shook her head. "Of course, you are here to see your brother. This is his house after all." She opened the door and he walked in.

"Is Steven home?" Daniel asked eagerly, and then glanced around the living room. It was a small living room, sparsely furnished with a couch, a loveseat, and a small coffee table. There were no pictures on the wall and no television set, which did not surprise Daniel. Many people in Fallow Creek didn't own TV sets.

He sat down when Stella pointed at the couch. She came and sat on the other end of the couch, and he stared curiously at her as she studied his face.

"What?" he asked, smiling.

She shook her head. "It's just that I remember you as the assistant leader of the security squad. Most people were somewhat afraid of you."

He raised his brows. "Afraid?" He shook his head and waved his hand dismissively. He didn't want to talk about the security squad. "Is Steven home?" he asked again.

"Oh, I'm sorry. He isn't home. He went to visit a friend with his wife and kids," she said.

Daniel gave a sigh of relief. At least Steven lived here and would be back today. His heart rate increased as anxiety gripped him. "Please, Stella. Tell me my brother and his family didn't travel out of town. Tell me they will be back today."

Stella chuckled as she looked at him. "You look so worried, Daniel. Yes, they should be back anytime now." Her eyes searched his face once more, and then she said, "You know, Daniel, you really look like your brother."

He smiled brightly. "Okay... and you look like your sister, Lily."

Stella blinked as her mouth tipped and she looked like she was about to cry. "Lily? Have you seen my sister, Daniel?"

Daniel immediately remembered that Lily had

been at the House of Refuge last year when Mike and his men had besieged the House. She had even come back months later to visit Rachel and Keith with her husband, Taylor. She had said something about searching for her parents and her sister. Daniel gasped. Maybe that was why Stella looked so stricken when he mentioned Lily's name. She didn't know where her sister was. He said to her, "I saw Lily earlier this year. She has been looking for you and your parents."

Stella looked like she was about to jump out of her skin. "Lily! I haven't seen her since she was driven out of Fallow Creek. You said you saw her earlier this year? Where?"

"She came to Fallow Creek, to the House of Refuge, to visit with Rachel and Keith. She's married to Taylor Archer, Rachel's brother. They stayed at the House of Refuge for a while."

Stella leaned closer to him. "Please, Daniel. Do you know where she is now?"

He shook his head. "I don't. But I am sure Rachel knows."

Stella wrung her hands. "I miss her so much. Every day I regret not going to see her at the Restoration House."

Daniel gave her a sad smile. "Stop blaming yourself, Stella. You didn't know she was going to be exiled from town."

"At least when I heard that she was going to be driven away, I should have found a way to go and see her. The last time I saw her was about two years ago." She looked deep into Daniel's eyes and said, "Please, I need to go back to Fallow Creek with you. You have to help me. John will not let me go anywhere, so I have to leave without him knowing."

Daniel blinked. "And where is your husband now?"

"He went to see his parents in Prospect, but he will be back tomorrow. I have only two days to leave and return here before John comes back, or I will be in trouble with him."

Daniel frowned. "Talking about parents, where are yours now? From what I remember, Lily has been going crazy trying to find them. Do you know where they are?"

"I did, but John separated us." Daniel frowned again, and Stella shook her head. "It's been like that ever since we got married. He hardly ever lets me visit my parents or any of the old friends I had before I married him. I only got to see them when they visited. When Lily was chased out of town, he became even more controlling. He said that our parents did not raise Lily and me right and that was why she turned rebellious." Stella laughed harshly. "He said she would be a bad influence on me if I went to see her before she left town. He also said my parents would be the same. I was angry, but there was nothing I could do since I'm just a woman. During the mass exodus from Fallow Creek, my parents came to our house and asked John if we were going to leave. He said we would, and my parents told him they were not yet sure where they were moving to but it would be a good idea if we all left together.

She stopped speaking and pressed her lips together as tears welled in her eyes.

Daniel began to reach out to place his hand on her arm to comfort her, then remembered it was frowned on in Fallow Creek to touch a married woman, or any woman you were not married to or who was not a relative. He reached into his pocket, pulled out his handkerchief, and handed it to her.

She thanked him, wiped the tears from her eyes, and went on. "John told my parents that they were right and we would leave Fallow Creek with them. However, when they left our house, he got me to pack up our things and we left town before my parents did. I tried to convince him to wait for them, but he refused to listen." She sighed. "Stubborn as usual."

Daniel felt anger burning in his stomach. "That's more than stubborn. That was cruel, what he did. He separated you from your parents, knowing full well that you would not be able to know where they went."

Stella continued. "We left Fallow creek, leaving my parents behind. Now I don't know where they are. A lot of people left town, right?"

"Yes, Stella," Daniel said. "Most people left, except for most of the women in the House of Refuge… and Mike Cadwell."

She looked surprised. "Mike Cadwell stayed in Fallow Creek? Rachel's husband? I heard she got married to someone else. I would have thought he would be the first person to leave"

Daniel narrowed his eyes as he remembered the terrifying incident with Mike last year: the mayhem, the fear, and Mike Cadwell's death. During the siege, on the day Mike and his men surrounded the House of Refuge, Daniel had thought that he and all the women in the house would be killed. But at last, Mike himself was the one who had died. He told Stella the whole story.

When he finished, she shook her head slowly with an astonished look. "Wow! And I thought that Rachel taking over as the leader of Fallow Creek was the worst that could happen there."

"Actually, Rachel's takeover is the best thing that has happened to Fallow Creek in a long time. And her name isn't Rachel Cadwell anymore. It's Rachel Thorn. That's her husband's last name."

"You're saying that Fallow Creek is much better now that a woman — a woman like Rachel — took over from Dennis Hamilton?"

He wanted to tell her that Dennis Hamilton was still in Fallow Creek, living on the goodwill of Rachel and Keith, the very people he wanted to kill because of his thirst for power, and Rachel's brother, Taylor. But he changed his mind. She didn't need to know that. He answered, "Definitely better."

She looked like she was going to cry again. "I wish we had not left. Tell me you are leaving for Fallow Creek today, Daniel, so I can go with you. Please, I have to go with you. I have to find out where Lily is."

"Stella, you don't have to beg. Of course I will take you along with me. I am sure that Rachel will be pleased to see you and will try to help you reconnect with your sister."

"Thank you so much, Daniel." She gave him a bright smile. "You know you are quite different from what I imagined you to be. You always looked so stern when you were in the security squad. Are there any members of the squad still living in Fallow Creek, or is it just you?"

He thought about the few men living with

Dennis Hamilton, but he said, "No, there isn't. It's just me."

"So there is no security squad anymore?" she asked him.

"There isn't. The town is totally different now. There's no threat or danger anymore, and no need for armed men like the security squad patrolling the whole town." He thought about the way the town was before Rachel had taken over and added, "Not that there was a lot of crime during Dennis Hamilton's time. He just liked having armed men everywhere to instill fear. It was all about control... controlling everyone in Fallow Creek and making sure they toed the line."

"You are definitely different than who I thought you were, Daniel."

"No, I probably was exactly who you imagined I was. But I am different now. I changed along with the rest of the town. Rachel and Keith changed me. God changed me. However, there is still one thing that needs to change about me that hasn't."

She lifted her brows quizzically. "And what is that?"

"My temper. It gets me into trouble more than it should, particularly now that I am not in the security squad anymore." He didn't know why he was telling her all this since they were not even close. Maybe it was because he was in his brother's house, his brother who he had not seen in ages, and somehow felt like he was in his second home. He was comfortable here, and therefore he felt comfortable talking to Stella about his life."

"I think you're right," she said. "Many of the members of the security squad seemed to have quick tempers and were always ready to punish anyone who stepped out of line."

He chuckled. "No, we were always ready to enforce the law. At least, that was what we were told."

Her eyes studied his again. "Do you promise to take me to Fallow Creek with you as soon as you see your brother and his family?" she asked.

"I promise. But even though your husband is not around, I am sure Steven and his wife will not let you go with me."

"Yes, you're right, Daniel."

"So I think we need a plan." He looked at the handkerchief he had given her. "Why don't you tuck this handkerchief under one of these cushion pillows here. After I see my brother, his wife, and my nephews, I will leave the house but wait for you outside. I believe I saw a huge tree opposite the house."

She nodded.

"I will stand behind that tree and wait for you. Just tell my brother and his wife that I forgot my handkerchief and you have to hurry out to give it to me. When you do, we can leave for Fallow Creek together."

She smiled. "Okay. But I have to write them a note first to let them know I'm leaving temporarily but will be back. I don't want them to worry about me."

"Okay."

She stood up and went to get a pen and paper. She came back less than a minute later and quickly scribbled something on the paper. She folded it and tucked it in her dress pocket.

"When did you say your husband was coming back home?"

"Tomorrow evening," she answered. "I have to get back here before then."

He couldn't imagine how she was coping, living with such a tyrant as a husband. He wished she could go back to Fallow Creek and stay in the House of Refuge with the other women. Those women had the freedom to do and be wherever they wanted. His mind immediately went to Vina and what she'd told him about her desire to leave Fallow Creek and find herself and her purpose outside their hometown. Pain rippled through him. This visit with his brother had to work.

Stella, curious about how Rachel ran Fallow Creek, began to ask him multiple questions. He tried as best as he could to answer her in detail. He turned around when the front door opened, and his heart soared with joy as Steven walked in, followed by his wife, Esther, and his two nephews, Jack and Freddie."

The two boys screamed when they saw him and immediately ran to him. He hugged them tightly and then looked up at Steven.

Steven walked slowly toward him, looking as though he had seen a ghost. His wife didn't look much different.

"Go out and play," Steven said to his children. When they ran out of the house, laughing, Steven stood before Daniel and eyed him. "What are you doing here?" he asked coldly.

"Steven, I know I have wronged you so many times and you are tired of hearing my apologies, but I came here from Fallow Creek to ask for your forgiveness." He looked at Steven's wife. "And yours, too."

Steven looked back at his wife and told her to excuse them. When she left along with Stella, Steven glowered at Daniel. "What are you apologizing for? You made it clear when we were in Fallow Creek that you cared more about other things, like your squad duties, than your own family."

"I know. I was wrong, and I am asking you to forgive me. Remember how close we were as children, Steven. I know I have been a lousy brother, but I think I have changed now. Besides, there is no more security squad."

Steven snarled. "No, there is something much worse. That woman Rachel who is now in charge of our town along with the man she's living with in sin."

Daniel ignored his brother's words. "I'm getting married next week, Steven. I want you to come to my wedding. I want you to be a part of my life, and my wife's life, and I want my nephews to be a part of our lives in the future."

"Never, Daniel! I am not going back to Fallow Creek as long as that woman is the leader." His expression softened, and he gave Daniel a tender smile. "I accept your apology. I wish with all my heart I could see you get married next week, but I cannot go back to Fallow Creek. Surely you understand why."

"No!" Daniel shook his head. "No, I don't understand why, Steven."

"How can you not understand? The whole town has been turned upside down. Why do you think everybody left? Well, everybody except for you.

I don't understand how you're still living in that town."

"The town is much better than now than it ever was." Again, he wanted to tell his brother that Dennis Hamilton was living there, but for some reason, he didn't feel comfortable about telling Steven. He pleaded, "Please, Steven. I really need you to come to my wedding. Forget about the leadership of the town and do this for your younger brother. You don't have to stay in Fallow Creek. Just come to the wedding and then you can leave the next day."

Daniel's heart began to race as Steven frowned and looked at him with a thoughtful expression on his face. He prayed silently. *Lord, please let Steven say yes. Please.*

"Okay, I will come with Esther and the kids."

Daniel's heart soared with happiness. "Thank you, Steven! This makes me so happy."

"But we will probably leave the same day." Steven groaned. "I cannot believe I'm going back to that town. I swore I never would."

Daniel pounded Steven's back affectionately. "You love your brother, that's why you are going back." He grinned. "You know you'd do anything for me."

Steven laughed. "Don't push it, Daniel, or I will change my mind."

They both laughed.

They started talking about Fallow Creek, and Steven asked Daniel to tell him all about how the town fared now and how different it was from before everyone left. Daniel repeated everything he had told Stella, but Steven had a much different reaction from hers. His remarks about Rachel were similar to Alan's. Daniel tried to defend Rachel and Keith, but Steven would hear none of it. Daniel finally gave up and changed the subject.

They talked about their childhood and their late parents until Esther came into the living room again. Stella came out as well. Esther asked him if he would stay for dinner, and he said he couldn't.

"Unfortunately, I have to go back to Fallow Creek this evening because my fiancée will be expecting me."

"I haven't even asked, Daniel." Steven put his hand on Daniel's shoulder. "Is the girl you're marrying anyone I know?"

Daniel thought about not telling his brother about Vina when he remembered Alan's remarks after he had told him. But Steven was his brother, and he would find out when he came to the wedding anyway. He exhaled and said, "Davina Brooks."

"Who is Davina..." His brother's mouth flew open. "Don't tell me you are talking about Davina Cadwell. Mike Cadwell's wife."

Daniel sighed wearily. He was tired of explaining to everyone that she wasn't Mike Cadwell's wife anymore. "I told you Mike Cadwell is dead, Steven. She's not married any longer."

Steven scowled. "Still, she is..."

Daniel held up his hand. "I know what you're going to say. Please, don't say it."

"All right then. Are you sure you cannot stay for dinner, though?" Steven asked.

"No, I have to leave." He glanced discreetly at Stella and said to Steven, "I will see you, Esther, and the kids next Friday?"

"We will definitely try to make it," Steven answered. He reached out and pulled Daniel into a tight hug.

After Daniel had said his goodbyes to Esther and the kids, he smiled at Stella and began to leave the house. "I will walk you to the bus station," Steven said.

"No!" Daniel shook his head anxiously. If Steven followed him to the bus station, his and Stella's plan to leave for Fallow Creek together would be jeopardized. "Don't worry about it," he said to his brother. "Stay here with your family."

"Don't be silly, Daniel. It's not a problem walking you to the bus station. The place is not far from here."

"Please, Steven. Stay with your family. Besides, I need to get some things from the store before I head to the station."

"Fine," Steven said, and slapped Daniel's back, grinning. "I'll see you in a week, brother."

Daniel sighed with relief, hugged his brother again, and walked out of the house. He looked back to make sure no one was watching him, and then quickly went and hid behind the tree a few feet away from the house. He waited for Stella to come out and gasped when a black truck passed by him and stopped in front of the house. He caught a glimpse of the man's face in the driver's seat and he looked like John, Stella's husband. Daniel had seen them together a few times in Fallow Creek and knew the man reasonably well.

But Stella told me he was coming back tomorrow. Daniel prayed he was mistaken, but when the man stepped out of the truck, Daniel's heart sank and he groaned. It was definitely John.

Stella's husband walked toward the house and reached the door just as Stella exited the house. She looked up at him, and the look on her face tore at Daniel's heart. She looked scared and devastated. They exchanged a few words, which Daniel could not hear, but he could see they were arguing, or more accurately, John was berating his wife. He took hold of her shoulders and turned her around. She looked back toward Daniel's hiding place, and when their eyes met, he mouthed, "I'm sorry."

Her husband pushed her into the house, and Daniel groaned again. She looked so sad that he wished he could rush inside, grab her, and flee with her. But he knew he couldn't do that without fighting his way through. He might be able to take her husband in a fight, but he didn't want to fight his brother, too. And without a doubt, Steven would support John and be mad at him for wanting to take a married woman away from her husband, even though that husband was treating her badly.

John looked back briefly and then entered the house and shut the door firmly behind him.

Daniel came out from behind the tree and stared briefly at his brother's. He thought about Stella and once again considered going in to try to get her. But he had to get going. His mission had been successful, but if he went into that house again, it would fail. He would tell Rachel and Keith about Stella and hope something could be done to get her away from John and reunite her with her sister.

He turned around and hurried to the bus station, determined to reach Fallow Creek before the sun went down.

TWELVE

Vina sat on the porch swing and struggled to concentrate on her lines. It was her last scene. Garret Fletcher sat beside her, and all she was supposed to say was "I have loved you since I saw you on my TV screen, Jared. I will do anything for you."

Just two lines. She had memorized and reread those lines about a hundred times the night before, and she knew them as well as she knew her name was Davina. But every time she tried to say the words, they suddenly evaporated. However, the reason that kept happening wasn't a mystery to her. Her mind was preoccupied with thoughts of her upcoming marriage. Fear and doubt had become her regular companions since she'd agreed to marry Daniel in such a short time.

Trent yelled 'Cut' as she messed up the lines. He asked her to do it again.

She looked at Garret. "I saw you the day I..."

"Cut!" Trent growled. He walked toward her and frowned. "What is the matter with you today, Vina?

You seem to be somewhere else. You played your other scene perfectly yesterday. This is your last scene, and you have just two lines to say. You are wasting everyone's time."

"I'm so sorry," she said to him. "I will do better now. I promise."

Trent sighed loudly and went back to take his seat.

After he asked them to do it again, Garret said his lines perfectly. He gazed into her eyes.

She took a deep breath. *Focus, Vina. You can do this.* She smiled and spoke her lines. Trent yelled 'Cut' again and her heart sunk. She'd actually thought she had said her lines right this time. Apparently, she had messed up again. She looked at Trent. When she saw he was smiling, she sighed with relief.

"Perfect!" he said. "We can take a break."

She smiled at him and then left the set to go back to the House of Refuge. She still had some errands to run for Rachel, but Rachel had kindly given her enough time to shoot her scenes in the movie.

For a couple of hours, she went around the House of Refuge delegating chores and making sure that Rachel's orders for the smooth running of the House were obeyed. She tried to forget that she still had to plan for her wedding, but it kept tugging at her mind. She did not want to think about the wedding at all.

If you're so afraid to get married, why are you going ahead with plans for a wedding? She kept asking herself that question as she went about her chores.

She tried to answer the question: She loved

Daniel, and it was what he wanted. She also wanted him to have the satisfaction of his brother being at their wedding. He'd been trying to find his brother for so long, and now that he had, she would not take away his joy.

She frowned as she walked into the storage room and saw that the huge bag of detergent she'd bought from Prospect the day before was almost finished. Someone was wasting detergent. She sighed and made a mental note to buy more as soon as she could go shopping again.

Her mind traveled to Daniel once more. She frowned. She hadn't seen him at all today. He usually came to the House to see her daily, but he hadn't stopped by today. The only time he stayed away was when they'd had a huge fight. But they hadn't fought yesterday. She had agreed to marry him in a week, and he had been extremely happy. So, where was he?

She finished unpacking the toiletries she had bought that morning and went down stairs. She planned to walk to Daniel's house and see if he was there. She started to make her way out of the House of Refuge and then her heart skipped a beat. Trent was passing through the gate. She paused as he walked toward her.

"I was coming to see you," he said.

Her heart pounded as he reached her. Why did he have this effect on her? She heard someone whispering behind her and turned. Two women were standing at the entrance to the House, gazing at Trent with dreamy expressions on their faces. She smiled. Of course she knew why he had this effect on her. It was the same effect he had on other women as well. He was blazingly handsome, and his job as a movie director only added to his charm and attractiveness.

He smiled at her. "We are through shooting all the scenes you are in. You've been great so far, and apart from that initial absent-mindedness today, your acting has been perfect. I think you are really talented, Vina."

She smiled widely, her heart soaring with happiness.

"Thank you," she said. She kept smiling. She could not stop. It was a big deal that the Hollywood movie director thought she was a talented actress even though her role was pretty small. She enjoyed acting; it would have been her chosen career if she had the choice to pursue it.

"You know what, Vina? I think you should actually pursue acting. You're really good at it, and it would be a shame to waste such talent."

She blinked in surprise. "Really? You think I am good enough to be a professional actress?"

"As soon as we wrap up shooting this movie, I have another project coming up. I am also producing that one as well. I would love for you to star in it. Not as an extra, but as one of the lead characters."

Her mouth dropped open, and she could not speak for a few seconds. Finally, she found her voice and said, "Really? You are shooting another movie here, and you want me to star in it?"

"No, we are shooting the movie in L.A."

She could not breathe. She stared at him, astonished. Was he really asking her to star in a major role in a Hollywood movie? She could not believe her ears.

"Vina? You haven't answered my question. Are you interested in starring in my film?"

"Yes!" she said quickly. A thought entered her mind. Trent was saying the movie would be shot in L.A. That would mean she would have to go there when she was supposed to marry Daniel next week. Would he agree to move to LA with her, or would she leave without him? She had heard about long distance relationships, but would a long-distance marriage work?

She immediately pushed the troubling thought out of her mind and concentrated on Trent. "I would love that very much. But are you sure I could succeed in Hollywood?" She became slightly nervous, thinking about acting in a major role in a Hollywood movie. She didn't know much about the industry or Hollywood except for the little she had learned from the magazines Leah showed her and the occasional secret internet surfing.

Trent assured her that she was a great actress and could take on whatever role she put her mind to. "Trust me, I would tell you if you were not good enough. I know acting and I know you can act, Vina." He began to tell her about the movie industry and what she could expect when she came to L.A. It all sounded so dazzling and interesting. She knew immediately that this was what she had been searching for all this time. This was her purpose in life and this opportunity would open the world for her.

But once again, the troubling thoughts about Daniel and their wedding filled her mind. His dreams to start a family with her here in Fallow

Creek intruded into her happy thoughts, and she had to hold back a weary groan. She had to believe that Daniel would keep his word and move to Hollywood with her to support her dreams.

A tiny voice whispered in her heart: *But what about his dreams?*

That was a huge problem. Their dreams were not aligned at all. Their aspirations and goals were totally different. How could they get married?

But she had promised to marry him next week.

"So, are you excited about playing a major role in my movie?" Trent asked her.

She nodded. "Yes. Very excited."

"Okay, then. I will try to send you the script in a week so you can go through it."

Happiness flooded her heart at the thought of this new opportunity. The doors to the world she had not known existed a few weeks ago had opened up for her. Soon she would embark on an exciting adventure in L.A. Daniel's face appeared in her mind, and this time she groaned loudly. Only Daniel would be an obstacle to her adventure.

"What is it?" Trent asked.

She smiled. "Nothing." There was no way she was going to tell him she was worried her fiancé wouldn't want to move to L.A. with her. "I'm so happy!" Her joy returned fully, and she couldn't hold back anymore. She threw her arms around Trent and hugged him tightly. "Thank you so much, Trent."

She pulled away, and Trent chuckled. He placed his palms on her cheeks and suddenly she could not breathe. The atmosphere around them crackled with their mutual attraction. His eyes were so tender as he looked at her that she felt herself getting lost in them. And then she gasped as his eyes moved to her lips. He looked like he was going to kiss her right here in the open. And with everything in her, she wanted him to. She didn't care who saw them.

She parted her lips slightly, anticipating his kiss, and then she drew in a sharp breath. Instead of the kiss, someone pulled Trent away from her and punched him in the stomach. Her mouth flew open, and she stared at Daniel in horror as he stood with fists clenched, glaring at Trent.

She yelled, "Daniel, what have you done?" She looked at Trent, who had doubled over and was groaning in pain and then turned back to Daniel. He glanced at her and then fixed his gaze on Trent, his eyes red with clear rage.

"Daniel, how could you?"

He blinked as he focused on her, and the rage disappeared from his face, replaced by shame and embarrassment.

She stepped up to him and glared. "Why did you do this, Daniel? Why did you hit Trent? He could sue you for everything you have." She shook her head and then laughed harshly in anger. "But you have nothing, do you? All you have is your stupid jealousy and uncontrollable anger."

He looked even more ashamed now and bowed his head slightly. "I'm sorry," he said .

"I'm not the one you should be apologizing to." She looked at Trent, who had straightened and was walking up to Daniel. Vina's heart raced in fear. No, he was actually storming up to him. He had a look of pure hatred in his eyes, and his fists were balled. Her eyes widened in panic, and she let out a scream as Trent threw a punch at Daniel.

"No, Trent!"

The punch landed in Daniel's midsection, and he stepped back slightly and held his stomach. And then he straightened, unfazed and seemingly in no pain. He lunged for Trent, and she winced as she heard a thud.

Trent landed on the ground on his back. He looked up at the sky, stunned. She watched as if in slow motion as Daniel attacked Trent again, and then she sprang forward and tried to hold him back. Thankfully, some of the production crew joined her and finally restrained him. A bunch of women from the House gathered around, and Vina stared at Daniel in shock. She went and knelt beside Trent to see if he was okay and sighed with relief when he sat up again.

"I'm fine," he said to her and the cast and crew who had gathered around to help him.

They helped him up, and Vina turned around and hurried after Daniel, who was already walking away. She caught up to him, grabbed his arm, and pulled him back. "Daniel, I have had it!"

He looked ashamed, but she had seen him look this way too many times and still lash out in anger because of his jealousy.

"I'm sorry," he said. "When I saw him place his hands on your cheeks and lean forward to kiss you, something came over me." He sighed. "But he should not have tried to kiss you, Vina. He knows we're together."

"Well, not anymore! And for your information, once we finish shooting this movie in Fallow Creek, I am moving to L.A. Trent offered me a role in another movie he's going to produce."

Daniel looked devastated, but she did not care.

"What about our wedding next week?" he asked in a small voice.

Anger rushed through her. "Are you serious, Daniel? There will be no wedding! The engagement is off. I am not even sure I still want to be your friend!"

"But my brother and his family are coming next week for our wedding. You promised we would get married so my brother and nephews can attend. What will I tell him?"

"You should have thought about that before you allowed your anger and jealousy to overwhelm your sense of reason. In fact, I don't think you have any sense of reason, and you totally lack self-control. You need to grow up, Daniel. You are not the assistant leader of the security squad anymore and your anger accomplishes nothing. No, actually it does accomplish something. It pushes away everyone who loves you." She frowned. "Including your own brother. That was why your brother cut off from you. Who wants to be around an angry man?"

Daniel blinked and stepped back, looking terribly hurt. She knew she had hit him below the belt, but she didn't care. She would never forgive him for how he'd humiliated her and what he'd done to Trent.

He started to plead with her again, but she shook her head. "Don't even try to apologize anymore! We are through, Daniel. You can find someone else in Fallow Creek to marry and have your dream family with. That person won't be me." Before he could say anything else, she marched away, fuming. This was the hundredth time she had marched away from him after a huge argument, but it would definitely be the last. There would be no more arguments. This was the last time she was ever going to speak to him again.

THIRTEEN

Daniel knew it was finally over between him and Vina. He had begged and pleaded with her to give him another chance, but she refused to listen, telling him there were no more chances for him. She had been annoyed when he'd come to plead with her, and she had warned him not to beg her to take him back again. Still, he had continued to plead until she screamed at him. "We are through, Daniel. Why won't you get that into your thick skull?"

He felt wretched. He had destroyed his relationship because of his jealousy. Why did he have to go in like a madman and attack Trent?

But what could he have done when he saw Trent trying to kiss his fiancée?

Ex-fiancée now… because of his stupid actions. He should have trusted that Vina would stop Trent from kissing her. But he had not done that. Instead, he had attacked Trent like a lunatic, and Vina had ended their relationship.

He stretched out on his couch and looked up at

the ceiling. Glancing at the clock on the wall, he groaned. He hadn't been able to go on his daily patrol since the day Vina had broken up with him. He groaned again. Today was supposed to be their wedding day, and any moment his brother and family would arrive in Fallow Creek. Shame and embarrassment had stopped him from sending a message or going to see Steven to tell him that the engagement was off. What was he going to tell his brother when he arrived in Fallow Creek? What was he going to do about the way his heart hurt? He felt like he had no more hope for the future. As if his breath had been sucked out of his lungs and he had no more life in him. Why oh why had he been so reckless and destroyed with his very hands the thing that meant the world to him — his relationship with Vina?

He was lucky that Trent hadn't sued him, Vina had said. But he didn't feel lucky. He felt wretched. He had to do something about his awful temper before it cost him something very dear.

He moaned. Actually, his temper had already cost him everything.

Not everything. God still loved him even though he failed the Lord every time, and his anger was something he was certain God was displeased with. Also, he still had friends like Keith and Rachel. He had to speak with Keith about this pain he felt now that he and Vina were no more. He didn't know if he could bear it for much longer.

Oh Lord, what am I going to do? he sighed heavily.

He kept mentally flogging himself for what he had done, how he had ruined his relationship with

Vina, and then he sat up. Why was he here mourning his separation from Vina when he should be trying to win her back? Yes, she had said they were over and he had run out of chances, but he loved her and somehow he knew that she still loved him. If not for his quick temper, they would have been getting married today. If only Trent Radar had not come to Fallow Creek and stolen Vina's heart. But he would win it back. They had known each other for years. Trent might be rich and handsome, with the dazzling job of a Hollywood producer and director, but he did not know Vina the way Daniel did. *Surely, he does not love her like I do.*

Daniel stood up from the sofa as a firm determination entered this heart. She had warned him to stop pleading with her to take him back, but how could he? How could he go on without her? He could never give up on their relationship.

He left his house and made his way to the House of Refuge. Hopefully, she would be there because if she wasn't, then she was probably somewhere in Fallow Creek, on the set of that movie, maybe, or worse, with Trent.

His confidence began to fail and misgivings filled him as he walked into the House of Refuge. What if they were truly over and nothing he did or said could change her mind. He pressed his lips together and then pushed the thought aside. He would not give up. Not as long as there was life in him.

He went up the stairs and knocked on her door. The door opened and her roommate Lisa looked at him.

"Vina, is she in there?" he asked.

"No, she has not been here since this morning,"

Lisa said.

"Do you know if she's in Rachel and Keith's apartment?"

"She told me she was going to the movie set when she left this morning."

"But I thought she was through with shooting?"

Lisa shrugged.

"She could be with Rachel and Keith," Daniel said.

"No. Rachel and Keith left Fallow Creek with Emily a few minutes ago. I think they said they were going to Prospect to get some things for the House. I don't think Vina was with them."

Daniel moaned and went back downstairs. He had to find Vina before Trent got his claws into her.

He went outside and found some women who were whispering about going to the location where the movie was being shot today. He frowned as he kept hearing them whisper Trent's name and giggle. He followed them until they arrived at the house that had been Dennis Hamilton's. As far as Daniel knew, even though Dennis didn't live in the house anymore, his wives and children still lived here. Why had this film crew been allowed to shoot their movie here?

He looked around, hoping to catch a glimpse of Vina, and then wished he hadn't. She was with Trent some feet away from the house. They were partly hidden behind a tree, but from where he stood, he could see they were kissing. His blood boiled with anger, and he bit his lip until the pain made him stop.

Calm down, Daniel. Don't do anything stupid.

He felt hurt and betrayed as he walked toward

them. It was hard for him to control his anger, but he had to. Even though everything in him wanted to attack Trent and beat the living daylights out of him, he could not do that. It would defeat the purpose for which he had come to search for Vina. And maybe this time, Trent Radar would actually file a lawsuit against him. Though that didn't bother him much. What concerned him was how Vina felt. If he was going to have any chance of winning her back, then he had to completely get rid of his anger.

They did not even notice him when he reached them. Vina's arms were wrapped around Trent, and she was kissing him as passionately as he was her. Daniel felt like throwing up, but he took a deep breath, gathered himself together, and then coughed to get their attention.

They immediately separated, and Vina glared at him.

He shuffled his feet and looked down as he tried to regain his composure. *Don't do anything stupid, Daniel. Please.*

"What are you doing here, Daniel?" Vina spat out.

"I came to talk to you." He sighed and looked up at her. She was glowering at him.

Trent chuckled and shook his head as he stared at Daniel with derision written on his face. "Why won't you get it into your head that you and Vina are through? She doesn't want you anymore. As you can see, we are together now." He reached out and pulled Vina close, and then he kissed her firmly on the lips.

Daniel felt like screaming in rage, but once again, he held himself together. He gave Trent a mocking smile. "I wasn't talking to you, was I?" He sighed and turned back to Vina. "Please. I won't take too much of your time."

"You need to get some self-respect," Trent said to Daniel. "Vina doesn't want you anymore. Why do you refuse to accept that?"

Daniel ignored him. He kept his gaze fixed on Vina and pleaded with her again to give him a minute of her time.

"Daniel, I'm sorry, but I don't want to talk to you. There's nothing you can say to change my mind." She looked at Trent. "As Trent said, I'm with him now. You need to accept that and move on."

Daniel narrowed his eyes. "Since when?" He turned to glower at Trent and then faced Vina again. "This guy has been gunning for you since he arrived in Fallow Creek, even when we were together. Now he has convinced you that he's better for you than I am. But look at him, Vina. Does he look like the kind of guy that can be committed to one girl? He doesn't love you — not the way I do. Once he finishes shooting his movie here, that will be it for you two."

Trent chuckled and Vina shook her head, a look of sympathy appearing on her face. "You're wrong, Daniel," Vina said. "Just like I told you before, Trent offered me a role in his Hollywood movie. After we finish shooting this movie, I am moving to Hollywood to be with Trent and start shooting another movie."

"If I just wanted something temporary with Vina, would I have asked her to come to L.A. with me?" Trent asked with a scornful smile. "And would I be doing this in front of everyone?" He took Vina's hand and pulled her out from behind the tree to the edge of the road.

Daniel followed, angry and curious. Trent took her face in his hands and kissed her again.

Daniel's heart nearly stopped beating as a car pulled up beside them. Steven got out of the car with his wife and his children. His eyes were fixed on Vina and Trent and a confused look was on his face. Steven's wife looked at him and then looked at Vina and shook her head, clearly astonished.

Daniel thought he was going to die from hurt and shame. He shut his eyes as pain filled him. Trent and Vina had made their point well. Now he knew it was truly over. Everyone in the town, including his brother, Steven's wife, and their kids knew it was over. He was never going to win back her heart.

Vina looked at Steven and then at his wife and children, and finally turned to face Daniel. Her eyes flashed with anger. If she could have strangled him, he knew she would have. He didn't understand why she looked so angry with him. He was not the one who had pulled her to the side of the road in front of everyone and kissed her, nor was he the one who'd made Steven, his wife, and their kids appear just in time to witness it all. In fact, it was the last thing he'd wanted to have happen. His family should not have seen that.

She bit her lip, pulled away from Trent, and stormed off.

Daniel turned to Trent, and he could not hold back his anger anymore. Because of Trent's stupid antic, Steven and his wife and kids had witnessed something they shouldn't have. So had he, for that matter. He swung at him, but Trent dodged his blow. Before he could swing his fist again, Steven hurried to him and grabbed him.

Trent shook his head, chuckled, and walked away.

Shaking with anger, Daniel tried to free himself from Steven's grasp, but Steven held on tightly. After a few minutes, Daniel got control of himself again. Once more, he had reacted in anger. Thank God Steven had been here to hold him back, or things would have gotten out of hand. A small part of him wished it had. That jerk Trent would have deserved the beating he would have got if not for Steven's intervention.

A still, small voice whispered in his heart, *He that is slow to anger is better than the mighty; and he that ruleth his spirit than he that taketh a city.*

He recognized the scripture from the Bible and groaned as shame filled him. He definitely didn't know the meaning of ruling his spirit. It was the other way around. His emotions controlled him. It had stolen his relationship with Vina. Would it also steal his relationship with God? If he didn't try to control his anger, how could he call himself a Christian?

"What was that about?" Steven asked him. "Why was Vina kissing that man, and who are all these people?" Steven waved his hand at the camera crew and the cast. His kids started to run toward the crew, but he ordered them back, and they obediently returned and stood beside their mother.

Daniel heaved a sigh and said, "Let's go into the House of Refuge and talk."

Steven, his wife, and their children followed

Daniel through the gates of the House of Refuge into the common room. Steven looked around the room as they sat and said, "This place has changed." He glanced at his wife and then looked at Daniel again. "So, this is no more a house of reformation for wayward women. It's now a place where everyone can come and go as they please. More like a party house now." He looked at a group of women who stood at the entrance of the common room laughing and giggling and shook his head, disgust written on his face.

Daniel ignored everything Steven said. All he could think about was how Trent had kissed Vina with that gleeful expression on his face. He tamped down his anger when he remembered the scripture that had flashed through his mind a moment ago and took a deep breath.

Steven waved to his sons, who were running around the common room. "Go out and play, boys," he said, then focused on Daniel. "So, tell me why your fiancée was kissing another man in the open where everyone could see them?"

Daniel covered his eyes and pressed his lips tightly together, shame smothering him. What could he say to Steven? Whatever he said would result in Steven scolding him for returning to Fallow Creek and deciding to marry a woman here. According to Steven, all the women in Fallow Creek were loose women.

"Daniel?" Steven put his hand on Daniel's shoulder. "Tell me what happened. I came all the way here even though I said I would not come back again just to attend your wedding. Now I find the woman you're supposed to marry kissing another man. Tell me why that is?

Daniel sighed and opened up to his brother. He told Steven everything that had happened in his relationship with Vina, from the time he'd asked Vina to marry him to the unfortunate incident that Steven and his family had witnessed. After he finished, he sighed again. "That's everything that happened. She is now with someone else, and the wedding has been canceled. I don't think Vina is ever going to accept me back."

Steven laughed harshly. "You see what happens when a woman takes over as the leader of a town?" He pointed, not discreetly, at two women who were sitting at the far end of the common room, chatting and laughing. "You should have expected foolish behavior from Vina since she lives here." He looked at another group of women at the entrance who were still in their pajamas and dragging their feet lazily. "Women become uncontrollable and start to do whatever they want when there is no man in charge to bring order. This whole town, this House — there was order when Dennis Hamilton was in charge. Men are the ones who are supposed to be leaders of towns and countries, not women."

His brow furrowed. "If Dennis Hamilton were still the leader of this town, or another man from here, your fiancée would not have dared to do all she's done. She would not even have thought of all that nonsense about wanting to find herself. And most of all, she definitely would not have kissed another man. You would probably be married by now." Steven gave him a sympathetic look. "You should not have returned to Fallow Creek, brother. You should have stayed away. I don't know why you decided to come back here when everyone had left. See what the woman who made you return to Fallow Creek put you through?"

He continued his tirade against women, and Daniel glanced briefly at Esther, his wife. Her hands were folded on her lap, her head bent slightly.

Daniel sighed as he thought about what Steven was saying. His brother was right. If Dennis Hamilton were still in charge, Vina would definitely not have had the stupid idea of going to find herself or even of leaving Fallow Creek. People couldn't just leave town whenever they liked. He looked at Esther again. Steven's wife was obedient and sweet. Just the way women were meant to be. If Rachel had not taken control of this town, maybe he would be married to Vina now.

He uprooted the doubts his brother had planted in his mind. As much as he would love to be married to Vina today, he didn't want a woman who was with him because she had to be. Vina had developed a self-confidence that she hadn't had when she was married to Mike, and so had many of the women here. It pained him that Vina had broken up with him, but he wanted her to be with him of her own free will. Unfortunately, her free will had led her away from him, but there was nothing he could do about that.

Besides, contrary to what Steven had said, if Dennis Hamilton were still the leader of Fallow Creek, Mike would probably still be alive today and Vina would still be married to him.

"I cannot live in a place like this," Steven said with repulsion as again he glanced at the women chatting and giggling on the other side of the common room. "I think you should come with me, Daniel. Leave this town for these loose women."

Daniel almost told his brother that even Dennis Hamilton still lived secretly in Fallow Creek, but he held that information back. There was no use telling his brother. He felt confused, hurt, humiliated, and most of all heartbroken. He had lost Vina forever. Maybe it would be wise to leave Fallow Creek with Steven. There was little for him here. How could he stay here and watch Vina carry on with that Trent Radar? He would not be able to bear it.

Steven stood up, went to the entrance of the common room, and called to his kids. They immediately came to him, and then he looked at his wife, who had already stood as well. "It's time to go. I can't stay one more minute in this place." He looked at Daniel. "Are you coming?"

Daniel blinked as Keith and Rachel walked into the common room. Rachel looked at Steven and smiled as recognition lit up her eyes. "Hey, Steven!" She glanced at Daniel and then turned back to Steven. "You came to see your brother. He's been searching a long time for you. He'll be so happy to have you and your wife and kids stay with us for a while."

Steven glowered at her and Keith and then faced his wife. "Let's go, Esther!" He looked at Daniel again and said, "Are you coming, Daniel?"

Daniel looked up at Keith and Rachel and slowly shook his head. "I can't," he said to Steven. "In spite of everything, I still love Fallow Creek, and I still believe in what Keith and Rachel are doing." He knew by not going with Steven and choosing to speak out in support of Rachel and Keith, he was risking his newfound relationship with his brother. Steven might decide to cut off from him completely. If that happened, he would miss his brother and his nephews, but at least he was confident he would be doing the right thing. And besides, he knew where they lived now. He would find a way to reconcile with them and then he could visit whenever he wanted, thanks to Keith and Rachel's new policy of allowing everybody freedom to come and go as they pleased. It would be hard to stay here when Vina was now dating someone else, but leaving would not make his heart less broken. The only thing he could do was to try to avoid them as much as possible.

Steven frowned. "You know where we live, Daniel. Soon you will understand that this is no place for people like us," he said, and glared at Rachel and Keith. He swept past them, and his wife and children followed.

Daniel looked after his brother and sighed audibly. Today was supposed to be the happiest day of his life. His wedding day. Instead, he could count it as one of the saddest.

Keith came to sit next to him on the sofa, and Rachel sat on the couch beside theirs.

Daniel covered his face with his hands. He felt like weeping. He looked up at Keith when Keith put his hand on his shoulder.

"What happened, Daniel?" Keith asked.

"My brother Steven came for my wedding today, but he witnessed Vina kissing that director, Trent, in the open."

"What?" Keith looked shocked.

Rachel's mouth was wide open. She blinked

rapidly and shook her head. "Did you just say that Vina was kissing the director? What has gotten into her?"

"Apparently they are now dating," Daniel said brokenly. "She told me that as soon as they finish shooting this movie, she's moving to L.A. to take a movie role that Trent offered her. She told me herself that they're now together."

"Oh, Daniel, I'm so sorry," Rachel said. She stood up, came and sat on the other side of him, and put her hand on his back. "I will try to talk to Vina."

"There's no use," Daniel said. "It's all my fault that she dumped me. My jealousy and anger got the better of me, and I attacked Trent when I saw them kissing yesterday and again today."

"You attacked him?" Keith stared at him.

"I punched him, and we got into a fight."

"No, Daniel. You should not have done that," Keith said. "He might just decide to sue you for assault."

"That was what Vina told me. But I really don't care about that. I just wish I had not done what I did because now I have finally lost Vina forever."

He shut his eyes as a sliver of pain went through him. A sob rose up in his throat, but he swallowed it. Soon Vina would leave Fallow Creek and that would be the end of their relationship. Already, she had moved on to another guy.

"I know it hurts, Daniel," Rachel said. "But one day you will find someone else who loves you and wants the same things that you do. You and Vina want different things in life, and I guess that is what actually tore you both apart."

"That and my quick temper, Rachel. Don't forget

that. Also, my jealousy and anger." He pursed his lips. "I don't want someone else. I want Vina."

Keith and Rachel looked at each other but said nothing. He knew why they remained quiet. Just because he wanted Vina didn't mean he would ever have her. It was the end of them. Everyone knew it, and he had to accept it, no matter how painful it was.

FOURTEEN

Vina looked out the window of her L.A. trailer and found it was already dark outside. The stars were sprinkled across the sky and it was a beautiful night. For a moment she thought about going out and sitting under the stars just doing nothing, but she had a ton of lines to memorize for her scenes tomorrow. The set was brightly lit, and she looked across at the trailers of the other cast members. Mark Durham and Johanna Barret, the lead actor and actress, were talking in front of Mark's large, luxury trailer. This time Vina was playing the supporting actress in this movie called *The King's Treasure*, the king being Mark; she, the treasure.

She closed the curtains again and once more concentrated on her script. She couldn't help comparing the hectic shooting schedule she had now to the one in Fallow Creek. She smiled in self-mockery. Maybe if she'd known how much she'd be working as an actress before she'd come to Hollywood, she would have thought twice about pursuing this path.

She chuckled. Of course that wasn't true. She loved what she did now, even though it was a lot of work. She just wished she had more time for herself. She had arrived in L.A. about a month ago and immediately started learning her lines and shooting her scenes. The little she saw of L.A. made her stare in wonder, but she had yet to explore the city. Since she'd come here, all she had done was rehearse her lines sometimes with her co-stars and show up to shoot her scenes. She'd hardly had time to go anywhere or do much of anything else.

The worst thing, though, was that she had not spent any time with Trent since they'd begun shooting the movie. He seemed to have forgotten completely about her. She only saw him when she was shooting her scenes and he was directing, but he was always too busy to speak to her for more than a minute after. She didn't blame him, though. She understood the grueling schedules they all had. She herself didn't have time for much else, but when they were in Fallow Creek, she'd dreamt of Trent taking her out a few nights a week and showing her the city. Now she knew better, but still, she yearned to steal a few moments in private with him in between shooting.

She continued to memorize her parts, and then her heart skipped a beat when she got to the part she had avoided since Trent had first given her this script. She had avoided even looking at this particular scene after she'd read it the first time. It was a steamy love scene where she had to make out with the lead actor. The scene was way more intimate and way more passionate than the one she'd had to play in Fallow Creek. If in Fallow

Creek she'd felt extremely uncomfortable when she'd discovered she had to kiss the lead actor, here she felt downright scared.

For a long moment, she stared at the couch in front of her, unwilling to continue reading. Finally, she forced herself to go back to the script. She began to read the part where she was to seduce her co-star, and she felt herself blushing. She couldn't play this part.

And yet she knew she had to. She had signed a contract that obligated her to play the role she was given, no questions asked. Even though she had seen this scene when she'd first been given the script and she'd shuddered at it, she had still agreed to take this role.

She had no choice. She had to try to put her discomfort aside, memorize this part, and give a great performance regardless of how she felt about it. Actresses acted steamy scenes all the time. It was just a part of the business of acting.

Daniel's face appeared in her mind like it had every single day since she'd come to Hollywood. She sighed loudly. Would she never forget about him? Even though her every waking moment was spent reading, memorizing her lines, and shooting her scenes, she still had time to think about Daniel and miss him terribly. What would he think if he saw her acting this part?

Which he just might, she told herself. Once the movie was released, Daniel would probably decide to watch it because she was in it, even though he hardly watched movies.

No, not probably. She had left him in Fallow Creek to come to do this movie in L.A. He would watch it, she was sure. When he did, what would he think? Would he be disappointed in her or thank God he did not marry her?

She thought about Rachel and Keith and felt ashamed. They would definitely be disappointed. She had learned so much about God and they had helped strengthen her relationship with the Lord through their teaching. But since she'd come to L.A., she had not spent more than ten minutes in total reading her Bible or praying. Not only had she been too busy, but every time she thought about praying, she had this nagging feeling that the Lord would not answer her because of the role she was playing in this movie and what she was doing now, especially with scenes like this.

She groaned. She was still procrastinating. There was no escaping this scene. She had to memorize it and make sure she acted the scene flawlessly. She couldn't keep avoiding it forever.

She looked out the window again, and her gaze fell on Mark. She hadn't even shot a scene with him yet. This love scene would be the first.

Stop procrastinating, Vina, and go back to memorizing your lines.

Guilt flooded her as she began to read out her lines. There was a bit of language. A word she had never used before and which even now made her blush.

Remember it's just acting. Get a hold of yourself, Vina.

She continued to read the scene, and then she lifted her eyes from her script. "How on earth am I going to act this?" she asked. She immediately imagined herself acting the part out with Mark, and guilt flooded her again. She tossed the script aside and groaned.

Her trailer door opened, and when Trent walked in, she blinked in surprise. "Trent! You're here!"

He smiled brightly at her. "I'm sorry I haven't had any time to visit you since we came back here. You know how busy our schedules are. Mine is even busier."

He sat beside her, and she nodded. "I understand, Trent. I've just missed you. I thought we would have a day or two alone together and maybe explore the city," she said.

"I have missed you, too." He reached out and ran his fingers through her hair.

"I want to have some alone time with you, too. Unfortunately, we still have a few weeks of intense filming before the madness lets up. I think after that we can talk about spending a full day alone together." He chucked her under the chin and then tilted his head as he studied her. "What's wrong, Vina? You look like you just had a fight with someone."

She smiled wryly. "Maybe I have. Not with someone, though. With my script... or more specifically, my lines."

"What's the problem?

She told him everything she had been struggling with; about feeling uncomfortable with how intimate the love scene was.

"I understand how you feel," he said to her. "This is the first time you will be acting a real love scene. I'll help you with your parts," he said. "Unless you want to rehearse the scene with Mark."

"No," she said quickly. "I would feel more

comfortable rehearsing it with you... at least for now." She gave him a curious smile. "Aren't you too busy, Trent? Do you have time to help me with my lines?"

"I am making time for you now. That's why I came."

She smiled. "Thank you."

"Now, show me your script and let's rehearse the love scene together."

They began to read and act out her lines and Mark's together. She read hers, going deep into character, and then paused when they came to the very passionate part of the scene. He smiled encouragingly and pulled her into his arms. When he kissed her firmly, she returned his kiss ardently, just like her character was supposed to. But when he started to undo the buttons on her shirt, she winced and jerked back.

"Vina, what are you doing?"

She shook her head.

"This part is also in your script." He sighed and smiled tenderly at her. "You're still feeling uncomfortable even though you are acting the part with me. How will you feel when you actually have to act it out with Mark?" He took her hand and squeezed it encouragingly. "You have to try to get over your fears."

"I know that part is in my script, and I am glad you are the one I am rehearsing it with, but I just don't feel comfortable." She looked down. "I am sorry."

"We are only rehearsing, Vina," he said. "I won't go past what is in the script. And isn't that why we are rehearsing it now? So you get used to it all before you actually have to act it out?"

"I know," she said, forcing herself to smile. "It's just that..."

"Just relax, Vina. It will all turn out right." He pulled her into his arms again, and they started kissing once more. He began to undo her buttons, and she stifled the urge to pull back. But when he undid a button more than he should have, she jerked back and blinked. "No, Trent!" She scowled at him. "That is definitely not in the script!"

He laughed. "I undid one more than it says in the script. Sue me." He shook his head. "I don't understand, Vina. Why are you so frigid? It's not like we're strangers. We are in a relationship. This," he waved his hands between both of them, "should be normal by now." She frowned, and he sighed. "I know. You don't believe in pre-marital sex. You have told me before, and I have tried to respect your values as much as I can. But I think if two people love each other, there is nothing wrong with expressing their love in whatever way they choose. I think it's time we took our relationship to the next level."

She blinked. She understood exactly what he meant by "the next level," but she wasn't going to do that. They weren't married, and that would be wrong. She told him so.

He didn't say anything for a long moment, and then he smiled. "I understand, Vina. It's just that... I'm starting to fall in love with you, and it's getting harder and harder to stop at just kissing you."

Her jaw dropped. She looked into his eyes. "You are in love with me?"

"Yes, I am," he said. He raked his fingers through

her hair. "You are so beautiful. I am such a lucky man." He drew her close again and kissed her.

She returned his kiss, but when he began to go farther than she was comfortable with, she pushed away once more. "I can't," she said in a small voice. "I'm sorry, Trent."

He nodded and touched her cheek. "There's no need to apologize. It's okay." He stroked her cheek. "I will wait for you until you're ready." He looked at her script again. "However, you need to rehearse your scenes and give a great performance," he said in his director voice. "Will you be able to do that, Vina? Or should we find someone to replace you?"

Her heart drummed in both fear and confusion. Was this really what she wanted? To be an actor? She thought again about Daniel, Rachel, Keith. About her friends in Fallow Creek. What would they say when this movie came out?

She looked into Trent's eyes. He was waiting for an answer. She had left Fallow Creek, broken her engagement with Daniel, and come here because she wanted this. The acting career, Trent, this life. The last thing she wanted was to be replaced and for her acting dreams to end before they had fully begun.

Trent frowned. "Vina, what is your answer?"

She sighed and said, "No, Trent. You don't need to replace me. I'll do it."

"Atta girl," he said, smiling. "Now, let's start from the beginning of the scene."

FIFTEEN

Daniel walked around Fallow Creek on his usual daily patrol. He had always enjoyed his job, which involved walking around the town he loved and making sure no danger lurked anywhere that would threaten the lives of the people who lived here. But today, he felt no joy or pleasure as he plodded around town. He did it mechanically. His heart felt dead, broken. Vina had taken his heart with her when she'd left Fallow Creek. He had tried to call her a couple of times, but she never answered.

He had to find a way to get over her, or he would never be able to go on with his life. Not that he had not tried to forget her, but he had not been able to. The pain of her leaving still tormented him, especially because he was to blame.

He got to the edge of town and groaned. Fallow Creek was as peaceful as it usually was these days. There were no threats and there was no point continuing with this patrolling. He was physically and emotionally weary. He turned around and began to head back to his house.

On the way, he stopped in front of the House of Refuge and looked up at it. Here, in this House of Refuge, he had proposed to Vina. He had been so happy when she'd told him she would marry him, and she had seemed happy, too. That day, he had dreamed of their future together, the kids they would have. He had pictured both of them living together in his house, happily going about their lives as a couple. A fresh wave of pain hit him as he thought about her. There would be no more visits to her room in the House, no more making sure that her roommate was around so they could stay in her room, no more kisses and cuddling.

He sighed sadly and moved on. Since the movie cast and crew had left Fallow Creek, the town had been quieter than usual. Or maybe it was just because Vina wasn't here anymore. She'd added vibrant colors to his life and made it lively with her presence. Now that she wasn't here, everywhere felt still and dull.

He reached his house and, for a short moment, stood in front of it and considered turning back to the House of Refuge. When he had decided to go back home at the edge of town, he had not thought about how lonely his house seemed these days.

He stepped back slightly. He dreaded going inside. He could go to the House of Refuge, spend time with Keith and Rachel, and try to forget his misery.

He sighed and changed his mind about that. They were probably busy, and he would only get in their way. Unlike him, they were busy with the running of the House and the whole town, with Emily, and definitely with each other. He went to their apartment almost every day now to spend time with them, but they were probably getting tired of him. He needed to let them spend time alone. Just because he and Vina were not together anymore didn't mean he could get between the time other couples should spend alone with each other.

He opened his door and walked in, and just as he expected, loneliness engulfed him as he shut the door behind him. He groaned and collapsed on the couch. When Vina was here, even when they'd fought, he'd never felt this alone. He'd visited her regularly and so had she. The awful thing was that, before they'd gotten together, he hadn't felt this alone either. He had gotten used to having someone to hold and love. Now they were no more. Would he ever get over this emotional pain he constantly felt? Would he ever stop thinking about her and how his stupidity had caused them to break up? Would he ever stop longing for her?

He groaned as Vina's face appeared in his mind and refused to be pushed aside. He had spent too many days and nights dreaming about her since they'd broken up. He spent every day hoping she would come back, even though he knew that wasn't going to happen. She had moved on with the rich director. He had been filled with remorse after she and the film crew had left the town as he remembered hitting Trent. He had asked the Lord to forgive him for doing that, but it had not stopped the jealousy and bitterness that rose up in him every time he thought about Trent. If the guy had not come to Fallow Creek with his film crew, he and Vina would still be together.

He turned on his couch and tried to take a nap,

but he couldn't. He sat up again as a thought ran through his mind. Maybe he had given up on Vina way too soon.

He groaned. There was nothing he could have done to keep her in Fallow Creek. He hadn't given up on her. She'd given up on him. She'd made it very clear that there was no chance of them getting back together. And that kiss out in the open between her and the director had cemented the fact that she had indeed moved on. She was all the way in L.A. now. There was nothing he could do to win her back.

Isn't there?

He frowned. Maybe he needed to go talk with Keith. He started to get up from the couch and then sat back down again.

Didn't you just decide that you need to give Keith and Rachel some space?

Keith was a pastor, and he clearly loved to help people out, but surely by now he would be tired of him. Almost every day, he was in Keith and Rachel's house whining about how lonely he was and how he missed Vina.

But Keith and Rachel had never complained or showed that they were tired of him. Keith could advise him on what to do. Even if there was nothing to do, maybe Keith could show him how to let go of Vina in his heart.

The thought of letting her go felt terrible. When Mike died and he and Vina were finally able to be together, he had known that nothing would separate them. If he'd guessed he would be the cause of their break-up, he would have done everything in his power to curtail his jealousy and temper.

He stood up from the couch again and quickly

left his house. Better to talk to Keith than stay here wallowing in self-pity. Even if Keith had no more wise words for him concerning what to do about Vina, he had to leave his house before he caved in on himself.

He got to the House of Refuge and climbed the stairs. As usual, women walked around, chatting or going about their business. Several of them greeted him, but he simply smiled and went on. He was in no mood to talk to anyone but Keith.

He exhaled. *As usual, Daniel.* Was he ever in a mood to talk to anyone except perhaps for those close to him, like Keith, Rachel, and Vina?

He remembered what Vina had told him some time ago. She had been talking about going after her dreams and finding herself again, and then she'd asked him what his dream was, what he really wanted in life. He had told her that she was his dream and starting a family with her was all he wanted. She had tried to get him to want more than just being with her. "Like maybe making more friends in this town," she'd said. But he had always been an introvert — though when he was with Vina, he came out of his shell a little. Being the leader of the security squad, he hadn't needed to interact too much with others except to bark out orders and follow Dennis Hamilton's when given.

He got to the front of Keith and Rachel's apartment and knocked on the door. He winced after he knocked. Here he was again about to bother this nice couple with his problems. But right now, they were the only friends he had. He had no one else to talk to.

The door opened, and Keith smiled at him.

"Come in, Daniel."

Keith walked into the living room, and Daniel stepped in and shut the door behind him.

Keith sat at the dining table and began to chow down on a plate of pasta. Clearly, he had been eating when Daniel had knocked. Daniel sat on the sofa and sighed.

"You're still like this, Daniel?" Keith said, and put a heaped fork of spaghetti into his mouth.

"I wish I could get over Vina quickly, but I haven't been able to. It's so hard, Keith."

"Have you prayed about it?"

"Every day," Daniel said.

Keith stood up from the table and came and sat beside him. "The only thing I can tell you now, Daniel, is that it will get easier as time goes on." His eyes searched Daniel's, and he added, "I can see that an idea is forming in your mind right now, Daniel. What is it?"

"Pastor Keith, I can never hide anything from you, can I?" Daniel shook his head. "I know what you will say, that what I have in mind is not a good idea, but I think it's something I have to do."

"Great!" Keith raised his brows as he stared at Daniel. "Another harebrained idea. Let me hear it."

"I'm beginning to think that maybe I shouldn't give up on Vina," Daniel said. "Maybe I should go to L.A. and try to win her back."

"Daniel! Are you sure that's the right thing to do? Remember you tried something extreme to win her back before and it didn't work out. She still broke up with you and moved on with that director. This is even more extreme than all the other things you've tried put together. I know you love her very much, but the likelihood of winning her back just because you went to L.A. is slim. And speaking about the director, are you sure they are not still together? If they are, your chances will be even slimmer."

"I have had a lot of time to think about how we broke up, and the part my anger and jealousy played." Daniel shut his eyes for a few seconds and then opened them again. "I know I'm mostly to blame for our break up. Vina was right. Apart from my jealousy and uncontrollable anger, I was overprotective and possessive. This time, when I go to L.A., I will go there just as her friend…at least at first. I will try my best not to be possessive or jealous. Even if she is with that director, I will grin and bear it. I will even be nice to the guy, and even though it will hurt like crazy, I will be by her side and support her as best as I can, even in their relationship."

Keith frowned. "How is that supposed to help you win her back?"

"I know in my heart that Vina still loves me. She broke up with me because of all my character flaws. If I am to win her back, then I have to learn to put all of that aside. I have to get rid of them all." He sighed. "And there's no better way to do that than to actually learn to control my jealousy and anger when she's with Trent Radar. If I can make her see that even though she's with a new man, I still support her and still love her, and if I don't act out in jealousy and rage anymore, then maybe she'll rethink her decision to break up with me. Hopefully, she'll begin to remember why she fell in love with me, and then we can get back together."

Keith shook his head and then laughed. "Daniel, Daniel, Daniel! Just like I said; a harebrained idea." The smile melted off his face, and he said, "Listen, Daniel, your logic is flawed. Supporting her, and even her relationship, when your plan is to win her heart back is not going to make her want to get back with you. The best scenario is that she might be happy you're not jealous or possessive anymore and you will go back to being good friends, but nothing more."

Daniel pursed his lips. "It is all I can come up with at this time."

"Are you sure you're ready to stay by her side even when you see her and her new man together? Are you sure you can stomach that? It will be hard. It will be very hard."

"I know, but I think I have come to a place where I would rather be just her friend than not be in her life at all. If that means having to bear her relationship with the director, then so be it. It will be painful, but I am ready to do whatever it takes to win her back."

"Well, I can see that you have made up your mind, Daniel. So when do you plan to leave?" Keith sighed. "I wish you didn't have to go. Rachel misses Vina so much, and now you're leaving. I will miss you, Daniel."

Daniel chuckled. "And here I thought you would be glad to get rid of me. I keep coming to your house every day to share my heartbreak stories."

Keith pounded his back good-naturedly. "No, I like having you over. Not that I enjoy listening to your 'heartbreak stories,' but I like talking with you, Daniel. I am glad that you want to work on your anger issues and your jealousy. It's important to do that. But going to L.A. to visit your ex-fiancée, who you are still in love with, while having to witness her new relationship with another man, is too extreme a way to practice controlling your jealousy and anger." He chuckled. "You should start visiting Dennis Hamilton with me instead. His constant condescending behavior will be good practice for you, and you won't have to go all the way to California."

In spite of himself, Daniel could not help laughing. "I thought you said Dennis Hamilton was a changed man?"

Keith shook his head. "Well, he is definitely better than he was before, but you know how bad that was. He has a long way to go still."

Daniel chuckled and said, "I think in order to get rid of this jealousy and anger, I need an extreme situation, like going to L.A. Though it might end up making it worse."

Keith grinned. "Okay. You haven't answered my question, though. When do you plan to leave?"

"Tomorrow," he said. He had just decided on that now. Tomorrow was the right time to go. He could not waste any more time wallowing in self-pity in Fallow Creek.

"Tomorrow?" Keith studied him. "Isn't that too soon?"

"I have to go immediately and start my quest to try to win back Vina's heart before she falls in love with Trent."

"And how do you know she hasn't fallen in love with him already?" Keith asked.

"You don't fall out of love so quickly and fall in

love with someone else just as quickly." He noticed the uncertain look on Keith's face and instantly knew what Keith was thinking. That Vina had fallen out of love with him before she'd left Fallow Creek. But that wasn't true. That could not be true. She still loved him; he was sure of that. At least she had when she'd left Fallow Creek.

How are you so sure? a voice in his mind questioned.

He pushed the voice away.

"How long do you plan to be away?" Keith asked.

"I really don't know. For as long as it takes to win Vina back, I guess. The earlier I leave for L.A., the better." He pressed his lips together and then added, "Before it becomes impossible to do so."

"I'll say it's already impossible," Keith told him, and then immediately apologized. "I wish you the best, my friend."

Rachel came into the living room carrying Emily in her arms. She looked at Daniel and then sat beside Keith. "Why do you both look like someone just died?" she asked.

"Daniel is leaving us for L.A.," Keith said. "And he doesn't know when he's going to come back. He is going to try to win Vina back."

"Oh, Daniel," Rachel gazed at him. "I know you really love Vina, but are you sure that's a good idea? I called her a few days ago, and all she spoke about were her acting scenes and Trent. They are really in a relationship now and it's serious."

Pain pierced through Daniel's heart, and for a brief moment, he began to reconsider his proposed trip to L.A. But he stood firm once more on his decision.

"I have to try," he told Rachel. "If I don't, I will always wonder. I have to try to get her back. Even if she's still in a relationship with that director, I think she still has feelings for me."

Rachel pursed her lips and then nodded. "Okay, then. But where are you going to stay when you get to L.A.?"

"I have a bit of money I saved from what I made when I was a security squad leader during Dennis Hamilton's time. I didn't want to touch that money because I felt it was not made honorably, and my plan was to give it away. But I think I need it now. I will probably rent a cheap motel room near Vina's movie set or wherever she is staying."

"And what will you tell her when you see her? She will not be pleased if she knows that you came to win her back. She complained about you being possessive, and if she thinks you came all the way to get back with her, she will believe you are trying to hold her back from her dreams."

"I will just let her know I came to visit as a friend. I know she has not been picking up my calls and said she would never talk to me again, but we have history. I am praying she will change her mind when I get there."

Rachel looked at Keith and then said to Daniel, "Since you've made up your mind to go, let us help you with your plane ticket to L.A."

"Really?"

Keith nodded. "Yes, we would love to do that for you."

Daniel felt overwhelmed. "You both have been so good to me. I was actually thinking of taking a bus to L.A. I have never been on a plane before."

Keith stared at him with a surprised look on his face. "Never?"

"Never."

Rachel did not look surprised. "He has spent all his life in Fallow Creek, Keith," she said. "He's had no reason to get on a plane before."

"Well, I'll pray for you while you are in L.A. I hope everything works out with you and Vina. But if it doesn't, know you can always come back here to us."

Rachel nodded. "We will be waiting with open arms."

Daniel stood up and hugged his friends tightly. Emily scrambled and fussed as she tried to free herself since she was squashed in the middle of their group hug. She succeeded in slipping down from Rachel's arms and everyone laughed as she tottered away.

Daniel caught up to her and ruffled her hair. He chucked her under the chin and she giggled. "I will miss you little one," he said to Emily.

She grunted and turned away.

They all laughed again, and then Daniel bid them goodbye, but not before Keith promised to book a ticket for him online. "We will drive you to the airport in Prospect," he said.

He left them feeling more hopeful of the future than he had since Vina had left. He wasn't sure what the outcome of his trip to L.A. would be, but he was excited to try to win the love of his life back. Most of all, he could not wait to see her again.

SIXTEEN

Daniel stepped out of the airport in L.A., then found a taxi to take him to the set of the movie Vina was shooting. Rachel had given him the address. That was all the information he had about where to find Vina. He didn't know if she was staying in a hotel somewhere in the city or living on the movie set.

He stared out the window for only a few minutes as the taxi raced down the road and then stared straight ahead. He'd heard so much about this city, but he wasn't particularly impressed. City life was not his thing. He preferred the sleepy rhythm of life in Fallow Creek.

Soon he began to think about what exactly to say to Vina when he saw her. His excitement began to build as he thought about seeing her again for the first time in more than a month, and then fear gradually began to take over. Would she even want to see him?

He groaned as conflicting emotions warred in his mind, and then he finally succeeded in pressing the fears away.

The drive to the movie set was a long one, but at last the taxi parked in front of an ornate black gate. Daniel paid the driver, got out, and lifted his suitcase out of the trunk. The driver drove away, and Daniel approached the gate.

A man in a security uniform sat in the gatehouse. He popped out his head through the small window and stared at him. "Yes, can I help you?"

For a second, Daniel pictured himself in his old fatigues, patrolling Fallow Creek's border to control who came and went based on Dennis Hamilton's orders, and then he told the security guy he was looking for Davina Brooks, an actress in the movie being shot here. The man shook his head and told him it was a closed set, and Daniel frowned.

"What is that?"

The man glowered at Daniel and waved his hand dismissively. "It means you are not allowed in."

Daniel glared at the man and exhaled. "Can't you just send a message to her or call her and tell her I am here to see her?"

"No. Unless you have an appointment with her, in which case your name will be written in the list of expected visitors." The man asked Daniel for his name, looked down at something Daniel could not see but which he guessed was a visitor's list, and then told him his name was not on the list. "You can't go in."

Anger flooded Daniel's chest, but he pushed it down. "I've come a long way to see Vina," he said. "I'm sure she'll want to see me."

"I'm sorry, but I cannot let you in."

He pointed at the phone on the desk in front of the man. "Why don't you call her or send someone to tell her I am here waiting for her."

"She's in the middle of shooting a scene right now," the man said. "I am not going to call her or send someone to get her. What you're asking for is impossible."

Daniel complained and then pleaded, but the guy refused to budge. He finally got tired of begging and complaining, carried his suitcase, and went to lean against the fence some distance away from the security gatehouse. Hopefully, Vina would come out sometime today. He was ready to wait here until she did.

He waited and waited, but Vina did not exit the gate. He began to grow weary and sat down on his suitcase. I'm so stupid, he thought. He should have gone to find a motel room before coming here. It was getting dark. What if she didn't leave the set at all today?

He stood up when he heard voices and footsteps coming toward him. Several people were coming out of the gate. The area was well lit, and he could see everyone who was exiting the gate. He groaned with disappointment. None of them was Vina.

There was silence again for some time, and once more he sat on his suitcase. About ten minutes later, he heard loud voices again. He stood up and faced the gate, and then his heart began to thud. Vina was walking out of the gate, hand in hand with a man. He fixed his gaze on the man's face and sighed. Of course it was Trent, the slick director. He sighed again and turned to look at Vina once more. She looked more beautiful than he had ever seen her. His heart raced, and he told himself to calm down. When Vina raised her face and Trent planted a kiss on her lips, Daniel groaned and turned away.

He heard footsteps coming toward him and turned to look at her again. She was alone now, walking toward him, but she had not yet seen him. His heart rate increased as he gazed at her, and her eyes grew round when she saw him.

She blinked and hurried up to him. "Daniel!"

For a brief moment, he held his breath, afraid that she might yell at him and ask why he had come here.

She reached him and stared at him as though she were seeing him for the first time. "What are you doing here?" she asked.

"I came here to visit you, Vina. I miss you so much." She opened her mouth to speak, but he held up his hand and quickly added, "I am not here to try to get you to come back to Fallow Creek with me or even to try to renew our relationship." He felt a sliver of guilt run through him. That was exactly what he had come here to do. He pushed the guilt away. "I came here as a friend. We've been best friends for years now, Vina. We don't have to stop being friends just because we are no longer together." He came closer to her and looked into her eyes. "I hope we can still be friends and that you don't mind my coming to visit and to support you… as a good friend." He smiled. "Your best friend."

She searched his eyes for a few moments, and then a smile broke out on her face. When she reached out and pulled him into a hug, relief flooded him. "I'm glad to see you, Dan," she said, and pulled away. "I love it here, but I'm truly happy to see someone from Fallow Creek after so long." She grinned. "And it's even better because it's you."

His heart soared with relief. He wanted to tell her how relieved he was that she was not sending him away, but he thought it was better to keep that to himself. Saying so might negate what he'd told her about being here just as a friend, and might give her a reason to suspect that he was here to try to win her back and therefore make her angry. "So where are you heading?" he asked her.

"I've been living like a hermit, or at least partially like one, since I came to LA. I just want to take a walk outside this place." She turned around and pointed at the gate behind them.

"Can I walk with you?" he asked.

"Of course you can," she said, and then blinked when she saw his luggage on the ground a foot away. "Is that your suitcase?"

"Yes. Don't worry about it. I will just leave it there."

"And where are you going to stay while you are in L.A., Dan?"

He shrugged. "Anywhere. I will find a motel somewhere and stay there until I leave."

"In a motel?" she frowned.

"Yes."

She sighed and then shrugged.

She began to stride away, and he fell into step beside her.

"So tell me, Daniel, how is our Fallow Creek?" she asked, turning to look at him. "How is everyone in the House of Refuge, especially Rachel and Keith? I miss Rachel so much. I haven't found time to call anyone since I left."

He smiled. "I left Fallow Creek just this morning, but I already know I am going to miss Keith and

Rachel very much. The town and everyone there are just like you left them. Nothing has changed really. Except, of course, that it is much quieter without the film crew and cast taking over the whole town." He smiled at her. "And it is definitely duller without you."

She stuck her hands in her jacket and looked down for a short moment. She looked up at him again and said softly, "And how are you doing, Dan? I'm sorry I haven't been answering your calls. I have been so busy." She turned away again, but not before he saw the guilt written on her face.

He stopped, and she stopped also. They stood on the sidewalk in a quiet area with just a few people walking down the street. He knew he shouldn't, but he couldn't help himself. He looked deep into her eyes and took her hands. "Vina, I miss you so much. These past few weeks that you have been gone have been hell for me. I've tried to stop loving you, but I can't."

She stared at him for a long time and then slowly removed her hands from his. "Daniel, we have talked about this. I told you to move on. I have. I'm with Trent now. I thought it was very clear to you when you saw us kissing in Fallow Creek that we are a couple now. Please don't try to convince me to come back to you. It's too late."

He looked into her eyes and knew that nothing he said would change her mind. "I'm sorry, Vina. Even though it hurts, I accept the fact that you have moved on. I don't know if I can move on so quickly, but I will try to. But know that I will try to support you right now with whatever you're doing, no matter what it is."

She pursed her lips and sighed audibly. "I think I should head back to the set. I still have one more scene to shoot for the day. I just came out here to get some air."

"Oh, I'm sorry. I did not mean to spoil your free time."

She smiled. "You didn't. I'm glad you came to see me. I just don't want to talk about your feelings for me anymore. Please, Daniel."

"I won't talk about it any longer," he said, his heart hurting.

"Thank you." She gave him a bright smile. "I have to go now, but I'll see you tomorrow?"

"Definitely," he said. He watched her walk away until she disappeared from sight, and then he sighed sadly. His emotions roiled with a mixture of confusion, hurt, and a drop of hope. At least she had not sent him away. She had said she was glad to see him. That would have to be enough for now.

***

Vina opened her eyes as her alarm went off, groaned, and shut them again. She covered her face with her pillow and grumbled when her phone rang. She gritted her teeth as the phone continued to ring, and she waited for it to stop so she could go back to sleep. When it did, she sighed with relief. It started to ring again, and she moaned. Sitting up in bed, she picked up her purse from the small bedside table and brought out her phone. "Yes?" she answered groggily.

It was the gate security calling. They told her a man named Daniel Bacon wanted to see her. "He was here yesterday," the security guy said. "Should I let him in?"

"Daniel!" She sat up immediately and rubbed her eyes. The memory of their walk the evening before came back to her. At first, he had told her he was simply here as her friend, but then he had once again gone on about his feelings for her. She didn't know for how long he planned to stay in L.A., and even though he had reiterated at the end of their conversation that he was just here as a friend to support her, she knew it wasn't so. Just like he'd done in the middle of their conversation, he would not be able to resist confessing his feelings for her after a while. Still, she was glad to see him. Hopefully, he would not make a scene here as he had done in Fallow Creek.

"Ma'am, should I let him in?"

"Yes," she said quickly. "Let him in. He will be a regular visitor, so whenever he comes you can just send him through."

"Yes, ma'am."

She hurriedly stood up. Daniel would be here any minute now. The film set security would show him the way to her trailer. She had to make herself presentable fast.

She pulled on a pair of blue jeans and a white T-shirt and then brushed her as hair as quickly as she could. She looked at her face in the mirror, and for a short moment, she thought about swiping on some lip gloss. And then she groaned. *What are you doing, Vina? Stop this right now!* She and Daniel were no longer together. She didn't have to try to impress him anymore.

She stepped out of her trailer and stood in front

of it waiting for him. She had been shocked when she'd seen him standing outside the gate yesterday, and then she had remembered how Daniel was. He was a passionate guy, and if he loved anything, he went after it doggedly. She just happened to be the major focus of his love and passion, and that explained why he had done everything to try to hold on to her. She was flattered by his attention and the fact that he had come all the way from Fallow Creek to see her and even to win her back, though he had said otherwise. But she had to be careful with him. She could not let him draw her back in. She would only go back to him trying to control her life. She'd had enough of his possessive ways, his jealousy, and his unbearable anger. He had never lashed out at her, but he had done so a couple of times to guys he thought liked her, like Trent, and all of his lashing out stemmed from his jealousy. She could not go back to that.

She smiled as he approached her. For a short moment, she studied him. He was tall and brawny, unlike Trent, who was just as tall but slim built. He looked like he could be a bodyguard for one of her co-stars or even Trent. It was not surprising that he had been made a leader of the security squad in Fallow Creek. He definitely looked like someone you would want to have in your corner when there was trouble. Unfortunately, she wasn't looking for a bodyguard. She wanted a boyfriend who didn't try to control her or dictate what she did with her life or her future. And she certainly didn't want a husband.

He reached her, and they hugged briefly. She opened the trailer door, and he walked in. She followed him in and held the door wide open and then smiled in self-mockery. Old habits died slowly. Unlike their relationship in Fallow Creek — where they had decided never to be alone in a room together or, if they had to be, to leave the door wide open — she always shut the door when Trent was here. But then, whenever Trent came to see her, they did nothing but make out, so the door definitely had to be shut.

She looked at Daniel, and her face grew hot. And then scolded herself. Why did she feel guilty when they were no longer together? Hopefully, Trent would not suddenly appear now that Daniel was here. She could not stand for them to start fighting as they had done in Fallow Creek. And a fight was sure to break out with Daniel's temper and Trent's condescending attitude toward him.

Daniel sat on the couch beside the bed. It was the only sofa that could fit into the trailer. She sat on the bed and faced him. "So, Emily is growing up so fast," Daniel said. Vina smiled widely, and he added, "She asked about you the other day"

Vina's mouth fell wide open and she shook her head. "Emily asked about me?"

Daniel laughed. "Okay, that's not true. She didn't. But I am sure she misses her Aunt Vina. You have spent a lot of time with her."

"I miss her, too," Vina said. "And I love spending time with that little girl. She's so cute."

"I can't wait to have a little one like her one day," Daniel said, and then he frowned and gave her an apologetic look.

She shrugged and changed the subject. She asked about some of the women she was particularly friendly with at the House of Refuge, like her roommate, Lisa. He told her that he had seen two of her good friends the day before he'd left for LA., and they'd asked about her.

"I really have to call everyone in Fallow Creek," she said.

After that they talked about their childhood, about growing up in Fallow Creek and some of the mischief they got into. Even though there had been strict rules in place, they'd still had fun times as children. Vina could not help noting how much they had in common as they talked and laughed.

She smiled as he started to tell her a funny story from his childhood, about how he and Steven had been sent on an errand to get some things from the store for their grandmother who raised them. They had spent the money on cookies instead, and their grandmother had decided to punish them by making them eat cookies every single day for a week. At first, they had loved every minute of their new diet, but then they'd begun to feel ill eating all that sugar, and by the middle of the week, they'd begged their grandma to give them some other punishment.

She laughed — not just at the story, but at the way he told it. She had forgotten how much fun it was talking with him, how much she enjoyed chatting with him and just being with him. Yes, they had to be careful when they were alone for a long time, but they were best friends and they could talk about anything and everything. He was looking at her now with the same admiration with which he had always looked at her, but it was different from the way Trent looked at her every time he saw her. She always felt like Trent was undressing her with his eyes. At first, she'd been a little flattered by that but also flustered. Now she just felt uncomfortable. She knew he was waiting for the time when she would agree to sleep with him, but she wasn't ready to do that. Not when they were not married. She just wasn't raised like that, and she believed it was wrong.

She laughed again when Daniel said something particularly funny. It felt so good to have a friend here from her hometown. She and Trent hardly had much to talk about except for work. They did nothing but kiss whenever he was here. She smiled at Daniel. She missed these fun conversations.

Vina, you need to be careful. She was enjoying herself way too much with Daniel.

She pressed her concerns away. She was just having a friendly chat with Daniel. Nothing more. Daniel was her old friend, and this was what good friends did. She wasn't going to let him pull her back in. He was just a friend now. Trent was who she was with. He brought passion into her life.

But as she continued to listen to Daniel and saw the way he looked at her, she knew as she always had that he would lay down his life for her if need be. She wondered if Trent would do the same?

"Vina?" Daniel studied her. "Did you hear what I just said?"

She blinked and focused her attention on him. "I'm sorry, Daniel. My mind just strayed for a moment." She smiled when he grinned. This was another thing about Daniel she loved. Another thing she could say to him that she could not say to Trent. She could tell him she had stopped listening to him, and he would not feel bad about it. If she told Trent the same thing, he would be offended and think that he wasn't interesting enough for her to listen to and give her undivided attention to.

She searched Daniel's eyes. He was gazing at her now. Confusion flooded her. His presence here and their fun conversations reminded her of why she had fallen in love with him, why she had accepted his proposal. But she could not stand his temper and jealousy anymore. His possessiveness. Trent was who she wanted to be with now. She was happy with her career and her relationship. Nothing needed to change.

"I'm sorry, Daniel," she said, realizing her mind had strayed again. "What did you say?"

"I asked how your movie was going. You haven't said anything about it since we started talking."

"It's going great," she told him. Her face grew hot with embarrassment when she remembered the love scene she had shot a few days ago with Mark Durham. She had forced herself to do the scene, and Trent had congratulated her after.

"You see. It wasn't so difficult, was it?" he had said to her.

She had nodded, but in fact, it had been one of the most difficult things she'd had to do.

They continued to chat and reminisce about their childhood, and then the production assistant came to tell her she was needed in hair and makeup in preparation for her next shoot. When the man left, she turned to Daniel. "I have to go. I've enjoyed talking to you, Dan."

Daniel stood up. "Can we hang out tomorrow? Just as friends?"

"Sure," she said.

"Okay, I will come here by eleven o'clock tomorrow morning," he said. "Will that be okay? If you have to shoot a scene at that time, I can come earlier or later."

"No, I am mostly free until about three in the afternoon. We can hang out around eleven o'clock."

He reached out and hugged her, and then he kissed her softly before pulling away again.

She sighed. "Daniel."

"I'm sorry."

When he left, she sighed and went out of her trailer to hair and makeup. She had already rehearsed for the scene that was going to be shot today.

Even though they were not strenuous, Trent insisted on them shooting more than the one scene they had previously decided on. They ended up shooting about three scenes, and Trent wanted each of them shot again and again. By the time they were through, all she wanted to do was sleep.

She started to head back to her trailer, but Trent called her name and she stopped. He caught up to her and gave her a warm smile. "Vina, we haven't actually gone on a real date since we started our relationship. I will be free at ten o'clock tomorrow. We can spend the entire day together."

"I would love that, but I have to shoot another scene at three o'clock."

He grinned. "Don't you worry about that. I know your boss. I will have him clear your schedule so we can spend the rest of the day together."

She laughed. "Well, then, I guess we will be spending the day together tomorrow." Her heart soared with happiness. Finally, she and Trent could have the much-needed alone time she'd been hoping for since she'd come to L.A. She started to tell him she was looking forward to their date, and then she remembered her promise to hang out with Daniel at eleven o'clock. She groaned and her excitement evaporated.

"What is it?" Trent asked.

She bit her lip. She could tell Trent she would not be able to go on their date tomorrow, but that would not be right. Since they'd became a couple, they had not even gone out on a real date. He was her boyfriend now. She owed him her time more than she did Daniel.

But Daniel was a good friend, and he would be really disappointed as he had come all the way from Fallow Creek to spend time with her here.

"Vina?" Trent tilted his head and stared curiously at her. "What's the problem?"

"Nothing, Trent. Just thinking about what to wear for our date tomorrow."

He smiled widely and then looked her over in his usual way. "Wear whatever you want, babe. You will look amazing in anything."

She forced a smile and nodded. "Okay."

He planted a goodbye kiss on her cheek, and then she left him and walked back to her trailer, feeling uncertain of her decision.

SEVENTEEN

Vina tried to shake off the guilt that gripped her as she prepared to go out for her date with Trent. She had called Daniel to tell him she couldn't go out with him today, and just as she'd expected, he had been sorely disappointed.

"Why are you canceling on me, Vina?" he had asked her.

She had not been able to bring herself to tell him she had plans with Trent. Instead, she told him that her schedule had changed and she would be busy throughout the day.

"Can't you just take out an hour for us to spend together?"

"I am sorry, Dan," she said to him, and reiterated that it was impossible for her to take time out of her busy day to hang out with him. She had promised to see him the next time she had a free day. "We will spend the entire day together. I promise."

"But when will that day be?" he'd asked her.

She hadn't said anything for a long moment, and

he'd called her name.

"I'm not sure when it will be, Dan," she'd said truthfully. "Sometimes, we have impromptu shoots because Trent might want to add or subtract something from the scenes we have already shot."

Daniel had sighed loudly over the phone. "Even if we can't spend the whole day together, when will I be able to see you next? If I can't see you soon, it will mean I will spend my days stuck in this cramped motel room."

Vina had pressed her lips tightly together and then said, "Explore the city, Daniel. You have even more time than I do to do so. I'm sure you'll find something to interest you. I have been in L.A. for more than a month, and I haven't been able to go anywhere yet. I wish I could have the time you do to discover the city."

He had groaned. "I'm not really interested in exploring the city. Except of course with you."

"I am sorry," she'd apologized again. There was nothing she could do. It wasn't like she could cancel her date with Trent just to hang out with Daniel. Still, she would have to figure out how to make time for him. Even if they could not spend a lot of time together, she could try to carve out an hour to spend with him, even if it was in between shoots. That day just couldn't be today.

She held up her small mirror to her face and began to apply a bright red lipstick. She had asked Trent what she should wear on their date, and even though he had told her she could wear anything, she knew enough to find something dressier than the jeans and T-shirts she lived in daily now. Trent was the kind of person who would say wear whatever and then take her to some glitzy place where, if she was simply dressed in jeans and a top, she would look way out of place.

After she had finished applying her makeup, she curled her hair, loosened the curls with her fingers, and smoothed her hands down her cream knee-length dress. She'd had to buy, or more accurately, Trent had bought her a whole wardrobe of clothes when they'd arrived in L.A., as he'd said the ones she'd brought from Fallow Creek were outdated and did not fully show off her beauty. Most of the clothes he'd bought her she had not worn, as she had mostly been wearing clothes from the movie wardrobe for her shoots. When she went out in the evenings for a walk, she simply wore jeans, a T-shirt, and a jacket. Today, she would actually be going into the city. Even though it was evening already, she was looking forward to it.

She suddenly wished that Daniel could come along and see the city with her, and then she frowned. How strange if would be if Daniel came along on her date with Trent. She smiled at the picture that came to her mind — Daniel and Trent on both sides of her while she held their hands.

And then her smile faded and she shook her head. The picture in her mind was wrong. Neither of the men could stand each other. It certainly would not be funny. More likely, a fight would break out between them as she tried unsuccessfully to prevent it. Some date that would be.

She finished dressing and left her trailer. Trent was waiting for her outside. He smiled when she walked up to him.

"You look amazing," he said.

She smiled at him. "Thank you. You look nice, too."

He was dressed in a white button-up shirt, a black blazer, and black leather shoes. His hair, as usual, was slicked back, his beard neatly trimmed. She held out her hand to him and he took it.

Some of the cast and crew were still about, and a few were also going out, taking the break Trent had given them today. Some were going to explore the city, others to visit loved ones. Vina walked with Trent until they reached his black Mercedes. He opened the door for her, and after she had entered, he got into the driver's seat.

As Trent raced down the road, she turned to him and asked where he was taking her.

"You'll see," he said, smiling.

She smiled back and turned away, not bothering to try to figure out where he could be taking her. She would find out soon enough. She looked out the window and marveled at what she saw. The city was beautiful, dazzling even. It was definitely different — no, completely different from Fallow Creek. It was everything she had ever dreamed a city, especially L.A., would be, and more. A wave of excitement washed through her as she thought about how far she had come. From a tiny polygamous town to living and working as an actress in this city she had heard so much about. This was her city now. This was her life.

She sighed and held back a groan when Daniel's face appeared in her mind. Why did she think of him every single time she got excited about her life now, her future? It wasn't enough that he had tried to keep her from going after her dreams and becoming all she could be. Even now, in this place of her dreams, she couldn't let go of the guilt that filled her when she thought about him.

And then she winced as she thought about the fact that she had hurt him terribly by breaking up with him. She had not allowed herself to think about it until now. That he had come all the way from Fallow Creek to Los Angeles just to see her and try to win her back did not help her guilt. The winning-back part would never happen, of course, but still, in spite of everything, she was glad they were still friends. However, she hoped he would not ask for something more again. They were through, but he didn't want to accept that.

She pushed all thoughts of Daniel out of her mind when they stopped in front of a building with a huge poster of a pretty model dressed in fur. The name Mario Perini was etched in big red letters across the picture. Her mouth fell open, and she turned to Trent.

"Is this what I think it is?" she asked, breathless with excitement.

"Yes. Mario's fashion show for his fall/winter collection. It's a pre-show before the New York Fashion Week next month."

She squealed with joy as they got out of the car. Mario Perini was one of the designers she had often seen in the magazines Leah had shown her. In fact, he was her favorite designer. She couldn't wait to sit in the Fashion Show and watch the models walk down the runway in his beautiful clothes. Most of all, she couldn't wait to see him in person. Before they got into the building, she took Trent's hand and beamed at him. "Thank you for bringing me here."

"You're welcome," he said. "And next month, we will go to New York Fashion Week."

"Really?"

"Yes."

She felt overwhelmed with emotions at his thoughtfulness. She'd only told him once about being enamored with the designer and the clothes she saw in magazines her friend had smuggled into Fallow Creek growing up. She'd told him briefly about some of the designers she liked, especially Mario Perini. It had not been a long conversation, but he had remembered. She smiled again at him, and he put his arm around her as they entered the building.

The show started with a show-stopping blue evening dress that caused Vina's jaw to drop.

"It's so beautiful," she whispered to Trent as the model walked past them on the runway. They were seated in the front row, and she could see very clearly and, if she'd wanted to, even touch the clothes. She felt incredibly special. She knew it was because of Trent's influence that they were seated in the front row. It was a privilege sitting here and being able to view the show like this. She took Trent's hand and smiled at him again in appreciation as the next model came down the runway.

Model after model sashayed down the runway in beautiful evening gowns and then trendy casual wear. Vina smiled constantly at Trent as the show continued. She was truly living her dream now; the dream she'd had in Fallow Creek to explore the world and to find her purpose. And she had a man like Trent, who was exciting and handsome and influential, beside her. What more could she want?

A magnificent white evening dress that looked like a wedding dress worn by a gorgeous model was the last down the runway. Vina could not take her eyes off the dress, and then her heart sank as she remembered the wedding dress Daniel had bought for her. He had been so excited when he'd given it to her, and she had loved that dress, too. Now that they were not getting married, she could only imagine how he felt. It had clearly been an expensive dress from the way it looked. She still wondered how he'd been able to afford the dress, but it had definitely been a gift that touched her heart.

Guilt pressed in on her as she thought about the dress sitting in its box in Rachel's closet, wasting away. She should have apologized to Daniel when she'd broken up with him. Even though his anger had pushed her away from him, she knew he truly loved her.

"Vina!"

She blinked and turned to Trent.

He stared curiously at her. "I've been trying to get your attention," he said. "What have you been thinking about? The show is over."

She glanced at the stage and shook her head in surprise. "How is that possible?" she said. "How come I did not even notice?"

The light in the hall came fully on just as the place erupted in loud claps and cheering.

She shook her head. "I didn't even notice the show was over."

Trent raised his brows. "You didn't see Mario come out on stage and wave to everyone?"

"No, he didn't," Vina cried. She stared at Trent. "I missed seeing Mario Perini even when I came to his fashion show?" How had that happened? Trent had brought her here, and the anticipation had been building in her heart to finally see the man who had created the lovely dresses she'd seen in magazines. She'd loved his dresses for years, and now she had missed seeing him. Why? What on earth had she been thinking about?

Daniel. She had been thinking about Daniel and, as usual, feeling guilty for breaking up with him.

People began to stand up in the hall to leave, and Trent stood as well. He took Vina's hand and pulled her up. He gave her a naughty grin. "If I had known you would miss seeing Mario when he was right in front of you, I would have arranged for a private meeting backstage. I just thought I would leave that for Fashion Week."

"You would have done that?" she asked, staring at him in astonishment. "Is that even possible?"

"Yes," he answered. "Anyway, until fashion week."

They began to walk out of the hall, and she apologized for her absent-mindedness. It was becoming a regular thing for her these days. Her mind was always straying. And ever since Daniel had come to L.A., it had only gotten worse.

When they finally got back to the set, Trent walked her to her trailer. He kissed her lightly, and once more she felt guilty for her absent-mindedness at the fashion show. Trent had taken out time and money and had pulled in his connections to take her there, and in a front-row seat.

She began to enter her trailer, and then she

turned around and said to Trent, "Do you want to come in?"

He smiled widely and nodded. He followed her into her trailer and sat next to her on the couch. Soon they began to kiss, as they always did whenever they were alone. The kissing became increasingly passionate, and Vina knew she should pull away. When she reluctantly tried to, Trent held on to her.

When things started to get out of hand, she silently screamed at herself, *Pull away, Vina!* But she didn't. And then her phone rang, and once more she tried to pull herself out of Trent's arms. But Trent didn't let her go. And then her door opened, and Daniel walked in.

EIGHTEEN

Daniel staggered back.

He had thought about what Vina had told him the day before about not knowing when she would next be able to see him, or when they could hang out. Because of that, he had decided to come visit Vina himself. He'd not considered the fact that she might be with Trent, and certainly not that they would be alone in her trailer making out. In fact, they looked like they were more than making out. His head buzzed as Vina and the director sat up and stared at him. Trent looked furious, Vina embarrassed.

Daniel felt rage rising up within him as he glared at Trent Radar, and then he took a deep breath and pressed his anger away. He apologized and quickly left the trailer.

He walked even faster as he headed toward the gate. The image of Trent and Vina wrapped up in each other's arms assaulted his mind. He couldn't get out of this place fast enough. He felt sick with hurt and anger, and the effort of trying to push down his anger so he would not do anything stupid weighed too heavily on him. He heard Vina calling his name from a distance, but he did not stop until he'd walked through the gate.

He finally leaned on the fence and took huge gulps of air. "Why, Lord, did you allow me to walk into that?" he whispered in a broken voice. He felt like screaming, but he held himself together, not only because he might get arrested if he gave in to the anger building up in him, but because screaming would be an expression of his anger, and he was practicing controlling it, or at least, not reacting negatively because of it.

He kept taking deep breaths until he finally rid himself of his rage, but his heart still hurt. He could not unsee what he had just witnessed between Vina and Trent. It was etched in his mind and it hurt like crazy.

He chided himself for coming to L.A. and believing that he could somehow win Vina's heart back. He had known that she'd moved on with Trent back in Fallow Creek, but he had still stubbornly come here.

He shook his head, trying to shake out of his mind the memory of Vina and Trent wrapped up in each other's arms, but he couldn't. He pressed his lips tightly together and shut his eyes. Why did he have to walk into the trailer just when they were together like that? But then, who knew for how long they had been like that and what would have happened if he had not come in just at that time. They both looked like they would have gone much farther than he had seen if he had not interrupted. The thought made him sick to his stomach. Vina was like him. Or at least, she used to be. They believed in waiting until after marriage for sex. That was why they had made the rule of not being alone together in a room or house. And yet, for Trent, she had broken that rule, and it had not taken long at all. Was this even the first time they'd been together in that way?

He groaned. If that wasn't a sign that there was no hope of him ever getting back together with her, he didn't know what was. He was wasting his time here. He needed to get back to Fallow Creek immediately.

"Oh, Vina!" He remembered what Keith and Rachel had told him. They had both been skeptical about his quest to come to L.A. to win Vina's heart back. He should have listened to them. He should not have come here at all. Now, the punishment for his stubbornness would be that he would carry this troubling memory of Vina and Trent together in his mind forever.

It was time to go back to his motel room, pack up his things, and leave first thing tomorrow.

His heart hurt as he thought about going back to Fallow Creek and trying to forget Vina completely. Would he ever see her again? He started to step away from the fence, and then he paused and looked back at the gate again. So he was really going to go back to Fallow Creek without Vina. He was going to have to put her out of his mind forever. Things had turned out completely different from what he had thought when he'd come here. He sighed sadly, turned around once more, and walked away.

He got to his motel room and began to hurriedly pack his things into his suitcase. A sob rose up in his throat, but he swallowed it. He had never felt so hurt and betrayed in his life. Not even after Vina had left Fallow Creek had he felt like this. But then, he had not seen what he saw now. Maybe it was why the Lord had let him see them together in that way. In order to let him know there was no hope of ever winning Vina back. He was through with trying. They needed him back at Fallow Creek.

He continued to pack his clothes, and then his hands stilled as he remembered the vow he had made to himself before he'd left Fallow Creek — to try to win Vina's heart back, no matter how long it took or what obstacles were in his way. Somehow, he knew she needed him here. As slick and charming as Trent was, he didn't seem to be the right guy for Vina; the kind of guy that would always be there for her, no matter what she did or didn't do.

That's because you think you are the right guy for her, he thought, mockingly.

He sat down on the bed and looked down at his suitcase. Would he just give up now? Would he throw in the towel and run away at the first sign of trouble?

His emotions roiled as he sat trying to sort out his feelings and consider what exactly he should do. There didn't seem to be any hope. The possibility of getting Vina back after what he'd seen was slim. Very slim. But he couldn't just give up. Despite what he'd seen, he still loved her with all his heart. He couldn't just give up. He was certain Trent wasn't good for her.

And are you certain you are? a voice in his mind whispered.

He shut his eyes as he considered the question. He

got easily jealous and angry, though he always tried never to direct that anger toward Vina. But she had complained about the jealousy too many times. As well as the possessiveness. Could he stop trying to make her see he was the one for her? She needed to decide that for herself. But he couldn't help himself a lot of the time. Whenever he was with her, all he wanted to do was wrap his arms around her and tell her how much he loved her. And he had done that the first day he'd arrived here, even though she had asked him not to. He was sure he would do it again if he remained in L.A.

You should go back to Fallow Creek, Daniel.

He sighed and looked at his suitcase once more. And then he began to unpack his things. He would not go back. Not now. He would not give up at the first sign of difficulty. He had to keep trying to win her, but he would do it furtively.

Without shedding his clothes or removing his boots, he lay down on the bed, shut his eyes, and tried to forget what he'd seen this evening as he began to fall asleep. But the picture of Vina passionately kissing Trent remained in his mind and made its way into his dreams.

***

Vina tried to pull away from Trent so she could go after Daniel, but he would not let her. He wrapped his arms around her and shook his head. "Why do you want to go after him? You're not with him anymore. You're with me. I don't know why you look so worried and ashamed. We've done nothing wrong. We are a couple, after all."

She blinked and nodded. "You're right," she said, sighing softly. It was wrong to even think about going after Daniel when she was here with her boyfriend. And yet she still felt guilty as she remembered the look of shock and disappointment on Daniel's face.

Trent tried to kiss her again, but she pushed him away. She could not shake the guilt that had gripped her. What would have happened if Daniel had not walked in on them? She did not plan to sleep with anyone before she got married. And she didn't want to get married yet. Even so, she had allowed herself to be carried away in a sea of passion with Trent.

She thought about Daniel again. If he was the one she was with now, maybe he would have pulled away when their kissing became too intense. He definitely would have let go of her when she'd tried to move away. But Trent did not have any of the scruples that Daniel did. He did not share her faith.

But Daniel does. So why are you with Trent instead of with him? a voice in her mind whispered. She sighed and ignored the voice.

Trent began to talk about their schedules for the shoot tomorrow, but she didn't want to talk about that now. She wanted to be left alone with her thoughts. Besides, she was tired and it was time to call it a night. She yawned, hoping Trent would take the hint, but he didn't. He put his arms around her again and pulled her close.

"You look so beautiful when you are deep in thought," he said, and kissed her once again.

She sighed wearily and pushed away from him.

He looked hurt, and she thought about apologizing but immediately changed her mind.

If she apologized to him, he would take that as an invitation to stay and start to kiss her all over again.

"Why do you keep pushing me away?" he asked, still looking like she'd punched him in the gut. "Don't you want me, Vina?"

She faced him and bit her lip. "It's not that." She hesitated and added, "I just wasn't raised to have sex before marriage. I've told you before. I don't believe in doing that. Besides, it is wrong in God's sight."

He laughed out loud, and she frowned "What's so funny, Trent?"

He stopped laughing. "I'm sorry, but didn't you tell me you were with someone who had a wife and you lived with the guy as his wife even though your marriage wasn't legal? Didn't you sleep with that guy you were with?"

Her face grew hot with shame and embarrassment. She had tried to forget after Mike died that she had been with him in that way. She had believed the lies she'd been fed in Fallow Creek that she was married to Mike in the sight of God, and so she had lived with him as a wife, doing everything a wife would do with a husband. She regretted everything, and yet it wasn't like she'd had a choice at the time. Nobody had asked her what she'd wanted when her marriage to Mike was arranged. She had obediently done what her parents had wanted without complaining.

"I know what I said." She bowed her head. "The marriage was considered legal in Fallow Creek, though that is not an excuse. I know better now. I know now that it is a sin in God's eyes to be with a man who is already married." She looked at him. "Or with any man I am not married to."

Trent put his hand on her back and smiled tenderly at her. For a short moment, he said nothing, and then he nodded. "I understand, Vina, and I will respect your desire to remain celibate for now. I will wait until you're ready."

She smiled, grateful that he'd decided to back away. The pressure to sleep with him had begun to get to her. "Thank you," she said.

He gave her a rueful smile and stood up. "I'll see you tomorrow."

After he left, she curled up on the sofa and then groaned as once again the memory of Daniel's disappointment and hurt haunted her.

NINETEEN

The film shoots for the day finally ended, and
Vina sighed with relief. She was tired and looking
forward to just going to bed. She began to make her
way toward her trailer, but Mark and Johanna, her
co-stars, stopped her.

"Vina, why don't you come with us?" Johanna
said. "It's been a long day and we need to let off
steam. We are going to get some drinks."

Vina raised her eyebrows. "By drinks you mean
alcohol, right? You know I don't drink."

The cast regularly went out together whenever
they were free for drinks and a night out, but Vina
never went with them. They'd asked her to go a
couple of times, but she always refused. They had
mostly stopped asking, which was a relief. Why
they were asking her to go out with them today, she
wasn't sure.

Mark laughed. "We know you don't drink alcohol,
Vina, but today we are going out to celebrate."

Vina frowned in confusion. "Celebrate what?"

"We are having a halfway wrap-up party.

Everyone has to come."

"Halfway wrap-up party?" Vina chuckled. "Is there such a thing?"

"If we decide there is, then there is," Johanna said. "Come on, Vina. We won't be long. And you can always order a non-alcoholic drink. They have those in bars as well, you know."

"It won't be right if you don't come." Mark smiled mischievously at her. "Besides, Trent will be coming along with us."

Vina shrugged. She really didn't want to go with them. Mark thought that letting her know Trent would be there would convince her to come with them, too. But that didn't make much of a difference to her. She would see Trent some other time.

Other members of the cast came to join them, and soon most of them were pressuring her to go to the bar with them. Shannon, one of the minor actresses gave her a knowing smile and said, "The director promised to come with us tonight."

Vina knew what the knowing smile was for. Most of the people on set knew she and Trent were dating, though they pretended not to notice. Shannon moved closer to her and said, "Trent is so dashing." Her voice turned sultry. "What is he like?"

Vina blinked and frowned in confusion. "What do you mean?"

"You know..."

Vina shook her head. "No, I don't."

The other girls nearby giggled, and Vina realized what Shannon was talking about. She felt herself blushing and looked away. So everyone thought she was already sleeping with the director. That was not good. She wanted people to judge her for her talent and not think she had gotten this role or whatever role she got in the future because she was Trent Radar's girlfriend — or worse, bedmate. She did not know whether to try to explain that what they were thinking was not happening or just ignore their insinuations. She decided there was no point trying to defend herself. She brushed aside her concerns, ignored Shannon and the other girls who were looking expectantly at her, and told Mark and Johanna that she was too tired to go out with them. "Maybe some other time," she said.

Trent began to walk toward them, and Vina sighed wearily. Hopefully, he would not try to convince her to go out with her co-stars. He reached them and kissed her on the cheek.

She pursed her lips and sighed again. *Great! More gossip fodder for my castmates.*

Mark said to Trent, "Will you please tell Vina how important it is for everyone to come to our halfway party? She doesn't want to go out, as usual."

Trent put his arm around her waist. "Vina, please come with us. We would love to have you. I would love to have you."

She groaned.

Trent said, "If you don't go, I won't."

Vina frowned. She didn't appreciate him putting her on the spot. She groaned again and then said, "Fine! I'll go with you guys."

They headed toward the gate, and at first, Vina stood where she was. She had thought they would have a bit of time to freshen up before leaving, but apparently not.

Trent looked back and called out, "Vina! Aren't you coming?"

She exhaled and hurried to catch up with him and her castmates.

The bar they chose was not far from the set, and they got there in under ten minutes. They chose a long table and sat down. Soon they were laughing and chatting while sipping their drinks. Vina drank the mocktail that Trent had ordered for her, while the others ordered assorted alcoholic drinks.

As the night progressed and the more everyone drank, the freer and more careless their speech and stories became. And the more vulgar. Vina ignored the thread of guilt that ran through her as she laughed at several of the bawdy stories. A scripture she'd been made to memorize as a child ran through her mind as she listened to a particularly coarse joke being told by Mark. *But fornication, and all uncleanness, or covetousness, let it not be once named among you, as becometh saints; Neither filthiness, nor foolish talking, nor jesting, which are not convenient: but rather giving of thanks.*

Troubled, she bit her lip and pressed the scripture out of her mind. They were just having innocent fun, and she wasn't the one telling the joke after all.

Soon, some of her castmates went out to the dance floor. Trent smiled at her and asked if she wanted to dance, and she shook her head quickly.

"No, I don't want to dance, Trent."

He looked at her empty glass and said, "I should order you another drink. A different one this time."

She frowned. "What type of drink do you want to order?"

"It will be a surprise, but I think you will like it." He beckoned to a bartender and ordered two mojitos.

"What's that?" she asked.

He smiled but said nothing.

She listened to the remaining cast members still seated as the topic of conversation shifted from film directors and producers they'd worked with, to the stupid antics of coworkers, to family members and exes. When Vina told them just a little about her life back in Fallow Creek, they were all fascinated and amazed at how different her life had been. She, however, stopped short of telling them about the polygamy practiced in Fallow Creek. They would think that was crazy and, in extension, that she was, too.

"So you didn't date anyone until you got married at twenty?" Johanna said, a surprised look on her face.

"Yes," Vina nodded. That was all she was willing to share with them about her marriage. She would not tell them that Mike had had another wife, or that they all lived together in one house. She had told Trent because he had come to Fallow Creek and had found out a little about their 'different' lifestyle. He had asked her about her life, and because she liked him, she had told him everything. Thankfully, he had told no one else.

Their drinks arrived, and she took a sip. She blinked and turned to Trent. "Are you sure there's no alcohol in this drink? I think there is. What did you call it again?"

"A mojito. I usually prefer something stronger, but I want to have it with you. There's a bit of alcohol in it, but not enough to get you drunk." He gave her a naughty smile. "At least not on your first glass."

"Trent! You know I don't drink! Why would you order an alcoholic drink for me?"

He smiled again, seemingly unbothered. "You have to admit that it's good," he said. "Take another sip."

"No." She glared at him.

He shrugged and took a swig of his drink.

For a long moment, she sat watching him and the others have one glass after another of their liquor. Though their speech was slurred, they seemed happier and more stress-free than she'd ever seen them. They were definitely happier at this moment than she was. She sighed, and then curiosity got the better of her and she took another sip of her drink. It wasn't so bad. She took a gulp and then coughed and spluttered.

Trent turned to her, put his hand on her back, and smiled. "A little at a time, Vina. You're just starting out."

She took another sip. Soon she finished the glass and felt slightly lightheaded but strangely lighthearted as well. She banged her hand on the table and turned to Trent. "I want more!"

Trent chuckled, beckoned to a bartender, and told him to get another drink for her. When the drink came, she drank and finished it much faster than the first, and then she asked for another.

Trent shook his head. "You've had enough, Vina. I think it's time I take you back to your trailer."

She felt him lift her up from her seat, and then he led her out of the bar.

She heard herself giggle as they walked back to the set, or more accurately, Trent walked back while she leaned heavily on him. She giggled again and asked herself what was so funny. She tried to tell Trent she wasn't ready to go back to her trailer, but she could not form the words and soon gave up.

He opened the door to her trailer and led her in. He sat her on the bed and then sat beside her, his arm wrapped around her waist.

"You're drunk, Vina. But not terribly. If you had had another glass, you would be out of it by now."

"I don't... I am drunk." She laughed. "Not... drunk." She leaned forward and planted a firm kiss on his lips.

They soon began to kiss passionately, but for some reason, Daniel's face appeared in her mind. "Oh, Dan!" she said.

Trent drew back from her. He looked like she had just slapped him.

"What?"

"You just called me Dan," he said.

She blinked and shook her head, trying to clear her foggy thoughts. "I did?" She hadn't realized she'd said Daniel's name out loud. She hadn't meant to.

Trent stood up, turned around, and walked out of her trailer. She called out his name but felt too woozy to go after him. She stretched out on the bed and closed her eyes.

She opened her eyes when she felt someone touching her hair. Turning around, she saw Trent standing over her, a smile on his face.

She licked her lips. Her mouth felt dry and she had a pounding headache. A faint memory of last night's events floated into her mind, and she sat up. She held her head in her hands, looked up at Trent again, and groaned.

"I am never drinking alcohol again," she said. "I remember acting like a fool yesterday." She also faintly remembered calling Trent Dan, and Trent leaving her trailer in anger. Guilt and embarrassment flooded her. "I'm sorry, Trent. I remember calling you, Dan." If only the ground could open up right now and swallow her. She turned away from him in shame and sighed.

"It's okay," he said. "You were drunk and didn't know what you were saying." He sat beside her and put his hand on her forehead.

She winced. Her head was still pounding.

"You have a headache," he said.

"Yes," she answered.

He stood up. "I will let you rest this morning. We have no shoots until later this evening." He planted a kiss on her cheek and left the trailer again.

When he was gone, she took a deep breath and gently climbed out of bed. She had to see Daniel today. Since she'd canceled their planned hang-out to go on a date with Trent, she hadn't seen him. Except of course for the brief moment when she and Trent were making out and he'd entered her trailer. A fresh wave of embarrassment went through her. In spite of what Trent had said that day, she still felt ashamed whenever she remembered the look on Daniel's face when he'd walked in on her and Trent passionately making out. She felt slightly reluctant to face him today, but still, she had to keep the promise she'd made to him and try to spend today with him, in spite of her pounding headache.

She found a painkiller in the top drawer of her armoire and took two tablets. Hopefully, she would be pain-free in a few minutes. She took a quick shower, dressed in a floral summer gown, grabbed her purse, and left the trailer.

Daniel had already told her exactly what motel he was staying at the last time they were together, and she decided not to call him. She would surprise him instead and pray he was still in his motel room.

Worry flooded her as she realized that he might have left Los Angeles after he'd seen her and Trent in her trailer. She had not even thought about that; she'd been too busy. Why did she just assume he would still be in L.A. after the sight he'd witnessed. She took a deep breath and prayed he hadn't left. For some reason, she really wanted to see him today and talk to him. She still felt ashamed, but she would not let shame get in the way of their friendship. She had thought when she'd left Fallow Creek that she didn't want to be friends with him anymore since they were no longer together, but the day he'd come to visit her in her trailer, she had enjoyed spending time with him. She yearned for their lighthearted conversations and reminiscing.

She got to the motel he was staying at and walked in. Contrary to what she had thought, it was a clean enough place and didn't look half bad. She walked over to the front desk and asked the receptionist for Daniel Bacon. As the woman looked at her computer, Vina prayed Daniel was still in L.A. When the girl picked up the phone and dialed Daniel's room, Vina let out a sigh of relief. *Thank you, Lord.*

But then her worries returned. *What if he doesn't want to talk to me even though he is still in L.A.?*

She exhaled and tried to calm her fears. If he'd decided he didn't want to speak to her any longer because he'd seen her and Trent making out, he probably would still not be in L.A. That would mean she would not see him now... or for a very long time. The thought did not sit well with her.

The receptionist dropped the phone and told her she could go up to room fifteen. She thanked the woman, relief flooding her again, and walked to the flight of stairs to her right.

His room was on the top floor of the motel, and as she climbed up, she realized her head had stopped throbbing. When she got to his door, she smiled. He was already standing outside waiting for her, and he looked happy to see her.

She reached out and pulled him into a tight hug.

They stood outside his room, hugging for a long moment. She could feel from the way he held her that he had missed her, just like she did him. His hug felt so familiar and so comforting that she did not want to pull back. She finally did, and they both entered his room. She smiled when he left the door open. It was simply out of habit, she knew.

She looked up at him and wondered if he'd really left the door wide open because of habit or knowingly. He was looking at her with an expression of both desire and sadness. Her heart raced. She looked deep into his eyes and remembered exactly why she had fallen in love with him. She could see how much he loved and cared for her; that she was safe with him, and that no matter where life took them, he would always love her. She had known this about him for a long time, but lately, she had forgotten, focusing on the aspects of his character that she disliked. She finally managed to pull her eyes away from his and then sat down on the single green sofa near the bed.

She looked around her. The room was small and the furniture was old but clean. So this was where he'd been spending his days, waiting for a time when she was free and could spend the day with him. He was mostly alone here. He would have left for Fallow Creek, where he had people he could talk to, if not for how much he loved her.

Her heart begun to pound as he came toward her, and then she blinked.

What's wrong with you, Vina? But she couldn't take her eyes off him. All the feelings she had for him, which she had buried, came rushing up. She had thought her feelings for him would gradually fade away the more time she spent with Trent and away from him, but from the overwhelming emotions she felt as they stared into each other's eyes, they certainly hadn't.

Remember why you broke up with him, she scolded herself silently.

He sat next to her on the sofa, and she turned to face him. "So what have you been doing with yourself, Daniel?" she asked, pushing away her confusing thoughts and emotions.

He shrugged. "Not much."

She began to tell him about the movie they'd been shooting. She enjoyed shooting her scenes, though she certainly didn't enjoy the hectic schedule. She told him what the movie was about and the parts she'd already shot, but she left out the steamy love scene. She suddenly realized he hadn't spoken since she'd started to tell him about her movie, and she studied his face. He looked slightly absent-minded, which was unusual. He always listened closely whenever they were having a conversation.

He clearly noticed her studying him and gave her an apologetic smile. She smiled back and realized why he was absent-minded. She knew him well enough to know what was on his mind. He was thinking about her and Trent in each other's arms.

She sighed, feeling sorry for him. The expression on his face tore at her heart. Maybe he should not have come to L.A. She would not feel so guilty now or he so sad. She had made up her mind not to bring up the thing with Trent, but she had to. She needed to clear the air.

"Daniel, listen, I know what you saw the other day when you came to my trailer was..."

"Don't!" he cut in. "Please don't say anything about that." He turned away from her, but not before she saw the tortured look on his face. "Please."

She frowned and put her hand on his shoulder. He turned back to her, and she smiled. "Okay, I won't talk about it. But please, Daniel, don't shut me out. Remember, you told me you came here as my friend and would support me no matter what. I need to talk to a friend. My best friend. That's why I came here. Remember, we're supposed to hang out. Unfortunately, I wasn't able to that day, but I'm here now. Can we just hang out as friends and forget everything else?"

"It's hard, Vina," he whispered.

She held back a groan. "I know."

She sighed with relief when he smiled at her. "Fine. We will hang out as friends only. We can go out later to get some lunch... or wherever you want."

She nodded. "I would love that."

Soon, they began to talk about Fallow Creek again, and he told her about being the assistant leader of the security squad. Since the inner workings of the squad were hidden from other people, she was fascinated by his stories of the squad's meetings with Dennis Hamilton, and the orders they'd received on how to "guard" the town.

"More like terrorize the town." Vina laughed.

"You are right, I guess."

They continued with their conversation, and though they had decided to go out for lunch, they ended up not going. They talked and laughed and talked some more. Every time they were together, they had so much to talk about. She could talk to him forever and never grow bored.

As they continued to chat, she completely forgot about the past, the things he had done that made her break up with him, his jealousy and anger. They unconsciously moved closer to each other until their shoulders were touching, and Daniel flung his arm around her.

She did not move away nor did they stop talking or enjoying each other's company. If she'd been alone with Trent like this, he would have kissed her, and then they would have spent the time kissing and nothing else. Maybe apart from the strong physical attraction, they didn't have much else in common.

It was not like she wasn't attracted to Daniel. They did kiss when they were together, but they had more than that. They had history and great memories that they had built together in their community. They were alike in so many ways.

She gradually became aware of Daniel's arm

around her, but she still didn't move away. It felt natural and right.

Daniel began to tell her another childhood story. He had hidden under the bed as a child one day in order to avoid going to the general chapel with his grandmother and his brother. His grandma had baked a particularly mouth-watering apple pie, and they were all supposed to share it after they returned from the chapel. But he had other plans. The pie was small, and his grandma had an annoying habit of sharing food with their neighbors and anyone who happened to stop by their house. He wanted a large portion of the pie for himself. He knew if he waited until they came back, he would only get a small slice. "That was why I decided to hide under the bed."

Vina laughed out loud. "How old were you at the time?"

"Umm... I think I was about five. Of course, my grandmother and Steven looked around the house for me and would not leave until they found me. I don't know why I thought they would leave if they looked long enough for me and didn't find me. But of course, they didn't leave. My grandma found me hiding under the bed, pulled me out, and made me go to the chapel with them."

Vina laughed again. "I remember how I used to love going to the chapel with my parents," she said. "Not the one during the week, but the general chapel on Sunday. You remember those delicious cookies they served after church and how all the children in Fallow Creek used to eat as many cookies and candies as we could?" She chuckled. "And then we played around the chapel grounds until our parents came to take us home."

He smiled. "I remember. I loved going to the general chapel as a child as well." His eyes softened as he gazed at her. "That was where I first noticed you."

She suddenly felt sad. They had loved each other for so long. How come it had all ended this way? Without thinking, she reached out and laid her hand on his cheek. When he leaned forward and gently kissed her, she briefly returned his kiss and then pulled back.

He looked stricken. "I'm sorry. I shouldn't have kissed you."

"No, it's okay." She stood up. She couldn't stay here with him any longer, reminiscing about their childhood, her feelings for him resurging like a flood. "I have to go," she said. She picked up her purse and, before he could say anything, walked out of his motel room.

When she got back to her trailer, she kept thinking about Daniel, about the day he had asked her to marry him, and about what her life would be like now if she had married him.

Maybe I should just give in and go back to Fallow Creek and become his wife.

But she couldn't do that. That was not her dream. She was living her dream now. And she was with Trent. She could not go back to Fallow Creek or leave her acting career. It was her present and her future, and so was Trent. She had to forget about Daniel.

Except that would be difficult to do, especially when she tremendously enjoyed spending time with him. Maybe she would insist that he went back to Fallow Creek. But knowing Daniel, he would do whatever he wanted to do, and apparently that included winning her back, no matter how many times she told him she did not want to be with him again.

But is that still the truth, Vina?

She had no answer to that. She groaned, and after considerable effort, she finally managed to press all confusing thoughts about Daniel out of her mind.

TWENTY

In spite of Vina's decision weeks ago to stop spending time with Daniel, she had visited him almost every day. Despite the rigor of their shooting schedule, she found time to go to his motel. When she couldn't, he came to the set to see her. If Trent knew how much time she spent with Daniel, he would not be pleased. She kept trying to convince herself that it was just two old friends spending time together. She was happy with Trent, after all. But deep down in her heart, she knew there was more. Every minute she spent with Daniel was special to her.

She sighed with relief when Trent yelled out, "Cut!" and quickly walked back to her trailer to prepare to go to Daniel's motel. She couldn't wait to see him, to continue their conversation from yesterday. He had been telling her about the events that had led up to Rachel and Keith leaving the small town they were living in to come to Fallow Creek. The miracles God had done for them, how He had opened the door for them to settle in Fallow

Creek and finally lead the place, were amazing and fascinating. Even though she and Rachel had been quite close for some months before she'd left, Vina had never really asked how she had managed to go from being a reviled woman who'd been sent to the Restoration House to have her mind renewed and then eventually chased out of town to the town leader.

She should have known it had involved a series of miracles. Keith had told Daniel everything in detail, and now Daniel was telling her the story. She'd had to leave yesterday in the middle of the story because it was getting late, but she had promised to come back today so he could continue. She couldn't wait to see him again so she could hear the end of the story. He told it in such a captivating way that she could not help marveling at all that had happened and what God had done.

Are you this eager to go to Daniel's motel just because of the story… or is there something more?

She sighed and brushed the thought aside.

She finished freshening up, brushed out her hair, and grabbed her purse from the sofa. Just before she went out the door, she checked her reflection in the mirror and frowned. *Maybe I should put on some lipstick.*

She smiled in self-mockery. And here she was trying to convince herself that she was only going to Daniel's motel room to hear him finish the interesting story.

She dug her hand into her purse and brought out two lipsticks, one red and the other nude. She studied them and chose to wear the nude lipstick. The red one would be too much.

She thought about the questions going through her mind and admitted that she was eager to go to Daniel's room not just because of his interesting story, but also because she enjoyed spending time with him. She enjoyed their conversation and just being with him. There was nothing wrong with that. Just because they were not together anymore and she was dating someone else didn't mean that she could not visit a good friend and spend time with him.

A good friend that you are in love with.

She blinked at the thought that had flashed through her mind. She wasn't in love with Daniel. Not anymore.

Are you sure of that?

"I am not in love with Daniel!" she exclaimed. She sighed again. Why was she trying to convince herself that she wasn't in love with him?

Because I'm not.

She shook her head as she stared at herself in the mirror. Who was she trying to convince? Maybe she needed to stop going to Daniel's motel room almost every day to see him. She moved away from the mirror and opened her trailer door to leave. She blinked in surprise and stepped back when she saw Trent standing at the door.

"You going out, Vina?"

She felt a stab of guilt in her heart, and then she squared her shoulders. She had nothing to feel guilty about. She wasn't doing anything wrong. "Yes," she said.

"Where are you going?" he asked.

She pursed her lips and then said slowly, "I'm going to see Daniel."

He frowned. "Why? Didn't you go and see him just a few days ago? How come he's still in L.A. anyway? Has he moved here?"

She shrugged. "I don't know. I promised I would go see him today."

Trent looked into her eyes. "Do you have to go today, Vina? In fact, do you have to go and see him at all? We're supposed to be together. You shouldn't be visiting your ex anymore... in his motel room. It's not right."

"Just because he's my ex doesn't mean we can't be friends. We were best friends for years before we got into a relationship. Now that we've broken up, we are still friends."

"Yes, and I am still friendly with a few of my exes, but not so much that I visit them at their homes every day. You might think it's harmless fun, but what would you think if I started visiting one of my exes regularly? Would you think it was okay? After all, what could possibly happen between us when we are just old friends?"

She sighed but didn't say anything.

"Let me answer the question for you. You would not like it, Vina. I don't think you should go. In fact, you should stop visiting him. We have to continue shooting this evening anyway."

She narrowed her eyes in anger. This was why she had broken up with Daniel. He had tried to control her. She wasn't going to let any man control her and tell her what to do and where to go, even if he was the director of the movie she was in. She looked Trent in the eye and said, "There's nothing going on between Daniel and me. Just innocent conversations. We have conversations about our childhood and about Fallow Creek. That's all. I miss my hometown and it's refreshing to talk to someone who is from there. I'm happy talking about Fallow Creek and reminiscing about our childhood. Would you take that away from me?"

Trent groaned. "I want you to be happy, and I don't mind you talking about your childhood and hometown. I just wish it wasn't with your ex. Daniel clearly still has feelings for you. Did you see the expression on his face the day he walked in on us kissing?"

"Daniel knows I am with you, Trent, and I'm happy." She took his hands, leaned in, and kissed him on the lips. "Please let me go. I promise I'll be back shortly." She let go of his hands and walked past him.

"Vina!"

She hurried away. He called out to her again, and she turned. "I'll be back as soon as possible. I promise." She walked away quickly and sighed with relief when she walked out of the gate.

When she got to Daniel's motel room, she reached out and hugged him. He kissed her hair and then pulled back and she sat on the couch.

He came and sat next to her and instantly continued the story he'd started yesterday. After the fascinating story, he began to tell her more stories; mostly stories that Keith had told him. Soon, they began to reminisce about their childhood again. Once more, as they talked, she marveled at how much she enjoyed talking with him and how different the time she spent with him was from the time she spent with Trent. And then she groaned when she realized she was comparing them. That was wrong.

As she and Daniel chatted, she lifted her feet off the ground and placed them on Daniel's lap. She smiled when he lightly tickled her toes while they talked. It reminded her of the old times, when he would visit her room at the House of Refuge and tickle her toes when she placed her feet on his lap. Lisa found it icky, but Daniel loved it. He would start tickling her toes and then it would turn into a tickling match between them until they both collapsed on the floor, laughing. Lisa would shake her head and go back to whatever she was doing.

They talked for a long time, and she kept telling herself she had to go so she would not be late for her shoot. But she was having such a good time with Daniel, she didn't want to leave. Just being with him made her feel so safe and so good.

She finally forced herself to glance at her wristwatch and she gasped. She sprang up from the sofa and said to Daniel, "I have to go now. I am late for today's film shoot." But instead of hurrying away, she waited for him to stand so he could walk her to the door.

He opened the door for her, and she stepped out. She stood at the door looking at him, hoping he would give her a goodbye kiss, just like he had yesterday. When he just smiled and told her he hoped he could see her again tomorrow, she smiled back and tried to hide her disappointment.

She got to the set and found they had already started shooting their scene. Trent glared at her as she walked up to him and mouthed an apology. He looked at her for a brief moment, shook his head, and went back to directing the scene.

She went and stood behind the camera operator and watched the scene being shot, feeling guilty. She understood Trent's anger. It was probably too late for her to shoot her own scene, which meant it would have to be done tomorrow. She would be costing him money and time to shoot her own scene separately. She would have to apologize again. Time had run away from her when she was with Daniel.

She walked away and went to her trailer. Fifteen minutes later, Trent walked in still looking angry. He sat beside her on the sofa and looked at her. "You promised you would come back quickly," he said.

"I'm so sorry, Trent."

He searched her eyes. "So, you have been with Daniel all this while. You never spend that long with me."

She bit her lip. He was gazing at her with not just an accusing look, but also a suspicious one. She knew what he was thinking, and she tried to put his mind at ease. "I promise, Trent. We just talked. Nothing more."

"Really?"

"Yes, really. I told you that we are just friends."

"And do friends kiss each other the way he kissed you the other day?"

Her heart began to race. She remembered the day Daniel had kissed her in front of her trailer. Trent had seen that?

Once again, she promised him it was not what he was thinking. Yes, Daniel had kissed her, but it was an innocent kiss.

You know it wasn't, Vina!

She sighed and pushed down the guilt that had

risen up in her. She was sick and tired of feeling constantly guilty. One day it was because she had hurt Daniel, the next, it was Trent.

She started to try to explain again, but he stopped her. "I didn't come for all that, anyway. As you know, we will soon wrap up shooting our movie. I have made a couple of movies, and I think this particular movie has the makings of a blockbuster."

"Really?" She beamed.

"Yes," he answered.

She felt exhilarated. If Trent was saying that this movie was going to be a blockbuster, then she trusted it would be. She smiled, extremely happy.

He kissed her on the lips and then pulled back again. "Everybody is already buzzing about you, Vina. At least everyone that matters. We have already shown the film we shot in Fallow Creek to some critics and industry giants, and they love it. And even though you had only a small role in that one, you were noticed. Your beauty and talent are undeniable."

Vina blinked, astonished.

He continued. "Soon, your life will really change. You, my dear Vina, are a great actress, and soon everyone will know it. I expect that within the next five years, you will have won an Oscar."

She laughed out loud and shook her head. "Trent, stop it!"

"I'm serious, Vina." He took her hands. "I've seen a lot of beautiful and talented women in this industry, but you're special, Vina. I never thought I would feel this way about anyone, but I love you, Vina. I want to spend the rest of my life with you."

She gasped in shock and her heart began to race.

Had he just proposed to her?

He went on. "I believe we will make a great couple. A power couple in Hollywood. Some magazines have already caught on to the fact that I am dating you. But by the time this movie is released, it will be the other way around. The front pages will say "Vina Brooks Dating Trent Radar.""

She shook her head as she looked at him in disbelief.

"I want them to say at that time that Vina Brooks is going to marry Trent Radar." He knelt before her, and she covered her mouth and nearly passed out as he pulled a box out of his pocket and opened it. Inside was a ring with a huge diamond. He said, "Will you marry me, Vina?"

She could not speak for a long while. She felt like she was dreaming. Here she'd thought he was about to break up with her when he told her he'd seen Daniel kissing her. Instead, he was asking her to marry him.

Her mouth fell open again. Trent Radar had just asked her to marry him. She didn't know what to say. Trent was handsome, and she couldn't imagine the fact that someone like him would want to marry her, a girl from a small polygamous town. If she accepted, just like he said, she would go further in her career than she'd ever imagined, and all her dreams would come true. But then, she'd told herself she didn't want to get married yet, and even if she decided to get married, did she love him enough to marry him?

"You haven't answered me," he said looking up at her.

"I don't know what to say," she told him.

"Say yes."

She bit her lip and looked down at him. Immediately, Daniel's face appeared in her mind. If she married Trent, it would really be the end of her and Daniel. She probably would not be able to hang out with him as friends the way she was doing. But then, Daniel couldn't make her dreams a reality, and Trent would. Wasn't he the one who had given her this opportunity to star in a major film in a major role? This was what she'd wanted for so long. To discover her passion, her purpose. To live her life fully?

Still, Daniel's face remained in her mind. She could go another way. She could go back to Fallow Creek with Daniel and marry him rather than Trent.

She pictured her life with Daniel in Fallow Creek. She had lived all her life there. That was not where she wanted to be — living in a small quiet town and having a bunch of children. She wanted fame and glamor. She looked at Trent and the huge diamond ring he was holding up to her. She wanted this.

No, I don't want to go back to Fallow Creek, and I can't marry Daniel. She would stay here in Hollywood and be a huge actress, and Trent could do that for her. She slowly nodded.

"Is that a yes?" Trent grinned.

"Yes, Trent. I will marry you."

He stood up and hugged her tightly and then slipped the diamond ring on her finger. He kissed her and said, "You've made me so happy. We will have such a great future together."

She smiled, and he kissed her again. She had no

doubt they would be great together in the future, but the happiness part she hoped with all her heart was true. For a brief moment, she wondered if she'd made the right decision.

Lord, is this what you want me to do?

But she heard nothing. She sighed and pressed her concerns away. Fully focusing her attention on Trent, she smiled and kissed him. She would be his wife and become a famous Hollywood actress. They would be a power couple, just like he'd said. That was her future, and she could not be more pleased with it.

TWENTY-ONE

Daniel hurriedly put on his shirt and a pair of jeans, preparing to go see Vina on set. She had told him when she'd left two days ago that she would be back the next day. But she hadn't come back. When he had tried to call her, she did not pick up his call. In the past few weeks, he'd gone from feeling completely hopeless about his quest to win Vina's heart to feeling quite hopeful.

He could still remember the look on her face two days ago, before she'd left his room. She had looked at him as though she'd wanted him to kiss her. There was nothing he wanted more, but since he wasn't sure that was really what she wanted, he had held back. Now, he wished he had taken the chance and kissed her.

But he had tremendously enjoyed spending time with her almost daily, and he was sure she did, too. Until yesterday, he felt certain that his plan to win her heart back was moving forward. But this seemed like a setback. Had he done something wrong the last time they were together, or had something happened to her?

He headed to his front door, still worried. He couldn't wait to get to the set and make sure she was okay. Hopefully, she was. He would ask her why she hadn't answered his call yesterday or this morning, why she hadn't come back to his motel room even though she'd told him she would.

Just before he got to his door, a loud knock sounded. He opened the door, and his heart soared with happiness and relief.

"Vina," he said, smiling at her. And then he frowned. She looked guilty, and her eyes did not meet his. His heart began to thud. "What is wrong, Vina?" he asked, worried again.

She walked into the room and sat on the couch. She looked at him as he sat beside her and then turned her gaze away again. "I have something to tell you," she said.

He studied her face. Why did she look so worried, so full of guilt?

And then his heart sank when he noticed the diamond ring on her finger. This one was much larger than the one he had given her, which she had taken off a long time ago. And it looked very expensive.

He could not breathe. *No, it can't be.*

She turned to him again, pressed her lips together, and sighed. "Trent asked me to marry him, Daniel, and I said yes."

He shut his eyes as pain ripped through him. He could not catch his breath as she began to tell him how Trent had proposed and how she had agreed to marry him.

She said, "Unlike the two of us, Trent and I are

on the same path and have similar dreams."

She gazed at him after she finished speaking, clearly expecting him to say something. But he could not speak. All he felt like doing was sobbing. He looked at her, and she bent her head slightly.

"I know you're shocked by my news, Dan. I came here to tell you personally because I didn't want you to hear about it from some other source."

He closed his eyes again as a fresh wave of pain and hurt rippled through his heart. And then anger began to replace the hurt, and he opened his eyes.

She put her hand on his back. "Dan, please say something."

He shook his head. He was so angry now that whatever he said would not come out right. He took deep breaths to try to let go of his anger and finally did. But the hurt he felt remained. He looked into her eyes and forced himself to smile, even though all he wanted to do was scream. He had told her he would support her in everything, no matter what. His heart was filled with pain, but he said, "Congratulations, Vina. I'm glad you found someone who is on the same path as you." He pressed down the feeling of betrayal rising up in him and added, "Trent is a lucky man. I wish you both the best."

She gaped at him. Clearly, she'd expected a different reaction from him. She pressed her lips together, looking even more guilty now than she had when she'd come into his room. He didn't feel like talking anymore. He wanted her to leave so he could start packing. Because there was no way he could stay here. He had been defeated. She was getting married to someone else.

"Dan, are you okay?" she asked with a concerned look. She put her hand on his back again.

He sighed and moved away from her. "I'm fine," he croaked.

"You don't look fine, Dan. Please talk to me. I know my news isn't easy for you to take, but maybe look at it in a different light. This frees you to go on with your life and find someone new. You're a great guy, Daniel. There are so many beautiful single girls in Fallow Creek who would love to be with you. Trust me, I know." She smiled sadly. "Whoever you choose to be with in the future will be extremely lucky to have a guy like you."

He groaned. "Stop, Vina! Stop telling me to find someone new. I don't want to find someone new. I love you, and I don't know about you, but you just don't replace someone you love so easily."

She winced and said again, "I'm sorry."

"Why are you apologizing? You fell out of love with me, broke off our engagement, and now you are going to marry a guy you have far more in common with than you have with me. It's the way of life."

"I wish things had gone differently. I still love you, but…"

He turned sharply to her again. "You still love me! Then why are you planning to marry Trent Radar instead of me? Tell me."

"Dan, you know we might have a lot in common because we grew up in the same town, but we're two different people who want completely different things."

"Really, Vina? You think we want different things? What I want is to marry the woman I love.

We have that in common. You're saying you love me and, clearly, you want to get married now. Why aren't you marrying me?"

"It is not as simple as that."

"I guess it isn't, because I don't understand. You told me you were not ready to get married. That was one of the reasons why you broke up with me. You said marriage was not part of the plan you had for your life now. Yet you said yes to Trent. You're going to marry a guy you've only known for a few months. I don't know why you are marrying him, especially since you just confessed that you still love me, but I want to marry you because I'm in love with you. That is enough reason to marry someone, but I guess you don't feel the same."

"I'm marrying Trent because I love him," she said defensively.

"Do you really? You just said you loved me. How can you truly love both of us at the same time? Unless you are not 'in love' with one of us, and I can only guess who that is."

She looked confused for a few moments and then shook her head as though to shake away the confusion. "I love Trent, and we are going in the same direction, so I'm marrying him."

"No, you are marrying him because of all you think he can do for you."

She glared at him and said defensively, "You just want to stay in Fallow Creek, have a bunch of kids, and live a quiet, uninspired life. I want more for myself, and there is nothing wrong in being with someone who can give you more."

He glowered at her and turned away.

"Daniel." She put her hand on his shoulder, and

he turned to her again. "I'm sorry. I hope we can still be friends. I want you to come to my wedding."

He flinched and felt as though she had punched him in the stomach. "How can you ask that of me?"

She stood up and apologized again.

"Stop apologizing!" His anger flared, but he quickly squashed it. "Please go, Vina."

"Goodbye, Daniel. I hope I'll see you soon."

He turned away until he heard the door close. He groaned and held his head in his hands. "Lord, why?" He should have seen this coming, but he hadn't. She had adamantly refused to marry him, saying she didn't want to get married yet. How was he to know that she would accept the proposal of a guy she'd known for less time than she and Daniel had been engaged?

He went to get his suitcase and began to pack his things, feeling both emotionally and physically drained. He recalled packing his things when he'd seen Vina and Trent making out, but he'd later changed his mind and decided to stay and not give up. But this time, there was no hope of winning her back. It was truly time to go back to Fallow Creek.

***

Vina entered her trailer feeling miserable after her visit to Daniel's motel room. He had been heartbroken because she was getting married to Trent. She'd expected him to be shocked and sad at her news, but the look in his eyes had torn her heart to tiny pieces. There was no doubt that he was still deeply in love with her.

Why do I feel so miserable when I should be

happy? She was getting married to the handsome Trent Radar, Hollywood producer and director. She should be over-the-moon happy. But she could not stop thinking about Daniel, about the look on his face when she'd told him she had said yes to Trent's marriage proposal.

She groaned. Daniel had not given up on trying to win her heart since the day she'd told him she didn't want to get married. Not only had he not given up, but he'd come all the way to L.A. and rented a motel room so he could stay until he won her heart back. Unfortunately, it had not worked out for him. She wanted to go back to his motel room and tell him she would not marry Trent and would marry him. She would go back to Fallow Creek, and they could have as many children as God gave them and raise them in the town they grew up in.

But she could not go back to Fallow Creek with Daniel. It was not the life she wanted for herself.

She shot her eyes and groaned. Would she ever see him again? She had seen the look in his eyes. He had finally come to terms with the fact that they were never getting back together. He had given up.

Maybe it's for the best, Vina. His presence here was a distraction. She seemed to enjoy going to his motel room to spend time with him more than she did the acting and the dreams she had come to L.A. to pursue. Definitely more than spending time with Trent.

She gasped. Was that true?

She knew it was. Being with Daniel was more exhilarating, more exciting than being with Trent. She felt happier when she was with him, a much better person. She had no guilt when they were together, and most of all, she felt connected with God, because unlike Trent, he shared her faith.

Stop thinking like this, Vina! You're going to marry Trent. You know you don't want to go back to Fallow Creek. She had come to L.A. to pursue an acting career, to find herself, and to live an exciting life.

She groaned. She had found all that, but it had turned out not to be as fulfilling as she'd dreamed it would be. And the initial intense attraction to Trent because of his exquisite looks and mysterious career was beginning to fade. She wondered if the love she proclaimed she had for him was real.

She stood up from the sofa. She had to stop thinking like this. She was living the life she had prayed and hoped for, and she was where she was meant to be. Placing her hand on her forehead, she groaned again. What about Daniel? He would be leaving L.A. soon.

Confusion raged in her as she paced her trailer. Had she made the right decision?

Her trailer door opened, and Trent walked in. He had a huge smile on his face, and he looked as handsome as ever. He reached for her, took her in his arms, and kissed her. "Hey, future Mrs. Trent Radar."

She mustered up a bright smile for him. "Hey, Trent!"

"I can't wait for you to become my wife." He kissed her again, and at first, she stood rigid. And then she kissed him back. Trent was who she wanted. She had to believe she had made the right decision. She would marry him and become Vina Radar. They would settle here in L.A., and she would make a life

for herself; one she would never even have dreamed
of if she'd remained in Fallow Creek.

TWENTY-TWO

Vina stepped into Trent's Beverly Hills mansion carrying two editions of The Ultimate Bride Magazine and a bag full of fresh strawberries that she had bought from a nearby store. She went to the kitchen and put the strawberries into the fridge and then walked into Trent's elegant downstairs den and sat on the sofa. She had been living in Trent's house at Trent's request since they'd wrapped up shooting *The King's Treasure* two weeks ago.

At first, when he'd asked her to move into his mansion, she had declined. She didn't want to live with him when they were not yet married. But after he took her to his home and she saw how huge it was, she knew they could live as though they were actually in different houses. His house was even bigger than Mike's. Her room was upstairs in another wing of the house, and Trent had been a perfect gentleman since she'd arrived here. He had never entered her room, and she was grateful for that.

Andrea, Trent's maid, came and asked if Vina

needed her to get anything since she was going grocery shopping.

"No, Andrea. Thanks." Vina smiled at the woman. "I just purchased some fresh strawberries. That was all I needed, really."

Andrea smiled and then left the den.

Vina began to riffle through the bridal magazines, trying to find inspiration for her wedding dress. She and Trent had set the wedding for July. That was in six-months' time. To her, it was more than enough time to plan a big wedding, but Trent had told her that for the wedding he had in mind, the time was short. He talked about vendors, wedding planners, and stylists. Jobs she didn't even know existed. She'd thought she was going to plan her own wedding, but Trent told her a wedding planner would handle most of it. Still, she wanted to purchase her own dress and be completely in charge of deciding what style she would wear.

She stopped at a page in the magazine and stared at the wedding dress on it. It was a beautiful mermaid-style dress, and it looked like the kind of wedding dress she would love to wear. But it would have to have a bit more 'bling,' as her co-star, Johanna would say, and the neckline definitely had to be higher.

Trent walked into the den. "You are back," he said to her. He bent down and planted a kiss on her cheek. "What are you doing?" he looked at the magazines in her hands and frowned.

"Trying to find inspiration for my wedding dress," she told him.

"No, you don't have to do that. Alexis Coleman will be designing your wedding dress. Why look for inspiration in these magazines when you have the wedding dress guru herself designing your dress?"

She stared at him. He hadn't told her that a wedding dress designer would be designing her wedding dress. She didn't know whether to be pleased or not.

He took the magazines from her. "All you need to do is present yourself to Alexis and she will handle everything."

"But I want to have some input into the type of wedding dress I wear," Vina said.

Trent sat beside her. "Don't worry your pretty head about that. I want you to look perfect on our wedding day, and Alexis Coleman knows exactly how to make that happen."

He continued to talk about their wedding — how he wanted it to be, his dreams for the perfect ambiance and venue. She soon unconsciously tuned him out as her mind traveled to Daniel and the wedding dress he had gotten her in Fallow Creek. She remembered the joy and love in his eyes when he'd presented the dress to her. Trent was going on about how he wanted her to appear before his guests, but Daniel had eyes for her alone. She was sure if they were the only two people living in Fallow Creek or anywhere else, he would still have gotten the best dress he could afford just to make her happy. Trent, however, needed other people around. Important people who would validate and congratulate him on his fine choice of everything, including his bride. She was just one of the people in his life that made him look good.

Stop thinking like that, Vina. But still, she could not stop thinking about Daniel. Just as she had guessed, he'd left as soon as she'd told him she was getting married to Trent. She'd tried to call him several times, but he didn't answer any of her calls. She didn't blame him. She would have done the same if she were him.

Overwhelming sadness settled on her as she remembered the day she'd told Daniel she was getting married to Trent. She could see he had been terribly hurt, but he had congratulated her. Though that was before he'd again declared his love for her and asked why she was marrying someone other than him.

That was her Daniel.

She bit her lip. Her Daniel! That was how she had always seen him... even when she was married to Mike. That was how she saw him now. He was hers, had always been.

And I am his... or should be.

An overwhelming sense of panic rose up in her. *Oh, Vina! What have you done?* She had followed a path she thought would bring her excitement and satisfaction, and for a while, a very short while, it had. She had followed the handsome director to the city of her dreams and to a career she had thought was so glamorous she could only imagine it. It had all seemed like a fairytale. But now the dream had faded, and she had woken up to reality.

She missed Daniel terribly; she missed Rachel and Keith; she missed being Rachel's personal assistant and helping her run the House of Refuge. She even missed Fallow Creek, especially the House of Refuge. Because she had grown up in Fallow Creek and had hardly ever left, she'd wanted to see the world, to experience something new. Now that she had, she couldn't wait to go back home. Fallow Creek was home. Daniel was home.

Her eyes widened. *Why then am I still here?* She looked at Trent, who was still talking, not even noticing that she had tuned him out. They had wrapped up the shooting of the movie with a big celebration, and then they had celebrated their engagement. Trent had told her *The King's Treasure* was definitely gearing up to be a blockbuster, and she had seen a gossip magazine with her and Trent on the front page. But none of those things held her heart or attention.

All she wanted now was her best friend. Daniel.

What have you done, Vina? she thought again.

Trent raised his eyebrows. "What do you mean what have you done? What did you do?"

She bit her lip. She hadn't realized she had spoken the words out loud. "Nothing, Trent," she said.

He stared curiously at her and then went on talking about the wedding.

Her thoughts strayed again, and once more she thought about Daniel. When she had told him about her engagement, the Daniel she knew before would have blown his top. The old Daniel would without a doubt have attacked Trent the day he's found them making out in her trailer. Instead, he had apologized and fled. He had controlled his anger and definitely his jealousy. Wasn't that the reason why she'd broken up with him? But he seemed to have grown. She had told him she didn't want to get married, but it was more out of fear than the fact that she wasn't ready.

She groaned. Why was she thinking about Daniel when she was planning her wedding with

Trent? She blinked and looked at Trent. And then she knew that if she married him, she would be making a huge mistake. She didn't want to marry Trent. She wanted to marry Daniel. He was the one she loved. She had never wanted anything as much as she wanted to be Daniel's wife.

She had seen the world, at least a small part of it, and she had followed a career she'd thought she wanted, but she knew now that the things she truly wanted, she'd always had. She wanted Daniel's daily company, she wanted to have his children, and live in his tiny house with him. And she yearned for the strong connection with God that she had enjoyed at the House of Refuge with people of like-minded faith.

"... you have to prepare for all the media attention that will come with our wedding," Trent was saying. "Soon you will be as famous as..."

"Excuse me, Trent." She stood up. She couldn't do this anymore. She couldn't stay here for one more day.

"What's wrong, Vina?"

"I have made a terrible mistake," she said. "Forgive me, Trent. I can't do this anymore." She removed the engagement ring he had given her and handed it to him. He looked shocked, and she bent down and kissed his cheek. "Thank you for everything you've done for me. I have to go now."

"Vina!"

She turned around. "I'm sorry, Trent. I truly am." She hurried out of the den and went to pack up her things.

***

Daniel left his house early to start his daily patrol. As he walked through Fallow Creek, he greeted the people he saw with a pasted-on smile, but his heart was not in his greeting. All he could think about, all that had occupied his mind since he'd come back from L.A. weeks ago was that he'd lost Vina forever. She was going to marry someone else. He could not believe it. And yet it was true. She had told him herself. He had gone to L.A. to win her back, but he had failed.

He walked past the House of Refuge, misery encircling him, and he decided to go in and speak with Keith. In the past, it had always made him feel better, but since he'd come back, he'd not been able to bring himself to speak with Keith and Rachel about Vina. Speaking her name had been too painful. But it was time he talked to Keith about her.

He entered the House of Refuge and went up to Keith and Rachel's apartment. When he knocked on the door, it opened immediately, and Keith beamed at him.

"Come in, stranger," he said.

Daniel sighed with relief, thankful that Keith was home. He walked into the living room and greeted Rachel, who was sitting on the couch, Emily on her lap. He ruffled Emily's hair and went to sit on the sofa facing Rachel.

Keith sat next to Rachel and looked at him. "I haven't seen much of you since you came back from L.A. What's up? You look awful."

Daniel shrugged. "Well, thanks, Keith."

Rachel gave him a sympathetic smile. "You haven't told us what exactly happened when you went to L.A."

He nodded. Keith and Rachel had visited him a few times and tried to get him to talk about his trip, but he never told them anything.

"We have been worried about you, Daniel," Keith said. "You have been miserable since you got back."

He sighed. He knew they had probably guessed he hadn't won Vina back or she would have come back to Fallow Creek with him. What they didn't know was that Vina was going to marry someone else. He still did not feel like talking about it, but he had to tell his friends.

He pressed his lips together and then finally said, "Vina is engaged to Trent Radar."

"What?" Rachel's eyes widened, and she shook her head. "How come?"

"Well, they were dating before they left Fallow Creek," Keith said. "But still, I didn't know she would be getting married to that director so soon."

Rachel still looked shocked. "But she said she wasn't ready to get married. Wasn't that what she told you, Daniel?"

Fresh pain filled his heart. "Apparently it's me she didn't want to marry. She came to my motel room herself to tell me she was getting married and showed me her huge engagement ring. She now has everything she ever dreamed of. Her career has been going well, and she's marrying a rich Hollywood director."

"Oh, Daniel, I'm so sorry," Rachel said. "I know how much you love her, and I thought she loved you as much. In fact, I was sure she did. It doesn't make sense."

"She has been restless for a while now," Keith

said. "I think it's because she has spent all her life in Fallow Creek and has never left town. She was stir crazy and wanted to experience something new."

"And now she has," Daniel said. "And someone new, too."

Rachel's phone rang, and she picked it up and answered. She beamed. "Lily, how are you? I have missed you." Rachel stood up, excused herself, and left the living room.

Daniel blinked as he remembered something. Rachel's phone call with Lily had brought a memory to mind. He said to Keith, "I just remembered now. I saw Lily's sister, Stella, when I went to Tucson to find my brother."

Keith's mouth fell open and then he closed it again. "Daniel, why didn't you tell us? You know Lily has been looking for her sister."

Remorse filled Daniel. "I'm so sorry. You know how worried and occupied I was with trying to make sure I didn't lose Vina. It totally slipped my mind." He felt awful. His obsession with trying to get Vina to marry him had made him forget something so crucial, so important. How self-centered was he?

Keith shook his head. "We have to tell Rachel immediately."

"Yes," Daniel nodded. "Stella would even have come to Fallow Creek with me if not for her controlling husband." He had detested Stella's husband the moment she'd told him about the man and how he'd separated her from her parents. She had suffered so much, and if he had told Keith and Rachel as soon as he'd came back from Tucson, maybe they could have gotten her out from the clutches of her wicked husband.

How could I have forgotten something so important?

But he knew how. His days had been completely preoccupied with Vina and how to win back her heart. There had been no space for anyone or anything else.

"Rachel," Keith called out, "come quickly! There's news about Lily's sister!"

Rachel rushed into the living room, her phone still to her ear. "What did you just say, Keith?"

"Daniel has information about Lily's sister. He knows where she is."

Rachel's eyes grew as round as saucers and she put her phone on speaker. She repeated what Keith had said to her, and Lily screamed over the phone.

Daniel told her everything that had happened the day he'd gone to Tucson, and Lily said, "I am getting on a plane today and coming to Fallow Creek. You will take me to my sister as soon as I get there, Daniel."

"Okay," Daniel said.

After the call ended, the three of them looked at each other.

"This was a pretty big thing to forget," Rachel said. Daniel started to apologize again, but Rachel shook her head. "Don't worry about it. At least you remembered now. Lily will be so happy to be reunited with her sister."

They talked about Lily and her quest to find her family, and then Daniel stood up again. He thanked Rachel and Keith for making time to speak with him and left their apartment. He continued to patrol the town, but this time, not only did he feel miserable about Vina's engagement to Trent, he also felt like a jerk for having forgotten to tell Rachel and Keith about Lily's sister, knowing how important it was.

Angry, jealous, and now forgetful, he scolded himself. But the Lord was already working in him in those areas. Through God's grace, he was becoming more adept at controlling his anger.

He headed toward the edge of Fallow Creek, his shoulders sagging. He sighed sadly. It was time for him to turn around and go home. He did not feel like walking around anymore. But just before he turned around, a car approached and zoomed past him. He blinked. The woman in the passenger seat looked like Vina. But that could not be. Vina was in L.A., planning her wedding to Trent. He smiled in self-mockery. He was beginning to see Vina everywhere.

The car suddenly backed up, and he frowned. It stopped beside him, and his heart began to pound when Vina got out of the vehicle.

Daniel could not move as the driver got her suitcase out of the trunk, left it beside her, and drove off.

Daniel stared disbelievingly at Vina. Why had she come back to Fallow Creek?

Her gaze was fixed on him as she moved toward him. He blinked. There were tears in her eyes. She reached him and the tears began to fall down her face.

"Vina?" he said slowly. "Why are you here?"

She bit her lip and looked into his eyes. "Daniel, I don't know how you will ever forgive me, but I want to ask you to. I made a terrible mistake when I broke up with you and left for L.A. I thought it was what I wanted. The glamour of being an actor in Hollywood, living in a big city, seeing the world..." she looked away from him, "being with Trent. But it did not take me more than a few weeks to know that I already had exactly what I wanted and threw it all away." She looked at him again as his heart raced. "I know it will be hard for you to forgive me for what I did to you, but I am asking, begging you to."

Daniel could not breathe as he looked at her. He could not believe what she was saying to him. She wanted him to take her back.

"Daniel, I will understand if you cannot take me back, but I know now that there's nothing more I want than to marry you, and have your children, and raise them right here in Fallow Creek."

He stared at her in wonder. And then he could not hold back his elation. He swept her into his arms and held her tightly. He kissed her hair, her cheeks, her nose, and then he held her away from him, overcome with emotions.

She began to cry, and he wiped away her tears with his fingers. He caressed her cheeks and shook his head. "Why are you weeping, Vina?"

"I'm so happy. After everything I did to you, I was afraid you would not want me again."

"I could never not want you," he said softly.

"So does that mean you will marry me?" She smiled.

"Of course." He grinned at her. "In fact, I want to marry you right now."

She laughed out loud and then blinked, a look of surprise on her face. She studied him and said, "You really mean that, don't you?"

"Of course I do." He chuckled. "Keith can marry us now. What's the point of setting a future wedding date? The wait would be pure agony for me."

She roared with laughter and nodded eagerly. "Yes, I think I want that, too. I love you with all my heart and you're my best friend. There's nothing stopping us from getting married now."

"So what are we waiting for?" He took her hand and laughed with joy. "Let's go and see Keith. He's in his apartment."

They headed toward the House of Refuge with their arms carelessly flung around each other's shoulders.

Daniel smiled at Vina. This was his best friend, and before the end of the day, she would also be his wife and forever companion.

A LOOK AT:
FINALLY HOME IN DESTINY

AFTER ESCAPES, LOVE LOST, HOPELESSNESS AND COUNTLESS MOVES, THE COUPLES REUNITE IN DESTINY TO TAKE ON THEIR NEXT CHAPTERS.

Fallow Creek, a once male ran-religious-polygamous town, has been left virtually deserted. A mass exodus prompted by a shift in power, has scattered families around the country.

However, the ex-leader, and elders of the former community, aim to take their town back and restore it to its former glory. Anyone who stands in their way will be dealt with.

COMING SEPTEMBER 2020

ABOUT THE AUTHOR

Like the characters in her stories, Emma Easter juggles a range of identities.

In the low-income community where she works, Easter is known as a family medicine physician who treats patients of all ages and backgrounds.

College friends see her as an accomplished musician, having studied and mastered five classical instruments—but behind closed doors, she's just as comfortable rocking an air guitar to Creed. And when she isn't giving her heart, soul, and sanity to her three young children she's indulging in her most secret identity of all: meeting new characters, crafting fresh plots, and exploring every corner of her imagination.

Across all these different roles, one cohesive thread has tied everything together: her faith and love of Jesus Christ.

Find more great titles by Emma Easter and Christian Kindle News at https://christiankindlenews.com/our-authors/emma-easter/.